CW01511420

# LA LUNA

**SYLVESTER MILNE**

*To Mother*
*(soz about the grotty bits)*

# <u>Chapters</u>

# 1

# TOUCHDOWN

A roller coaster jolt slapped my face against the cabin window, rousing me from a bourbon-induced coma, self-administered at thirty thousand feet. My beady half-drunk eyes opened to the ghastliness of our 747 jumbo locked in a full kamikaze nose dive. The plane was in full roar, the cabin banking sharply from side to side, eagerly shaking itself into a spastic fit. Emergency lights pulsed over snarling faces, all contorted by fitful states of pandemonium. Warning indicators beeped a sharp and steady rhythm, searching for order in the chaos. There was a high pitch of screeching metal twisting into new forms. This was countered by a vacuous hollow spot made by the absorbing cabin pressure, which somehow rendered this violent, raging miasma of despair into something silent and otherworldly. Oxygen masks splayed outward from the overhead luggage racks. Great lengths of red and yellow cable dangling freely like the gutted entrails of some dying mechanical beast. We were plummeting out of the sky without compromise. The other passengers were whipping themselves into a hysterical frenzy of expectant, imminent, death. There were fearful cries of mercy. Utterances of renewed reverence to God. And a few outlandish promises for a wholesale change in lifestyle. Together it formed a piercing chorus of last-minute plea deals with the All Watching One.

Sat in front of me was a heavy-set bearded man whose initial incomprehension of events reflected my own muddled state of alarm. He repeatedly punched his headrest whilst rattling off a slurry of menacing words, strange ramblings that felt eerily close to the garbled calls of a gypsy curse. An old lady sat to my right. A ghostly white pensioner with marbled black and grey hair. Her face weathered to the point of scarring, her skin crumpled and creased like the cover of a well-thumbed bible. The old relic wore a soft black dress, adorned with a golden crucifix that she clasped between forefinger and thumb. Her eyes - filled with an electrifying panic - fixed on me. A raw, merciless fear poured from her soul into mine.

Waking up to that level of terror is a cattle prod to the nervous system. As I jackknifed awake, I began taking stock of my own forthcoming and impending doom. I scanned the plane again for any signs of reassurance. *Perhaps I was half dreaming an exaggerated sense of peril*? But every face remained etched with the same manic desperation to live. A brief check of myself revealed my groin showered with the sad crumbs of in-flight pretzels and peanut dust. My white t-shirt daubed with smatterings of low-quality claret. Bamboozled by the whole concoction, I had nowhere left to turn but back to the old grey widow. For reasons unbeknownst to me - whether I was trying to confide or seek refuge - I flashed the old lady a wild grin. One that came off not born from reassurance but laced with a devilish, twisted kind of malice. She didn't flinch, instead slapping her hand down on top of mine and gripping it with the strength of a python.

Then relief. The plane's nose lifted and steadied, while the landing gear rumbled ominously into position. The wings fluttered and flexed. Somebody yelped. There was a moment of anxious weightlessness before the wheels made a sudden, thunderous impact, squealing down fiercely onto the asphalt runway of Mexico City airport. The relief was palpable and speechless. There was no round of applause. My neighbour's hand clamp had turned my fingers white. She was strong for an antique, but they built them to last in those days. Far behind me, someone made a terrible gurgling noise like water being sucked down the plug hole. I wanted off that plane at once.

Inside the airport, I hurriedly made my way through customs, eager to get a lungful of fresh air and dig out my snouts. My mouth was paper-dry as I headed down the various corridors. Miles of flickering white fluorescent lights strobed my approach like an epileptic nightmare. It was a plank walk toward salvation, flanked on all sides by indecently sweaty Mexican officials. Reaching the immigration booth, I nonchalantly waved my mahogany British passport. It was still encrusted with the late Queen's royal seal; the ticket that allows free entry on all the rides. Or so I thought. However the official, in his shabby glass cubicle, apparently hadn't gotten the memo. He lifted a chubby sweat-glistened palm, catching me in my stride as I was about to round him. He stared not at me, but at my passport.

"Jack Marden?"

"That's me."

"Why you come to Mexico?" he said, staring only at my celluloid mug.

*Affirmation of existence? Fiendish debauchery?* I wasn't quite sure, so I opted for: "Leisure."

I was too tired and tetchy from the flight to feel the necessity of expansion. My customs officer apparently wasn't as tired and looked at me for some elaboration.

"To celebrate... *Cerveza*... uhh, party?... Day of... Dia of - the Dead," I said, finally amalgamating a series of words that might be deemed passable.

"*Dia de los Muertos,*" he said sourly, waving me through.

Outside the airport, I was greeted by a warm tropical fug. A soupy playground for a million mosquitoes swirling around in the early evening air. It was a far cry from flights arriving back in London, where the cold misty vapours wrap around your body upon exiting the airport. England is a seasonal funeral parlour, and it likes to embalm you as soon as you return.

I reached for my Camels and lit up, casting off memories of home. The sticky humid air reminded me of why I left, the harsh dry smoke from my cigarette reinforcing the feeling of those shackles now removed. The sun was beginning its descent, blaring crimson on the horizon and partially hidden by clumps of bruised and blackened thunderclouds that swelled like vast blood blisters, threatening to erupt under the fiery intensity of the burning orb. The airport's perimeter was defined by a wall of black palm trees silhouetted against the mauve skyline, all swaying rhythmically like hula girls in the gentle dusk breeze. To my left, a line of forlorn dented stock car taxis, parked in a line that should have led straight to the scrap heap. Alongside them stood their owners, appearing to be equally in need of a good service, huddled together in a thick fog of cigarette smoke. The nearest and keenest tossed his cigarette to the ground as I approached and beckoned me toward the boot of his car. I prefer my baggage in touching distance, so I gestured this with a double tap on my canvas duffel and climbed into the back seat. Once we were both seated, he stared at me in the rear view; evidently, it was time to give him a destination.

"La Casa Roca?" I ventured, and upon puzzlement, I added an address in the downtown district. With neither reply nor hesitation, he pulled away the old knackered taxi in stuttering jerks of acceleration. We corkscrewed around the airport's spaghetti slip lanes in an unfeasibly low gear. It was only once we reached the freeway that the car stopped rattling and eased itself into a comfortable, listing bob. The steering wheel and column had been ripped out of the driver's side and gaffer taped into position in the opposite footwell. My driver was effectively sitting in the passenger seat, while I bobbled about in the rear. Whatever model the original car had been was hidden now by the varying torturous mechanical hacks it had endured over the years. The windscreen had been heavily impacted in the bottom corner, the size of which I guessed roughly matched an adolescent human skull. From the impact spot, a set of disorientingly splintered glass lines ran away in all directions. This created a kaleidoscopic effect where certain objects appeared far away in the distance, but then leapt suddenly forward at you with an alarming irregularity. A few nervous minutes later and my driver began rummaging around inside his top shirt pocket, producing a little black wrap of twisted plastic. He gnawed at it with the feverish persistence of a stray animal attacking a bag of garbage. Eventually he pried it open, dabbing inside with the edge of a brass cent, before bringing it back out covered in white powder and rorting hard across the coin's surface. He caught most of it, pinching his nose to hold back any strays. Only the odd sprinkle fell out and back down to earth, as gentle as the first snowflakes of winter.

"Coca? Coca, amigo?" he asked, looking at me in the rear view.

A delightful offer, but one surely anchored to some future, potentially more threatening advancement of narcotic indiscretion. One minute you're doing taxi lines, the next, blowing monkey dust up each other's bum holes. The customs ink was barely dry in my passport, the memory of obdurate police officials fresh in my mind, casting a shadowy spectre that made me reluctant and coy. After the plane ride that I had just experienced, I wanted nothing more than the safety and confines of a well-equipped hotel room. But then, *wasn't that the whole point?* To escape the comfort zone rather than rush back into its ever-warming embrace? I was jacked from the flight, which made my cigarette taste all the sweeter, so why not go one further? Time to do only what feels good, forget the future, live in the now, and all that other stoic mumbo jumbo. It had been ages since I had taken anything stronger than ibuprofen, yet I found myself leaning toward the idea. An apprehensive assessment was required, however, on the quality and authenticity of the drugs on offer. The trust given to a dealer usurps that of a doctor or mortgage adviser because it can be hard to retrieve a lost mind. Bad financial advice won't lock you into a nightmarish seven-hour trip where the faces of your loved ones morph onto the bodies of decaying animals. *But more on that later.*

My formula for narcotic dalliance is simple: if the dealer is on the drugs himself, then he can be trusted. On this score, my driver gave me very little cause for concern. Eyeing his face again in the rear view mirror, I noticed pock-marked cavities in his cheeks, the mottled skin that bore all the hallmarks of rugged poverty and long-term drug familiarity. He had a wart-studded nose like a mangled stick, with curly slick hair falling on either side. In his youth, he may have been regarded as handsome, but those years were long overtaken by a lifetime of barbiturate dependency. He had thick black caterpillar tufts for eyebrows, sponges for his unnaturally sweaty brow. He gave off a feeling of unthreatening criminality, one more conspiratorial than confrontational, a victim rather than a perpetrator. Perhaps it was the youthful menace that still sparkled in his eyes. I was his partner, not his foe. I leaned forward between the two front seats and he loaded the coin again, offering it to me over his shoulder. I brought my nose down hard on the coin and snorted over it and his fingers, an eager dog picking up the scent. In turn, he loaded himself up once more, before packing it all away and tucking it back into his shirt.

"Gacias, gracias amigo," I said, sliding back into the rear and twinkling my nostrils. The hit was instant, light, and sparkly, rising effortlessly into the recesses of my mind like the intoxicating whispers of a forbidden siren.

"De nada," he replied, before checking his side mirror and launching us into the fast lane.

"What's your name?" I asked.

"Ang-hel" he said, in a thick, gloopy Spanish accent, speaking to the air as much as speaking to me. "Ang-hel, 'cos you see, amigo, I died. I died cinco - cinco times," he continued, holding up his five fingers for emphasis. "On d'table. D'doctoro's? Meth. Overdose. I die, cinco times en d'table."

Unsure quite how to process this revelation, I instinctively reached for my cigarettes.

"Camel... eh, cigarillo?" I said, offering him one.

He took it in silence, not speaking now or for the rest of the journey. He just tuned in the radio and tuned out the world, perhaps finding some halfway house in his mind where he was back on the hospital table, existing forever more in the gateway between life and death.

Gazing out the rear window I saw a massive urbanised shanty sprawl descending upon us on all sides. The sun was almost gone, nothing more now than a blood-red teardrop in the murky smog of Mexico City. The houses that flew past the window seemed to be an endless iron and brick jungle. A maze of corrugated poverty, all stacked one upon the other, co-supporting a fragile house of cards. In the gaps between houses stood various dejected souls, clumped together and half obscured by darkness. The occasional street lamp turned on, casting a jaundiced glow into pockets of the ghetto, lighting up sickly corners like cancerous spots in a diseased lung.

I felt deflated by the slums, but conversely positive from the cocaine. Angel was absorbed in his driving and we shared another smoke as we reached downtown and closer to my hotel. The city here was brighter, more civilised, with cafes that resembled home, and smiling faces all bathed in pure light. Yet the grime was for the most part papered over, populated by the same forlorn figures from the shanty districts, lurking in the shadows, hawking around on street corners waiting for some kind of opportunistic criminal event.

*Ang'hel* dropped me off outside my hotel and hadn't asked for any additional coke money, just the fare. I rounded this up to ten bucks, and as I turned to leave he asked if I wanted any more "coca amigo?". I returned to the driver's window, which was the passenger's side, and leaned in. He wrote something on a scrap of paper and handed it to me.

"Y'ew call me, OK?" he said.

"Si, thanks Angel, will do," and I turned and went into my hotel.

Inside the lobby, not a creature stirred. At first glance, it felt generously awarded its two stars. The walls were a gross magnolia cream, offset by pine timbers stained in a marmalade orange varnish. I approached the desk and banged the little brass bell on the counter which ruffled up a miserly concierge who looked to be on the wrong end of a three-day-straight shift. He mumbled a gruff unpleasant sound, then tossed over the key. Getting up to the room and throwing my bag down onto the sturdy bed, I felt a liberating sense of freedom. The weight of my world now coincided with the contents of that bag. For a few months at least, maybe a year, all I could carry was all that defined me. I gravitated to the mini-bar where my choice was made all the easier by the lack of it, just two beers, both Modelo. I grabbed one and headed out onto the balcony to peruse my new kingdom.

The city was slowly coming alive with the noise of car horns, dogs barking off in the distance, and early fireworks announcing the arrival of the *Dia de los Muertos*. Directly below I heard two men locked in a deep lyrical discussion that sounded somehow sinister, yet joyful. I went back inside to grab my Camels, noting their number and the need for more. I popped the lid on my beer and supped back all its delicious coldness, holding the bottle briefly to the back of my neck to cool down against the still, sultry night air. Lighting my cigarette, I held the flame alive a touch longer than necessary, letting the wildfire dance momentarily in my mind's eye. I thought back to Angel, suspecting it wouldn't be long before we spoke again. Absentminded, I reached for the number he had written down, bringing it out of my pocket and back into the light of the hotel room. It was simply a mobile number written beneath a scrawled drawing of a crucifix.

Heavens above.

# 2

# ROLANDO

Ruminating on whether to call Angel, I thought of home; Blighty, His Majesty's Green Isle. Pubs and villages and hills and rolling meadows. Sun-shy skies, 60's architecture nestled amongst Tudor gables, weekend kebabs slapped flagrantly against shop windows, and nighttime city buses swaying under the weight of violent drunks. Ex-girlfriends, rent, traffic, box sets, and goose feather pillows wrapped in Egyptian cotton. A comfortable asylum. Each week my soul slowly ebbing further into the digital mire. Emails. Always emails. Disgruntled work colleagues, just like me, desperately bailing out the sinking vessel until Friday afternoon came to wash it all away. I had become a piece of paper, folded too many times. My twenties had evaporated, and I was limping, gak-footed, into my thirties. The prospect of another decade of aimlessly wandering from one job to the next, never owning anything, washing all my pennies down the pub urinals, filled me with an ambivalent self-loathing. Friends were starting to get proper jobs, and wives, even kids. Whereas I drank with teenage enthusiasm and corralled with mates of the more delinquent leaning.

My job was the type that when explained, made your eyes glaze over like ringed doughnuts. The type that you stumbled upon on a job hunt and read the description thinking "not only could I not get that job - I don't even understand what the fuck it is". Yet somehow I had gotten it and had been doing it for long enough that even I almost understood what it was that I did. It involved online analytics, algorithms, and code. I think.

Then one day, my mind collapsed.

I always had my phone turned on, naturally, meaning work flowed into me all through the night like an intravenous drip of mildly worrying data. I hadn't even realised it was happening at the time. A slowly mounting pressure building every day. Every communication via the phone meant a diluted teaspoon of stress. A work call, a missed deadline. An email, an annoyed client. A text, my disappointed girlfriend. My brain had become a fuse board where someone had taken all the wires out and plugged them into the wrong connectors. So when the phone rang one innocuous Wednesday morning, my brain reacted with entirely the wrong signal. Whatever the intended message, my brain received something akin to; *A fucking lion is about to kill you!*

I went into a full meltdown and spent the morning breathing into a paper bag. I was a quivering mess as I made my way into the office, unaware I was about to receive a second dose of seemingly fortuitous fate. I had barely progressed a few meters beyond the foyer when I was stopped in my tracks. There was a young Mexican kid emerging from the caretaker's closet.

"Hey, where's Rolando?" I inquired.

"Ah, I'm afraid he passed away. He was my father," the young man said, solemnly.

"Oh I see, I'm sorry…" I muttered, walking slowly away.

The exchange of words was no more noteworthy nor dramatic than that, but the impact upon me was seismic. Rolando was as old as the building itself, working thirty years as the cleaner, without time off, forever trapped within those walls. He embodied the capitalist dream, suffering in the present, for dreams of future happiness. Yet somehow he found joy in the everyday mundanity. He had found a way of projecting into that future state of bliss, so that really he wasn't suffering at all, everything was working toward his dream.

"Come on Rolando, what's the secret, how come you always seem so happy?" I would ask.

"It's simple, I'm not really here, I'm in the Baja, in the village I was born in, San Felipe. That's the village I'll go back to after this. If my family asks me how my day was, I say '*excellent*', because we are one step closer to Baja. Have you ever been to Mexico Jack?"

"No, never."

"You really should, life there is pure."

But Rolando never made it back to his true home. A few days shy of retirement, he died. He was always keen to impart his wisdom upon me, telling me about his dreams and his fantasy life back home on the Baja. Our talks were a welcome respite from the stifling confines of the office grind. He was so close to his nirvana, the light at the end of the tunnel, twinkling in his eye. Yet he never made it, and his dreams died with him. We spend our lives at the coalface, then die from exposure to the sun. Here was his son, filling the role of his father, perpetuating the cycle of false promises. I didn't want to find out his name. I didn't want the curse. I couldn't even walk another inch into that tower of lies. I quit my job that morning, verbalised to nobody, I just quietly turned away and headed to the nearest pub. I sat at the bar, brooding over my pint with a feeling of peculiar detachment and foreboding as if watching my life from above. My working self had been reduced to an online avatar, a digital being, a glossy apparition. I existed in filtered Instagram pictures of sausage legs and well-laden bagels. That was the world where I really existed. Not in a grimy flat roof pub surrounded by the daily regulars, gruff men with faces like trampled pouches of tobacco. That scene was dangerously un-Instagramable.

I drank a lot that afternoon but found there was a taste in my throat that no booze could quell. An acid reflux from the pit of my stomach, one which raged to break free from the whole system. I had already been writing notes on scraps of paper, left lying around my flat or car, ready to be found by my future self, warning him of the dangers of these modern trappings: "Gasoline your work clothes", "Dance naked in the fire", "The Wild is Calling You", "You have a Navajo heart", "You Are Free". And now I had another note for the pile, "Rolando Lives". I left that note scrawled onto a beer mat, then booked the next flight to Mexico City.

Five thousand miles later, a gut load of in-flight libations, and there I was, standing in the hotel room with my hand placed on the telephone receiver. I had half a cold Modelo in my left hand and a Camel smoking in the ashtray. A thousand work-related calls flashed before my eyes like a haunted flick book. Business calls, business voice. Upset clients, tempers, suppressed rage, and desperate cries for help and understanding. An email chain of exasperated disapproval and missed deadlines. *You Are Free.*

I quickly lifted the phone, washing away frightening visions of the past. I dialled the number and listened to only two rings before it answered midway through the third. There was no sound on the other end.

"Angel?" I inquired.

"Si," came the response. However, it was not Angel.

This man was older. Firmer. Somehow less trustworthy, perhaps because he had begun the discussion by not being the person he claimed to be. Slightly thrown, my right hand instinctively came around and hovered over the receiver, ready to terminate the call. I listened. Nothing. If there was any faint breathing, then it was *very* faint. A second more and I would hang up.

"Amigo?" he said.

Yet more silence, my turn now. I pondered, and eventually endeavoured, "Si, is... Angel there?"

"No, no. No Angel. You want amigo?" he replied.

My finger now rested firmly on the terminating nibs. "Where's Angel?" I asked.

"He no here, he tell me. You want? I bring for you," he said.

*Perhaps this is just how business is done out here. Simple. All one merry band, show the cross and get what you want. One religion, many gods.*

"OK, fine. How should we do this, shall I meet you? You bring, something... for me?" I said, losing my thread somewhere amongst my pigeon English and mounting distrust.

"Si, si, you know bar La Luna?" he said. "Plaza Jardin, Coyoacan. You come there, one hour." The phone clicked dead.

I moved back across the room to my cigarette and picked it up from habit, distant, my mind pondering the circumstances behind the call. I drank back a deep gulp of beer and the sharp tang brought clarity to my senses. I stepped back out onto the balcony and inhaled deeply on my Camel, exhaling a big plume of smoke into the night sky, allowing my fears to escape alongside. I grinned to myself. The same grin I had stuck to the old lady earlier on the plane. I wondered what to wear:

incognito pale shirt, or the Hawaiian print, aka Latino drug mule. The latter image of a freewheeling Tony Montana was soon replaced by visions of a police mugshot, holding up a placard with the scrabble letters spelling out my name, date, and incarceration centre. The dishevelled fall from grace captured in the permanence of polaroid. The inky bruised eye with a glossy sheen, my gift from the local law enforcement. I quickly washed this image away with the remaining swill from the bottom of the bottle, flicking my smouldering fag butt down into the city below. Beer number two made me opt for the tropical shirt.

Why? Because *The Wild is Calling You.*

# 3

# LA LUNA

I stepped confidently out of my lodgings, La Casa Roca, and headed along the narrow avenue of Franciso Soza. The city buzzed frenetically with cars moving busily along, their headlights casting a murky din from the kicked-about street dust. A beggar half-heartedly approached me but lacked the aptitude to halt my stride. I simply tapped my shirt pockets, shrugged an empty gesture, and walked briskly by. The end of the street opened out onto a large boulevard with a central grassy thoroughfare bordered by two lanes of traffic on either side. The central island housed tobacco stands and park benches replete with sleeping drunks, people milling around chatting in small groups. I crossed over to this central section, leaving the darker side streets where the shuttered doorways were decorated with suspicious looking characters. Ahead of me some guys on benches were playing Spanish guitar, mostly locals joined by a backpacker who was eager to impress them with his playing. Opposite them sat a moon faced indigenous-looking Mexican with his head down, pouring coffee from two giant flasks. His trade was regular and when I approached he offered me an espresso-sized plastic beaker for a pittance. I opted for the sugarless brew, which tasted citrus-sharp and alive, with a raw earthy quality. I watched the musical bench opposite. They played well, with passion and energy. I thanked Moonface, tossed my beaker into the trash next to him, and continued on down the central aisle. It was nighttime proper, the street lamps showering a yellow tinge over the darkness, the rutted pavement shining Aztec gold beneath grubbed up patches of filth. The cobbled path was bordered by palm trees that looked centuries old, their leaves a deep midnight green against the amber mist. Benches with motionless bodies wrapped in newspaper. Men stood under trees, almost out of sight. Women in fishnet stockings poked out of side streets, calling to me and others, beckoning us over, luring us into the darkness. There were Day of the Dead decorations in shop windows and giant skeletons hanging from the overhead power lines, covered in yards of silver tinsel. Black and orange paper butterflies were tied to a tree, the base of which had been decorated into a shrine of candles and flowers surrounding a photo of a smiling young boy. A car rushed past me, honking, the passengers all dressed as the dead. One of them, laughing at me, ran a slicing finger gesture beneath his throat. I flipped him the bird.

A barrel-chested local dressed in a carelessly buttoned white linen shirt came sauntering down the main strip. His open shirt revealed a bright medallion nestled amongst mounds of thick, matted chest hair. He passed by me smoking an intoxicatingly rich, chestnut brown cigarette. He was flanked on either side by beautiful women a quarter his age. They wore satin evening dresses that clung delightfully close to their bouncing, wobbling breasts. I rounded them, briefly engulfed by the waft of his cigar tobacco, my senses bombarded by a powerful incense akin to a sultan's brothel. I smelt the faint aroma of sticky, sweaty sex, recently consummated. The kind you can't help but envy.

There was something about the eerie street life mixed with the swill of Latino music that resonated with me. That slight edge of danger that keeps the mind awake, each passing lurker seemingly woven into the fabric of the city. They approached with the usual sheepish hunched gait, offering coke or weed or chicas, anything you could want it seemed. I batted them back with confident indifference as I already *had a guy*. My only problem was, I still didn't really know *who* that guy was.

As the main boulevard came to an end, I crossed over to some sandy-coloured stone fortifications demarcating the entrance to the medieval part of town. I walked through a large walled gateway leading to a pleasant neighbourhood populated by alfresco dining. The buildings were all rendered in bold pastel colours, striking marine blues contrasted against opposing reds, yellows, and greens, all interconnected like the body parts of a jungle caterpillar. The alleyways grew tighter, yet carrying an air of charm and tourist friendliness. I took a couple of wrong turns before finding Plaza Jardin Centenario, which was headed by a fountain spraying water over two dancing coyotes. From here I spotted bar La Luna down a side street, one that meandered away from the better lit tourist hot spots. The bar had a green neon sign out front and under the lettering, an illuminated moon. The door was solid oak with large brass handles. I held one of these and hesitated for just a moment, before swinging it open and wading in.

There was a scattering of people inside the bar, mostly odd-looking misfits, the type it's not polite to stare at. The room was long and thin, with the right hand side dominated by the bar top, a plastic cream coloured marble mock-up, lit brightly from beneath. The bartender was absent, leaving an unobstructed view of the mirrored wall decorated with rows of tequila bottles, all topped with melted candle wax. The wall was fringed with hand-sculptured masonry shaped into gargoyles, with wide cavernous rock openings, all painted a hellish red and daubed in fake spider webbing. The narrow footprint of the place left only enough space for three round, high tables in the middle of the room, the furthest of which was occupied by a pot-bellied man in his 50s wearing aviator sunglasses. His face was expressionless and he sat in front of a beer that looked untouched. Near to him was the jukebox, a beautiful neon relic from the jive days. Leaning over it was a skinny old man with dark brown skin, a rustic peasant's tan the colour of freshly painted garden furniture. He swayed to Long Tall Sally, loosely shaking his body around in his oversized workers' denim. I had him down as a permanently drunk Guatemalan farmer.

Toward the back of the room, the moon logo shone iridescently beneath a pair of archways leading off into separate alcoves. To the right, a tight corridor labelled "Banos". I could hear chatter drifting from there, an American, prominently voiced. I headed over to the bar, realising that it was occupied after all by a shadowy man at the far end, picking at his beer bottle label like an irritant scab.

I saddled my stool and was about to tap the bar for action when miraculously the bartender appeared from behind a hidden doorway in the mirrored wall. He approached with the stride of a man who had walked these planks many, many times before. He appeared to be saving his smile for his regular customers. He stared at me.

"Cerveza?" I asked.

Duly he turned, grabbing a glass and pouring. What he handed me back was a frothy, beastly looking pint glass where the ratio of beer to foam was skewed in his favour. I reached into my pocket for a dollar when I heard the American voice getting louder, approaching from the side corridor. He entered alone, walking his conversation from the rear into the bar. He was wearing an extra large navy blue football shirt made of a silky mesh fabric that highlighted the physique of a modern alpha male, pinching at the biceps, pecs, and gut. Free flowing but bursting with testosterone, he walked with a jock's swagger. He had a dark grizzled beard left unmanicured, creeping up his face where it almost touched the baseball cap that had been wedged down tightly over his brow, shielding his eyes and the angle of his gaze. His head was craned over his shoulder as he entered, bellowing back his words to the person he had seemingly just left.

"...well exactly man, exactly - and the chick had a bigger fucking dick than me!"

He stopped walking at this point, contemplating a return to finish off the debate, but then thought better of it, fly-swatting the air casually. "Ah fuck it, you live and learn man," he said, addressing the bar now, and keenly looking around for his new audience. "I'm doing OK, I'm doing OK aren't I, man?!" he said.

I was unsure to whom exactly this was directed, but it appeared I was the only one in true acknowledgement, therefore obliging me to accommodate. I think the shadow at the end of the bar mumbled "Gringo" into his bottle, but other than that the response was nil. Taking pity, I raised my bottle to the American.

"Exactly man!" he said, approaching, "and I'm supposed to pay the chick even when she's got a fucking Tinder surprise?" He waved a forearm between his legs. "Fucking thing, it was bigger than mine dude, and that - I do take exception to."

He sat on the stool next to mine. Instinctively I necked a good third of my beer, buying myself some response time, expecting us to be soon embroiled in manly mirth.

"Sounds pretty fucked up," I ventured.

"Ah fuck it, one of those things, don't ever go to Asia. Barman!" he said.

"Noted. Nobody likes a girl with a giant dick, that's just showing off." I said, unsure of where and why I was becoming entangled.

"Exactly," he said, slapping my back, "Beer?"

I gulped my remaining third, nodding while doing so. The barman reappeared and went about his business with the same muted regularity.

"Eric," the American said, offering me a hand.

"Jack," I said, offering him mine.

We sculled down our first beer before the barman had barely had time to retreat. So for the next round Eric told him not to disappear too far; to "keep 'em coming". I couldn't find any counterargument to this approach and soon we were waxing lyrical, slaying Modelo's by the brace. I found myself caught up in Eric's raucous tales, regaling the moment such-and-such a song was on when such-and-such was having a suck-and-fuck at a friend's house. A moment like this was developing, Eric now off his stool and gyrating against the farmer who had knowingly or not selected Sexual Healing as a backdrop. Eric

29

was telling me how he'd been fucking an ex over the bathroom basin of a friend's house when it had collapsed and fractured the water main. Whether the farmer was enjoying the story or enjoying being dry-humped, I couldn't quite tell, but he was grinning wildly and trying to waltz Eric with gay abandon.

"There's fucking water flowing fucking everywhere," Eric continued, gesturing a spraying motion with his hands all over the jukebox farmer's face and body, whilst bending him over as a dummy stand-in for demonstrative benefit. "But I don't stop. I can't, right? So I'm pounding and pounding... it's like a plumber's wet dream, man."

Suddenly, I was snapped out of Eric's story when a hand clasped my shoulder from behind. I span around to find a sullen-faced Mexican man in his late forties, positioned right in my grill, eating up my shadow.

"Senor? You called?" he said, sternly.

For a few seconds I was totally lost, I hadn't called for anybody. But then it hit me, and I remembered why I'd gone there in the first place. "Ohh yeah," I said, still smiling and glowing from the first few pints, "Angel's guy!"

He glanced briefly and awkwardly around the bar when I said this and I took the opportunity to quickly assess the features of a serious-looking

Mexican that I had seemingly just irked. He had charcoal hair and a silver handlebar moustache, with a nose as sharp as a hawk. He looked back at me, briefly across at Eric, and then said "Come," before walking off toward one of the rear archway booths. I was like a naughty school boy, giggling to myself and starting to "Shhhh" as I went over to Eric who seemingly hadn't noticed any of this, instead now telling his story directly to the bemused peasant.

"Eric... Eric..." I whispered, between adolescent giggles, "I gotta go sort something out quick. Just wait here."

"OK," he said, swaying a bit, half-listening.

"Hey, what happened to your mate?" I said.

"What mate?" he said.

"The guy. The guy you were talking to earlier, about the chick dick-" and I gestured a thumb into the same recesses where my guy had just disappeared, wondering if Eric's mate might occupy one of the booths.

"Oh him? Fuck knows – pussy. Think he left earlier."

"OK, right, look just gimme a minute," I said. I was about to add that he should grab another round of drinks when he squared himself up without asking and started heading back to the bar with purpose.

"I'll get some more in," he said.

31

I smiled and turned to leave but then he called out to me as I walked off, "Hey, get me one!"

The booth was a semicircle of worn black leather surrounding a round central table with a snow globe white moon lamp hanging in the middle. The hawk from the bar, an apparent associate of Angel's, was sitting in the booth wearing a look of general impatience. His features were mostly hidden by his vintage tash and bushy black eyebrows, but his eyes shone through the dark hairs like searchlights from a watchtower. He had high cheekbones decorated with wiry grey hairs that as kids we called 'Bugger's grips' - something for the buggerer to hold onto while rogering the buggeree from behind. Beneath the strong bone structure, his cheeks sagged downward with cracks and crevices in his skin, the way a river carves through a canyon. His crow's feet were deep chiselled lines, and in his ears stood sprigs of virgin white hair that offered the only signs of endearing humanity. This was a face that had stared down the sun and remained thereafter etched in the permanence of that moment. He was every bit a gaucho cowboy, missing only the bolo tie with blue rune stone centrepiece.

I slid into the sofa opposite him and offered my hand, "I'm Jack". He gripped my hand with the strength of ten pack horses and I felt immediately soft and emasculated.

"Carlos," he said, smiling only by squinting one eye, pinching together some of the crow's feet. Then the barman appeared next to us, as proactive as he had been all night.

"You want a beer?" Carlos asked me.

"Yeah, why not," I said, scanning the volume of my current bottle, which looked empty enough for justification. The barmen made an about-turn.

"Angel, said you wanted something?" Carlos said, straight down to business.

"Yeah, where is Angel? Where'd he get to?" I asked.

"He works late, amigo. He works... for me." He said.

Just then, I caught Carlos half-glance across to where the adjacent alcove opened out to the bar. Almost beyond my line of vision, I could see the knee of the old aviator-wearing guy who had been sitting at his table, quietly not drinking all night. He was there still, not moving. The memory of him made me strangely nervous. Carlos clicked back into action. "How many you want?"

"How many? Well... I dunno, it's the same stuff Angel had earlier?" I said.

"It's always the same. Angel works for me."

"How much are they?" I asked.

"Ten dollars for one. It's less - you buy more," he said.

Wow. I couldn't believe the price. I had heard it was cheap in Central America, but this was supermarket bin-end madness. Suddenly I wanted it all, like a crazed shopper on Black Friday deals. "Three?" I said, then immediately corrected myself, "Eh, four." Then I remembered Eric wanted one; "Let's say five. For now."

"Good, amigo," said Carlos, pleased with my buying approach. The barman arrived and Carlos gestured something and asked for some nuts. A moment later the barmen returned and dropped a tray of nuts on the table.

"So how much is five?" I asked.

"For you, friend of Angel, we say forty dollars, OK?"

He grabbed a few nuts from the bowl, revealing as he did, a small bundle of cardboard wraps nestled beneath the surface. It was either a deft sleight of hand, or the barman had planted them there, his venue being in on the action. At that moment, I felt an uneasy movement out of the corner of my eye. The aviator man adjusted his seating, just a touch, but it was as much movement as I'd seen him make all night. My heart rate spiked. *Was this a sting? I still hadn't taken the coke - I could back out now and deny all knowledge. Or maybe that moment had passed?*

Carlos eyed me suspiciously. He was a man I didn't want to disappoint, and he was letting me know this. I felt a little sweat trickle down the back of my neck.

"Yeah, fuck it," I said, plucking up the courage and reaching for my wallet.

"Hey, hey," whispered Carlos, flapping his hand under the table, a gesture that requested a touch more caution from my grabby pocket dive. He was slowing the pace, like an experienced lover taking control. He supped his beer, a slow deliberate gulp, relaxing the mood. He was dimming the lights and lubing me up. I slugged mine and replayed my first manoeuvre, slowly this time, cautiously revealing my wallet by my side and pulling out some notes under the table, then delicately passing them to Carlos. I reached into the bowl and fished out my grams, eating a handful of peanuts before tucking Carlos' white load into my back pocket. He looked pleased, the deal consummated.

"Good, amigo," he said, before leaning again to glance down the archway opening, toward the aviator man. "You and your friend should leave. The man, on the table..." he said, gesturing with a dart of his eyes.

"Yeah, I... I know the one," I stuttered, my voice rife with mounting panic.

"Policia."

"What?!" I said.

"S'OK, amigo, he's no policia, not today, no ahora… Pasado, policia. But, I don't think he like your friend."

"He's not my friend," I said.

"Doesn't matter," said Carlos.

We had reached the extent of what he was prepared to divulge, nothing left to elaborate. He just sat back and gulped his beer. It was my move now, stick or twist. *Take Eric or leave him? The guy was a liability, but I felt safety might come in numbers. Why was the aviator man an ex-cop? I bloody knew he was a cop from the moment I saw him! But why? Is he in on the deal too, the whole venue is sweet to it… You get busted as soon as you get outside? Or had Eric pushed it so far that they pick and choose who gets busted and who doesn't?!* It was too much to figure out, but I knew one thing because Carlos had said it: *it was time to leave.*

"Gracias amigo," I said to Carlos, nervously pulling myself out of the booth.

"You have my number," he said, not glancing at me.

I rounded the archway and saw Eric at the bar, he was locked in conversation with the barman, his hand on the back of the barman's neck, pulling him inward and yelling a story into his ear. The music was loud, full-frontal Latino. Aviator man's gaze fixed on Eric, his teeth gritted, his nostrils flared with the scent of American blood. I walked directly to the bar and started settling up the bill.

"Come on, we're leaving," I said to Eric. "Barman, how much do we owe?"

"What?! Come on man-" Eric began, but I shut him off.

"-Fine, you stay. But *I'm* leaving, and I advise you to do the same." I didn't want to glance back at the aviator man because the last thing I wanted was Eric catching the eye line of an ex-cop while I had a pocket full of super-strength cocaine. But I must have inadvertently looked in that direction as Eric's head turned, following my line of sight. I stopped his head turn with a serious and direct tone. "I'm leaving Eric, you should leave too. Right now."

"Fifteen bucks," the bartender said.

Eric looked at me and knew something, he just didn't know *what* he knew. When a new compadre turns suddenly serious, you know something is amiss. I gathered from Eric's persona that he had probably found himself in a few bar scrapes and grown familiar with the calling signs of trouble. "OK," he said, throwing down some money. We both turned and marched to the door without saying anything more. Sometimes when it's time to go, it's time to go.

# 4

# RAT PACK

Two hours after leaving La Luna we were sitting outside in the main plaza having wolfed down some chimichurri steaks, two bottles of punchy red, and a river of beers. The waiter was bringing over trays of tequila shots in between our regular trips to the banos to powder our noses. Surrounding our table were various diners, most dressed in funeral costumes, with the carnival atmosphere starting to get into full swing. Eric and I were bathing in the night, in a jacuzzi of sordid pleasure, our egos basking in the euphoria of high-quality cocaine. Eric had suggested we get more coke "just in case", and made me phone Carlos. There was no answer so I texted the address of our bar, my first name, and nothing more. The last thing I wanted was to explicitly reference drugs in the text, for fear of riling the man. Eric also asked me to message Carlos about getting some prostitutes. I pretended that I had but actually excluded this detail, it was not an avenue I planned on pursuing, and figured Eric might be better off discussing those things directly with Carlos.

Next to us, a mariachi band circled the tables and behind them I saw two sheepish looking guys approaching. One was tall, with a pencil tash and beady eyes. The other stubby, full in the face, with a pea-shaped head that squashed in his eyes like an overstuffed bean bag. He wasn't that fat necessarily, but try telling that to his shirt. They looked fairly young, and a bit skittish. The tall one scanned the crowd and soon spotted us. He grinned unpleasantly before heading over with predatory precision. He offered a hand as he approached, "Jake?" he asked.

"No, Jack actually. This is Eric," I said, smiling suspiciously back at him, trying to gauge the trustworthiness of the individuals seemingly sent down to act on Carlos' behalf.

As I introduced Eric, I felt a little tinge of inner delight. The prospect of how and when this encounter would turn sour for some reason delighted me. It was Eric's brash manner that suggested an inevitable clash against the cagey looking dealer. The pleasantries would soon expire, I guessed, but for now there was a little calm to enjoy, made all the better by the anticipation that things would likely spiral. I had taken an instant dislike, or at least distrust, toward the thin dealer, and projected forward to the time when we could tell him to go fuck himself. All of the coke and booze had made us impenetrable to fear, wanton of destruction, untouchable, even immortal.

"Ah I seeee, Eric, and Jack!" the thin one said, continuing the introductions. "I'm Marco - nice to meet you both… and this is Bernard," he said, pointing down at the tubby one. I didn't like the look of either of them and trusted them less, but for now, we needed them.

"Here, grab a seat," I said, pulling some around. Eric had given the helicopter finger to the waiter, so a fresh round of beers was duly prepared.

"So, motherfuckers, what's the score? You got drugs? Where's the pussy?" said Eric.

I winced with glee. It was a bold opening gambit. I also wholeheartedly agreed with his assessment of them being motherfuckers.

"Ha, ha, ha," laughed Marco unconvincingly, before offering up a toothy, snarling grin. "I come to help my amigos! My man said you needed help, you wanted something... motherfucker?"

"Sure thing," said Eric, reining in his tone, knowing there's only so far you can push a dealer before you have your hands on the product. "I'm just fucking with you man, come on, come on, sit round. You too Bernard. Now, get this, we want some coke-"

"No problem," interjected Marco, still grinning falsely.

"And..." Eric continued, pulling out some cigarettes and offering them about, "some Pussy."

Marco leaned forward and pulled a cigarette out for himself, ignoring Bernard who had to reach for his own. Marco looked up from the deck and said with deliberate calm, "No, problem. In fact, I have some, mi casa." Before once again bearing his sinister grin.

The beers arrived with Eric beaming smiles back at Marco. Hookers aren't my thing, so I left them to negotiate their price in a whispered huddle. From what I could gather, Eric didn't fancy committing to a price until he'd seen the goods, which seemed reasonable to me. We sank another round of beers and then Eric became impatient for the girls to be brought down. A phone call or two later and Marco informed us that they were not keen on coming outdoors to the main plaza and that it was best we go up to the apartment. *Shy prostitutes, who'd have known?*

"Oh wait, I love this song!" said Eric, beckoning the Mariachi band over to us. "Is this Bueno Vista?"

The band nodded. More drinks arrived, seemingly unordered, and the plaza started to spin. I broke free for a toilet break and a customary banos cubicle nose-beer. When I returned the scene lit fireworks in my eyes; Eric, Marco, and Bernard all singing along to Dos Gardenias in full voice, accompanied by the five piece mariachi band. Bernard was sitting on Eric's knee. Each man looked like he was exactly where he needed to be in life. I pulled out a smoke and watched this one from the sidelines. Some things are best spectated.

A round of applause later and we were on our feet getting ready to leave. The band helped us sweep away the final pints, with Eric looking wildly excited at the prospect of imminent whoring.

"Wait, wait, wait," Eric said, gathering himself. "The band - the band *have* to come!"

"Erm, Eric, I'm not sure that's their thing..." I said.

"Bullshit, man!" said Eric, like a child whose toy was about to be taken away. "Guys, you wanna come with us tonight?" He continued, and to be fair they looked keen, although none of them spoke. "How much do you make in a night?" And before waiting for an answer, "I'll give you 50 bucks to hang with us tonight."

They all nodded in unison and like a coin in the slot, began immediately playing a new song. Eric reached both hands to the sky praising God, his cigarette clamped in his mouth and booze sweats racing down his temples. I came over and hugged him around the waist, knocking over several chairs in the process. We all marched off across the square to the sound of our own beat.

Marco's place was just outside the old town neighbourhood of Coyoacan. A modern apartment block with grey-rippled concrete slabs dividing layers of dark windows, not a single one lit. The block looked derelict, abandoned, if not by people then at least by hope. The band wasn't impressed with our choice of venue, agreeing to stay with us but opting not to come inside. We said we would not be long and headed through a flimsy side door while the band played us out with a farewell tune. The lift was broken so we had to walk up to the fifth floor. Once there I could still hear the band tinkling away at street level and I wondered how long they would maintain. Eric had given them the fifty bucks already, yet they all looked warmed by the beer and shots, seemingly content to stay on a good thing.

As we entered Marco's apartment I felt a brief pang of realisation cut through all the stardust. We were off the golden cobbled streets laced with Latino music and spiced rum, and thrust into the neon glare of a semi-functioning whore house. The hallway was painted dark green, with grime seeping through the wallpaper in streaks and spots. The ceiling bulb was naked, flickering intermittently, crackling with surges of electrical current. We passed a crime scene of a kitchen, a room packed with old silvery-brown saucepans glued together by layers of scum. The corridor became darker the deeper we descended, occasionally blacking out completely when the ceiling bulb went off, as if unsure about its own desire to reilluminate. A bright shard of light came from the end of the corridor. A sanitised, unforgiving streak of brightness. This was the lounge, inside which there were only three points of interest: a black three piece sofa, a king-size TV showing Japanese Anime, and a round table scattered with various items of smoking paraphernalia. There were no pictures on the walls, no paintings, nothing to create the feel of a home. Instead, this was an apartment squatted in for the sole purpose of shady business.

"Here, sit," said Marco, gesturing to chairs around the table. "Beer?"

Before waiting for an answer he went back to the kitchen to fetch some, mumbling a brief conversation with Bernard. They had become engaged shopkeepers, opening up especially for our custom. I hesitated on taking a chair, wondering how long we needed to stay there. Marco went into a back room and began rounding up his staff in a frustrated manner.

"Hey! Hey Isabella, get out here!" he said, following up with some incomprehensible Spanish.

Bernard appeared from the kitchen with two beers, followed reluctantly by a pair of girls dressed in feather bowers, high heels, and black plastic, gimp-Esq onesies. I offered an awkward "good evening" as they entered, but it couldn't hide the elephant in the room - here were paying customers who had just walked up five flights of stairs with the express intention of ramming their cocks into you. I cringed as I smiled. I personally had no intention of fucking anyone there. But they didn't know that, offering weakly enthusiastic smiles back in return. Eric bounded over and greeted them like old friends, or at least like a creepy, rapey uncle might greet his niece at a family gathering. There was an immediate weirdness in the air. I took my phone out to check the time, contemplating heading back downstairs to hang out with the band until Eric was done.

"Here, here, come, sit," said Marco, beckoning me deeper into the lounge and pulling more chairs out.

It was only once seated that I noticed movement from a high-backed leather chair next to the sofa, which faced the wall. It span suddenly around on its axis as the man revealed himself to the room. He was a Mexican dressed in a skeleton tuxedo, the black fabric highlighted by the painted white bone outlines of the human body. He wore a matching black top hat, with a spring of colourful flowers in the centre held together by a voodoo skull. His face was painted black with a matching white skull outline. His eyelids were also painted black so that as he sat with his eyes closed, it created the appearance of a hollow skull. He opened his eyes to reveal their bloodshot glory, smiling with his lips sealed to accentuate a true deathly malice. The sight of him shook me, like stepping out in front of a car, then being saved by the jarring horn. The jump made my phone skip from my grip and go plummeting to the floor.

"Fuck!" I said, reaching down to pick it up, the screen now black and cracked.

"Ha, Diego you Motherfucker!" said Bernard, laughing and throwing a lighter at him.

The guy, Diego, picked up the lighter and used it to light a silver pipe, sucking heavily on the end. I cursed him internally for giving me the fright that broke my phone, but conversations resumed in the room without much notice given to my minor plight. Diego leaned back in his chair, pressing in the rear rim of his top hat, lifting it up to reveal a shaven head, painted black. Beneath the makeup, I would have guessed him being in his early twenties. He had no facial hair and spider-thin eyebrows on a head shaped like a bowling ball. I reluctantly gestured my beer in his direction. He let his hat fall back into position and sucked the pipe smoke deep into his lungs. Bernard and Marco joined me around the table. I glanced back over my shoulder in time to see Eric leaving the room with his arms around the girls.

"Hey Bernard, get some music on my man," said Marco.

"What've you got?" I said, rising out of my chair to join Bernard by the CD player. I needed to keep moving, my body pulsing from all the coke we had consumed. Staying active meant a better chance of making this stop-off as transitional as possible, not allowing the night to grind to a halt.

"I'll make a joint," Marco said, "Bernard, vamos, weed."

Bernard, seemingly lower down the pecking order, hopped out of the room to get Marco's

47

supply, leaving me to casually browse the music selection.

"What's the deal, where'd you guys meet?" I asked.

"What, Bernard?" said Marco, fiddling around for papers amongst old beer cans, "... joint?"

"Yeah, sure," I said. With all this energy flowing through my blood I was beginning to get digital, glitchy, and I needed some mellowing out. "Good idea."

"Bernard?" continued Marco, absently licking Rizlas together, "I don't know, man. I know him from about two years ago. I think he was an orphaned or some shit. He's like, half-Colombian, but raised in France or some shit like that. Yeah that's it man, lived in France. And then here. Parents dead. In France I guess. Like when he was a boy, maybe... car crash."

I got the distinct feeling Marco didn't have a fucking clue about Barnard and was just adding in whatever felt good. The guy in the armchair, Diego, eventually exhaled a vast cloud of acrid smelling smoke into the room. Doing so, he ventured a long "Heeey", before closing his eyes and disappearing back into his ghoulish nirvana.

"Hey," I replied, unsure if he could really hear me from his warped transcendental state. I cast my voice out like a fishing line, a long call into the depths of his altered dimension, like trying to converse with a spirit from another world.

"Dieeego," he said, his eyelids drooping towards closure again.

"Hi, Diego," I said, candidly, as if welcoming a new recruit into the Alcoholics Anonymous circle.

"Ha ha, fucking Diego man!" Bernard said upon reentry, tossing some weed to Marco, before throwing himself down onto the main sofa.

"Hey, Bernard - fucking music, man!" Marco said.

Bernard jumped back up and took over selection, while Marco continued to roll. Some unsettling Mexican rap music poured out of the stereo, the lyrics confined to mostly one: "gasolina". The beer was icy cold, and when the joint fired up, I finally started to relax. Bernard borrowed Diego's pipe and started losing himself amongst the cushions of the sofa. After a few pulls on Marco's joint, I started questioning again how long I fancied staying in this pop-up drug-slash-whore-house. The ambience was far from cosy, feeling more like a place where dreams come to die. My relaxed state was gradually losing ground to a mounting sense of uneasy paranoia. I necked my beer. *Beer was my only hope for survival.*

"Where's the toilet?" I asked.

"Oh down there, on the left," said Marco. "Hey man, you want more coca?"

"I dunno, we got more left…from what we bought earlier? I think we do, I think we should be OK," I said.

"Yeah you do man, but your friend has it," Marco said, raising a thumb back in the direction of Eric.

All three of the guys burst out laughing. Bernard let out a yelp of excitement and curled himself into a ball. It was becoming clear to me now why he hung around this apartment; for the very same reasons Eric and I had come: coke and clunge. I guessed the coke wouldn't last long with Eric and the two girls, so reasoned that more coke could only be a good thing. It would ensure we had the necessary drive to get out of this place before we became part of the sordid fabric.

"Ha, OK sure thing," I said, grinning sheepishly back at Marco. "Why don't you grab us a couple more? Two more."

Marco gestured at Bernard who made his way to a wall-side cabinet dresser. I turned and went down the hall looking for the bathroom. I reached the first door on the left as directed and opened it, revealing the sight of a complete and total fuck bonanza. It was a bedroom lit by a sole standing lamp fitted with a lurid red bulb. It was bright with fiery intensity, which made me recoil as if standing too close to a bonfire. It was essentially a photography dark room. A black and red inferno, which no other colours were able to penetrate. The characters inside were captured in the stillness of a pornographic negative, the photo hanging there before my eyes, slowly developing. Eric had one girl bent over a circular leopard skin bed, fucking her from behind and pulling her hair back taut so that her chin faced up to the ceiling. She had nipple clamps connected by a metal bar and her face was awash in agonising pleasure. The other girl wore a black dog collar around her neck, long forearm-length rubber gloves, and her torso was wrapped in elasticated rubber bands. She was on the floor behind Eric, bent over, with the thick base of a black dildo visibly protruding from her arsehole. Her black-gloved hands were either side of his butt cheeks, her face buried deep into his butt crack. She was struggling to match his rhythm as he thrust aggressively into the other girl. Eric was naked, apart from a pair of eye-and-nose combination snorkelling goggles, which appeared to have coke sprayed up the inside of the polarised lenses. When he noticed me mildly aghast in the doorway, he roared like a lion, then nonchalantly beckoned me to come and join in the festivities.

"Come on, man, it's cool," he said.

"No, no thanks!" I said, edging backward.

There was a carnal voice inside me crying out to get involved, but tempting as it was, the scene had advanced too far to just go wading in. *I could just watch - pull up a pew for the final act? No, no!* The Fear was telling me to keep moving. My head was rattling like a chemist and I needed some air. "I just needed a piss," I said eventually, after a few more absorbing seconds of observation.

The girl licking Eric's bum hole paused from her thankless task, pulling her face out and leaning around his butt cheek to look at me, "Next door on the left."

"Okay! Thannnk you," I said, closing the door with a crazed, half-envious look of bewilderment slapped all over my face. A helpful multitasker she turned out to be, but the whole affair was instantly playing back in my mind with a worrying resonance. I was grinning internally but also locked in a rising weed panic. I upped the pace to the toilet. Reaching the bathroom and shutting the door firmly behind me. I took a shaky piss and looked out of the window, down to the pavement far below. I couldn't see any sign of the mariachis. I splashed my face with water, making sure not to look at myself in the mirror. A few deep breaths and I would formulate an exit strategy.

I went back into the lounge, passing the door where cries of ecstasy came from tortured harpies, finding Marco and Bernard sitting with two extra grams of coke and looking keen for payment. I paid promptly and started opening one of the wraps, needing the buzz to right the wrongs in my head. I skulled a brew they had left out and offered around the gear. It did the trick, and I started to feel better. *Must maintain, stay high and everything will be dandy.*

"So, we were thinking, there's this party that Diego's going to, maybe we can join if you and your friend want to come, you know..." said Marco.

"Yeah bro, dope party," added Bernard.

"You keen?" Marco said.

"Yeah, yeah, I guess so. I mean, I'd have to check with Eric.. but yeah, count me in," I said.

I was already sharper, back on point. I liked the idea of the party, mostly because it was somewhere other than here. This was the sort of flat that swallows up the hours and spits you out in daylight. Eventually, Eric appeared from the bedroom walking the exuberant swagger of a man who's just had his rectum licked clean.

"Eric! The boys are talking about going to a party, you keen?" I asked.

"Fuck yeah!"

When we got down to street level, we found the band was still there, sitting on some nearby steps, chatting casually. I wondered if they had any idea what things took place on the fifth floor.

*Fuck it, they were probably regulars.* We asked them if they fancied the party too, and one of them pulled out a bottle of tequila while another strummed the guitar.

"Ole!"

"Let's get taxis. We all here?" Eric asked.

I did a quick head count: one Mexican coke dealer, his French sidekick, a Baron Samedi lookalike, an American sex tourist, two local whores, and a five piece mariachi band.

*Yep, we were all here.*

# 5

# THE WALTZ

Half of us piled into Marco's truck, a modern metallic-blue, open-backed Ford pickup, with white leather seats and sparkling alloy wheels. The other half of the gang split evenly into a large taxi, a girl in each vehicle and the band divided up likewise. I was in the front cabin of Marco's, wedged in between the guitarist and Eric, who was keying up lines for everybody. Bernard and one of the girls were bouncing around in the open tailback. The party was almost an hour's drive out of the city limits, enough distance to warrant a roadside stop for whiskey and cigarettes. Eric regaled us with tales from his recent sexual exploits. I tried to remind him that I had seen most of it but he insisted that was just the matinee performance. Occasionally the others would drive alongside us on the quiet midnight roads and someone would wave a beer at us, rattle a maraca, or flash a tit. Eventually, we were driving side by side in a race, the taxi driver laughing and pounding the gas while drinking from a stubby bottle. The pipe-smoking voodoo priest, Diego, dangled himself out of the passenger window, holding aloft in his hand a bright red flare. His eyes were closed, lost in a supernatural trance. Their taxi eventually sped ahead, leaving us to follow in the trail of smoke, which filled our cabin with a blood-red fog.

We pulled off the tarmac road and onto a narrow dirt track with thick palms on either side, the leaves of which slapped against the side of Marco's truck like mop heads on a drive-through car wash. Eventually, the track led us to a large wooden farmhouse, clad in slatted white timbers in the style of a Mississippi plantation manor. It was brimming with activity. There were around twenty cars and trucks parked out front, and more off into the shadows behind. Music was blaring out of the house and people were piling in and out of the surrounding forest. The *dia de los muertos* was in full swing, with everyone dressed as various ghouls and ghosts. A cluster of people were smoking on the porch, next to a guy juggling large kitchen knives. A woman wearing a Victorian dress sat on top of a car, writhing and swatting at invisible insects that seemingly plagued her. Dogs roamed freely, chasing each other's scent. We pulled the truck up to the rear of the house searching for a space. As we parked, the headlights settled on a fence post upon which where two cats were fucking. We all sat there for a moment admiring the cat fucking and cheering on our favourite.

The eleven of us corralled up outside the main steps and bowled in together, making a grand entrance, with the band playing us our own walk-in music. Marco, Bernard, and Diego led the way, the latter knew the host and was keen to get established. Inside, the house party was a manic cluster of people all writhing around to find space between the hall and living room. It was dimly lit but appeared to be a decent quality country home, certainly of higher stature than many of the characters who were filling the rooms with bong smoke. The walls were decorated with cardboard UV zombies and skeletons, the rising dead glowing iridescently on all sides of the house. Smoke blew from faces, the walls and the people becoming one; a living cemetery of feverish celebration. When people saw the mariachi band they would cheer and raise drinks and force tequila down our throats. Diego was looking strangely more sullen, peeling off upstairs with Bernard in tow. Marco also disappeared in search of the host, leaving the girls hanging with Eric and I. They looked confused, unsure if they were now tied to Eric, or free to work new clientele. The road vendors we had passed only had neat spirits for sale, so Eric shouted to me over the heads of the many in the hallway, "We need mixer!".

"Kitchen!" I shouted back, pointing up ahead.

The kitchen was a welcome respite, with more breathing space and free stuff to raid. We found some mixers and started knocking up robust rum and cokes. We drank and chatted freely and toasted drinks with the girls. For a moment, I forgot which one I had seen licking out Eric's poop shoot only a short while ago. Then I remembered, the one with the sad eyes and the smudged makeup.

"Is this a fucking party or what?!" shouted Eric, wrapping his arms around the girl with the smudged face.

"You got those cigarettes?" I asked him.

He passed some around and we all smoked and shot the bull. Eric and I did most of the talking, with the girls struggling to follow our English, but they seemed to be enjoying themselves. Pooface finished her drink first and gleefully called us "*cock sucker motherfuckers!*" for not drinking fast enough. I admired her grit and sank mine, clinking glasses with her on the finish. Another round of rums and Eric racked some lines for kickers. Drugs seemed commonplace, the people next to us were doing triple headers; a hot knife of weed over the cooker's gas hob inhaled through a sawed-off coke bottle, followed up instantly with a line of powder and then a swift shot of tequila. Each person's legs buckled by the final stage. It looked like fun and mentally I joined the queue to get involved.

"Hey! The chicos with a band!" shouted a guy entering the kitchen, striding toward us.He was slim built and wearing a silk maroon shirt, with a neat thin beard and a Panama hat. "I'm Chichi, welcome, welcome."

"Ah, it's your house?" I said, extending a hand.

"Fuck no, you think I can afford a house like this? C'mon, man! Hey - Chichi..." he continued, introducing himself around the circle.

"What's up, Chichi?" said Eric, "You like my band? I just signed them, I'm flying them back to LA, they're gonna be fucking stars!"

Eric locked an arm over Chichi's neck and pulled him into his usual combative grip. Marco appeared behind them, along with some fine looking chicas dressed in sexy funeral garbs. They were accompanied by a mountain of a man, at least 6 foot 6", with a tombstone head that was thick, flat, and carved from stone. He had a strong black beard that hid any expression. His eyebrows were gnarled and moody, like thunderclouds that twisted and knotted above his unforgiving eyes. *A man that size must eat chicken for breakfast.*

"Awoooo!" Marco wolf cried over to us, snapping me out of fearful admiration for the man-beast behind him. "There's my boys, how'd you like the party?" he said.

"Fucking sweet bro," Eric said.

"Yeah man, fucking sick," I said, peeping a half-glance again at the giant behind him; *imagine the size of his shits!*

"Good, good, OK let me introduce you around..." said Marco, trailing off when the bearded Gigantor touched a shovel-sized hand on his shoulder and started whispering in his ear.

I had started warming to Marco. Despite the fact his motive was to ply us full of gear for his own financial gain, it certainly *felt good.* Maybe it was just the afterglow from tearing through so much high-quality cocaine that it had become impossible to see anything wrong in the world. We were introduced to the giant Mexican, Anton, who was both party host and seemingly Marco's boss. I assumed if he was Marco's boss, then in turn also Carlos' boss, and by proxy, Angel's. So all the gear that I had eagerly consumed since touch down, a mere few hours before, had begun here upstream and I had now reached the source. Eric and I thanked him for the party, and I wanted to thank him for the coke but thought better of verbalising my conclusions. Even Eric was biting his tongue, thankfully. We both sensed Anton was someone not to displease.

"...And this is Felix," Marco said, continuing his introductions, pointing to a guy wearing black square-rimmed glasses who was licking two papers together. "This is Freddy, my cousin. Edwardo. This is Tutty..." he said, pointing to a girl at the kitchen entrance, who looked about as interested in us as a dog is with its own shit. "And..." he said, reaching back to find her, "Catrina! Come here, Cat!"

*Wow.* Now, this girl was drop dead gorgeous. About 5'8, with a dynamite body. She had a plump rack pressed snugly inside a tightly strung corset. She was appropriately dressed in the classic Victorian lady costume of La Calavera Catrina, and she really made it sing. Her face was painted on one side with a black skull, the other full of radiant colour. Down her arm and torso, she had a dragon tattoo that disappeared under her garment.

"Hola chicos, it's Sammy, actually. Although today, I'm Catrina!" she said, pinching her floppy hat and offering me the downturned hand of a lady, complete with silk lace gloves.

"Hi, hola, hi, I'm Jack" I fumbled, my brain sounding off alarm checks - *Who was she? Anton's girl? Or maybe a prostitute? After all, Eric said basically all attractive South American women were prostitutes... Shit, Eric, he could really fuck this up. And fuck, how long have I been holding her hand?* I twinkled her gloved hand, which made her giggle.

The man-beast Anton eyed my every movement, so I quickly dropped her hand. He mumbled some neanderthal-like words to Sammy and Marco, then turned and left, with Marco darting out after him.

"Right, who wants a drink?" Eric boomed.

A cheer went up, and soon Eric and I were mixing and pouring drinks for everybody in the kitchen. I was pleased to see Sammy had stuck around, even if her body language was a little apprehensive. I had a bad feeling she was Anton's lady but didn't know enough at that stage to stop myself from showing off and hoping she was available. The problem was, every time I got close to her, I imagined the shadow of Anton towering over me. Or I couldn't think of anything worthwhile to say, or I got drowned out by one of Eric's stories. After a few joints from Felix, the room started to spin like a waltzer, and I desperately needed some air. In my head, I was going to ask Sammy to join me, but the proportions of my approach became too complex to calculate. I felt the burning need to regroup and plan my next moves from a safe distance. I mumbled to Eric about getting some air, but he was talking American politics with Felix. Eric was jabbing his finger into Felix's chest as he made his points and each point he made seemed to confirm the counterargument Felix had initially raised. I opted to grab some air solo, glancing across desperately as a final call for Sammy, but she was talking to some other guy so I bailed before eye contact came. There was also a worrying taste in the back of my throat that seemed like vomit rising. I bolted.

Stumbling out of the back door I walked straight into a guy's beer, squeezing it up into his chest. "Hey Puta!" he said, brushing me off effortlessly. I apologised and rounded, slamming into his friend's beer. The little group then cleared a path of least resistance and I cascaded down the rear porch staircase and into the back garden. My head was doing cartwheels, lost in a circus of narcotics and alcohol. I needed to level off. Maybe sleep it off, but a voice of reason spoke to me from some distant recess of my conscience - *do you really wanna wake up in that hedge tomorrow, the party's over, Sammy's gone, your wallet's gone, your ride's gone, your bum's tender?* I gathered myself as best as possible, dry retching my way over to a hedge. The puke urge gradually subsided and instead, I decided to piss in the bush. I was losing my balance, trying to hold onto the bush to steady myself but it made the situation worse as the bush was too lightweight to act as an anchor, instead just becoming my wrestling partner. I swayed about wildly, pulling off branches and leaves with my bare hands like some kind of prehistoric gardener. Then I heard a familiar voice.

"Hey, man. Jack, right?" It was Diego, the skeleton pipe smoker from Marco's apartment. It seemed he was just lurking around in the shadows, which actually made partial sense to me, especially in my inebriated state.

"Heeey, Di-Di-Dieee.." I attempted, before becoming distinctly aware of my own level of drunkenness by my inability to formulate words, let alone sentences.

"Diego," he said, damply.

"That's it," I said, pointing a pissy finger in his general direction. "That's exactly it. How are you, brother?"

"Bueno amigo, bueno," he said, approaching me with a wry grin. "Dude, you piss everywhere."

I looked down and he was absolutely right. Fucking everywhere. Some on the bush, the floor, the side of the house, and a good portion over myself. I looked back at him and grinned inanely.

"Come on man, we go back in the house," he said.

"Sure, sure," I said, zipping up. "Hey! Yo, I just remembered, there's a girl, this girl... Cata, catar, no wait... Sammy! Mate, you gotta see her!"

"OK amigo, OK," he said.

"No I'm serious, Diego - she's perfect," I said, trying to centre him with my glossy eyes.

"Pfft, tu es muy borracho! You drunk, man!" Diego said. And I felt he had a point.

"You're right, you're right. I'm fucked. But I gotta get with this girl - Sammy!"

"Yeah, I know Sammy. She ain't the one for you, homes! Just look at you!" he said.

"I know, I know, but I just... I just I gotta level off. You gotta help me out," I said, trying to straighten my shoulders out.

"Look ese, I guess... Fuck! You want something?" he said, apparently crumbling against his better judgement to recommend anything stronger than tap water.

"What ch'u got?" I said, holding back a hiccup.

"Man, you wanna it or not?!"

"Will it do me any good? I mean, will it sort me out?" I said.

"It works for me," he said, loading something into the little silver pipe I'd seen him with back at Marco's. "Look, like this. Just hold the flame and breathe it in."

Diego was effectively telling me how to smoke a pipe, but even this I was struggling to master. So, exasperated, he held the flame there himself, and the pipe, and all I had to do was suck. I took a long hard hit. The longer I drew on the pipe, the more drawn out time seemed to become. It took instant effect, so the one draw started to feel like minutes, not seconds. When I eventually relinquished control of the pipe, it could have been the following day. Time had become a mechanical construct whose rules no longer applied to me. I felt a rising euphoria filling my mind with an ever-swirling multitude of colours. Exploding firecrackers fizzled in my frontal cortex, a hypnotic steam swelling and raising me off my feet. I felt like a travelling showman fired out of a cannon, my head the cannonball and my body trailing through the cloud of rainbow coloured confetti.

"Dammmmn Diego!" I said, "What was that?"

"It's better you don't know," he said. "But you owe me five bucks."

Back inside the party, I was walking with new legs. There was a fire burning inside of me that made me want to jump out of the window and fly head-first into the moon. I saw Eric on the dance floor so I stormed up to him, grabbed his head, and lion-roared into his face. It was the first time I saw fear in his eyes. I laughed the way lunatics laugh. I scanned the room for prey and there she was - Sammy. She was dancing with a skinny dude with an afro. The beast in me howled and I moved like a mad panther across the dance floor, scraping people off me with windscreen-wiper arms and flailing them to the floor. I could hear faint cries of disapproval, but they were behind me, in the past, and I existed only in the moment. Shock and awe were working, no one dared stop me. I hit the dance floor hard, bouncing up and into Sammy's space, just me and her now. I must have slammed afro-boy off his feet as I saw Sammy smile and lean around me to check he was OK. She showed great kindness, which confirmed in my mind that she was *The One*. I didn't check the kid, instead working through each move in my disco repertoire. I was shaking spade hands at the floor, kicking heels above heads. Crazed dancing, pirate dancing, hula, cossack, Bavarian lederhosen table topper. The full ensemble. Sammy seemed impressed and frightened in equal portions. She whispered something in my ear. It was something containing the word coca. I didn't hesitate a beat, pulling out my wrap and tapping a bundle onto the back of my hand. She laughed, shaking her head.

"No, no! Tu, too much cocaina!" she said.

She was implying one of us had done too much coke. *She didn't know the half of it.* I was confused. I didn't like her preachy attitude and if I stopped long enough to truly evaluate my position in the world then the whole system would fail. I didn't speak, flaring my nostrils I flashed her a wicked smile. I tried communicating again by pushing the coke-piled hand in her direction. She took the bait, plunging her face down into my hand-mound of dazzling arctic white powder. She came back up looking five years younger. I finished off what was left, licking the remnants up with long, flaccid tongue strokes. We danced now, closer, not a gnat's wing between us. She whispered weird little things in my ear. I nuzzled her ears. She vibrated. Her skin trembled like a bongo. Jazz heels zipped across my ear lobes as someone used my spine like a xylophone. Then time spliced and we were in the kitchen talking through a barrel of smoke. On the porch, kissing. In the hallway, talking excitedly with strangers. With Diego in the bathroom, smoking his pipe. Then on the dance floor again. A blue pill sat on a red tongue. The tongue came out of a skull, the pill sitting proudly on the moist surface. *Was it her tongue, so fleshy and raw?* The tongue and I became one. A jade coloured mist rose around my ears. Chinese New Year dragons leapt up my back and swooped in front of my face. The last thing I remembered was the dragon's shimmering emerald skin and the intoxicating aroma of wild eastern spice as I plummeted into a cauldron of never-ending ecstasy.

# 6

# WAKING THE DEAD

What I woke up to the next morning was an apocalyptic fuck festival. I was in a white room with broken slatted blinds letting in various prisms of dawn light to illuminate each new disaster. The floor was awash with beer bottles and cans, wine bottles filled with fag butts, ash, litter, and detritus of every kind covering every surface. I was in bed with Sammy. I glanced across at her and knew there was a problem. An icy chill ran over my heart. My organs seized. My blood froze. She lay motionless. Photograph still. She was dead, and I knew it, although it would be a few more moments before I *really* knew it.

*She couldn't be?!*

Became; *she could.*

Became; *she was.*

Dead.

Her body was still and silent. Her eyes were open, empty. The colour was gone from her body, which lay as motionless as a marble statue. Her beauty had transformed into something muted and mournful, like a winter's lake shrouded by a murky fog. My world was tearing apart, but all in the background. The time to truly comprehend would come later, but for now, Her time was gone. Something in the recess of my mind told me I was naked. An odd thought, and for a moment I felt her as naked too, our bodies being one. I looked down at the bed sheet and it covered us both. I looked back at her face and its stillness dove again beyond the level of my reasoning. I noticed blood had bubbled up in her nostrils, little volcanic craters, dried and crusted. Her neck was stained purple where the skin was stretched and twisted. Her makeup remained from the night before, the cheek facing me decorated with colourful flowers, leaving me grateful not to be facing the side painted with a skull. I reached over to her mouth, vainly hoping to feel some breath. As my hand touched her lips, her chin sagged open and collapsed to one side as if I had just welted her with a hammer. The bone was completely fragmented, her gaping mouth screamed silently at me from the underworld. I leapt out of bed, taking half the bed sheet with me and knocking over a bottle. I had uncovered more of her naked stillness now, and a life-altering howl came surging through my soul.

On the far side of the bed, a body rose from the floor. It was Diego. *What the fuck was he doing here?!* His face, painted like death, staring back at me. I started shouting internally at him to reveal himself, to reveal his true self. We looked at each other, and then down at the dead girl. *Sammy, she was still Sammy.*

Diego slowly rose, saying only "Fuuuck". He then absently started gathering up his clothes from the floor. I just stood there, naked and bewildered. My hands came up behind my head, raking through my hair. Then a noise, a little way off from the house. The sound of a car approaching up the driveway, tyres screeching to a halt and doors thudding. Diego went to the window and looked out.

"FUCK!" he said.

"What?!" I mustered, surprised at the sound of my own voice.

"Policia!"

The moment was becoming a series of worsening slides for which I had no control, a carousel of catastrophe. I had no idea why the police were there, but surely Sammy's dead body was the reason. And if not initially, then it would pretty quickly *become* the reason. I was strangely pleased to hear their arrival. They could help put this whole disaster into some kind of perspective. Diego was rapidly dressing, pulling his skeleton-print tuxedo back on with an alarming lack of self-awareness.

"What are you doing?" I asked. He didn't reply. "Hey!" I whisper-shouted at him.

"I'm leaving," he said, matter-of-factly, half under his breath.

I took a while to process this, instead looking back at Sammy and wondering why, wondering *how?* It was only as he passed my end of the bed, heading for the door, that the reality of the words sank in. I grabbed his suit jacket as he passed me.

"Hey! What the fuck?!" I said.

"Fuck you!" he said, struggling. "You wanna fucking stay?! You wanna fucking stay - you stay! Fucking gringo puta!"

"You can't go!" I said. "Listen, man, I know. I know this is fucked. This is *really* fucked. But we gotta stay. We gotta speak to the police and figure this out. We... we... fuck!" I was running out of calming words. Everything was so fucked I couldn't think of words to convey the levels of unfucking required. All I knew was that he had to stay. I needed him to stay. I couldn't work this out alone. He had to stay; that was the only thing in that room that made any sense.

"You fuck her, man?" he asked.

"Wha-a-t??" I stammered.

"Did you Fuck her?" he repeated.

I gripped his jacket tighter now, my confusion rapidly turning to rage. He tried to squirm free, but my grip was unrelenting.

"'Cos if you did, the cops will find it, man. So? Did you fuck her?" he said again.

The question bore a hole into my head. There was a wrapping of nightsticks on the front door. *Did you fuck her?* He may have said it again, or was it just swirling around in my mind? *Did I fuck her?* I honestly couldn't say at that point, but if I had to hazard a guess, *Yes.* My grip on Diego's jacket lessened as the horror show entered the final act.

"Someone fucked her, maybe me, maybe you," he said, brushing my now flaccid arm off his shirt. He went over to the bed and pulled back the bed sheet fully, revealing her naked legs crossed over each other. He grabbed an ankle and tossed it to one side, the way a butcher handles a loin of pork. "Look, you see that," he said, pointing to her lifeless vagina, "that's cum, man."

The window on the front door smashed downstairs, followed by rampant shouting.

"You fucked her," he said. "Fucking gringo," and he started making his way passed me once more. Again I grabbed him, not as fiercely this time, but there was still no way I was letting him walk out of there.

"What?! Fucking Puta! You fuck her?!"

"Stop saying that!" I said.

"You fuck her and you use a condom? No?! Maybe that's your cum?!" he said.

I scanned the room for condoms and saw one on the floor, it looked used but too translucent to contain any semen. I rummaged through my fractured mind for accurate memories but it was still painful to think and the whole scene was making me want to vomit. Then an image of me and Sammy came into my mind, of us locked in a lover's embrace, my hand clawing down the dragon tattoo on her back. I vomited instantly. My stomach and my heart were being vacuum-sucked through the shell of my body. When I came round, Diego was at the bedroom door with his hand resting on the handle. I raised an arm in a plea to make him stop.

"Fucking puta," he said. "You think I'm gonna hang around here so the cops can find me - next to a dead girl - cum all over her? Full of drugs? Fucking gringo!"

I heard rummaging downstairs as the police began turning people and place upside down. Diego prised the door open and looked across the landing and down the staircase to the ground floor. Then without glancing back, he simply slipped out and pulled the door closed behind him with a gentle click. It was just me and Sammy left. I was in the corner, my hands on my knees, staring into a pit of utter despair. On the bed, a beautiful young woman cut down in the prime of her life. There was no running for me. Time to face the music. I must answer for whatever part in this I had. But just as quickly as that decision was made, a new image flooded my mind: one of me in a Mexican jail for all my remaining years, Diego having never been caught. The whole thing hung solely on my head. Me gibbering in court. Tales of a second man, a local drug user. Diego, long gone. Dust. The judge, hammering the gable. Families in hysteria. Diego sunbathing and drinking cocktails. Me being gang-raped by Mexican bull queers. *Was that the right ending? Was it justice?* Maybe it was. Probably, it was. But the Diego question would haunt me forever - what if he was the murderer, and you just let him slip away? That was an extra sentence I just didn't know if I could handle. But any which way I framed it, Diego was right, that if I stayed here, I was finished.

*"Diego."* Just saying his name aloud led me to start following in his footsteps. My motions turned automatic. I was a spooked getaway driver, his hand instinctively going for the gear stick, the key slotting into the ignition. Slow movements designed not to attract attention. I slipped on clothes; jeans, shirt, boots. My eyes were on Sammy the whole time, hoping she would somehow make a last minute miraculous recovery. It seemed unlikely. Something in my head - a raging level of cowardliness that I was previously unaware I possessed - took control of the situation. *Get out now, put this whole scene into perspective once it's in your rear view and you're doing 100 mph in the opposite direction.*

A moment later I was at the door. I opened it and glanced down the stairs. The sound of police movements echoed up, but without a uniform in sight. I took one final glance at Sammy but I couldn't hold her stare, all I could look at was the cave-like opening of her saggy broken jaw. I reached over and pulled the bed sheet back over her body and head, then scuttled wearily out of the room, across the hall landing, and through the opposite door. I was in another bedroom, one equally filled with party filth. Revellers lying strewn across furniture and people asleep in bed. I tiptoed around the various bodies, heading for the bathroom en suite which was open on the opposite side of the room. The bathroom had an open window, carrying all the hallmarks of Diego's escape route. I moved slowly at first until the sound of footsteps hurrying up the staircase became alarmingly audible. I dashed for the bathroom in a late panic, knocking over a side table. I felt eyes watching me. I looked over and saw one of the mariachi band members lying half-upright against the side of the bed. Two other members were in the bed, dead to the world. But this one was awake, it seemed. But just how awake, I really couldn't tell. His eyes were open and yet strangely vacant. His face had no facial expression, yet I felt his eyes panning the room with my movement. I tried to ignore him, reaching the bathroom and shutting the door behind me. I started to cross toward the window, but the basin mirror caught me. More eyes watching me, my own this time. I couldn't hold their gaze. I would decompress later, not now. I did, however, catch enough of a glimpse in that mirror to know my person had changed forever. That look on my face would be the reflection of murderous guilt that was mine now and for eternity. I would be haunted by my own image. I knew it then, as clearly as I know it now.

When I reached the window my movements were sluggish with remorse. Taking the next steps would resign me to the life of a wanted criminal. And wanted for murder, no less. These thoughts rooted me to the spot. The image of Diego's face, laughing psychotically through a whirl of pipe smoke, restored my momentum. A fire burned in me. Whatever happened, I wasn't going to let him get away from me. From Her. From the whole horrific mess. We would face justice together. I grabbed the window frame and forced it up to allow more space. Peering out, I could see directly beneath was the corrugated tin roof of a log store. It would make a loud bang if I hurled myself onto it so instead, I set about climbing out one leg at a time.

A noise - bang! A door being flung violently open. Cops yelling. They had entered the bedroom of the mariachi band. They must have instinctively turned right at the top of the stairs, *or maybe seen my daring escape?* There was the sound of shouting, people being commanded awake. After this, they would check the next room - Sammy's room. They couldn't have checked it yet, the voices weren't of a worrying enough pitch. These cops shouted more like parents clearing out unwelcome adolescents. I panicked when I thought how close the cops were, cursing myself for not locking the bathroom door. I dropped out of the window onto the metal roof below.

Bang! It made a terrible noise, worse than I had imagined. I prayed it was lost amongst the sounds of the police raid. I didn't hang around to find out, sliding off the roof into the dirt below.

Parked near the log store was Marco's blue Ford. I scrambled over to it, using the rear trunk as temporary cover. I paused, hunched by a wheel, hugging it like a life raft. I cautiously glanced around the rear of the truck up to the bathroom window. I saw no movement. This was not a time to linger. I scanned the trees at the end of the garden, looking to see which way Diego had run.

Then, in the front seat, a body moved; Diego. He had been fiddling with wires under the steering wheel, priming for a hot wire escape. I was about to creep down the side of the truck and join him via the passenger side, when another police car careened up the driveway and skidded to a halt outside the house. I was exposed now, so retreated back to the rear of the truck. I watched Diego over his shoulder. This would be a foolish time to fire up the truck, to make his presence known. Better to let them get inside the house first, then make your getaway. I scanned the bathroom window again. No sound, no movements. One of the newly arrived policemen entered the front door of the house, while the other remained in the car, rabbiting into the radio. Diego stayed out of sight, skulking beneath the dashboard. My best chance of remaining concealed was to avoid the truck's door, choosing instead to climb into the open tail of the boot. I found an old crumpled canvas tarpaulin in the back, which I pulled up over my body. My weight rocked the truck, alerting Diego to my presence. He sat up slightly to eye me through the rear cabin glass. We exchanged fierce looks and he mouthed "motherfucker" at me. Then the front door of the house burst open, spewing out the bodies of an arresting mass. Three of the policemen surged out of the door with a man in handcuffs. A big man. Anton, the giant bearded Mexican I had met the night before. The spare officer finished his radio call and dashed out of the squad car to assist his colleagues in wrangling the behemoth into the back seat. The officers then became locked in a heated discussion around the car. Their body language was overtly fraught and anxious. *They've found Sammy*. The alarm on their faces suggested as much. Anton for his part too, looked deeply ashen.

The policemen filed quickly back up the steps to return inside. Before they had all fully entered the house though, Marco's truck ignited. Diego had chosen to wait no longer. He was partially upright in the driver's seat with both hands engaged in the starter wires. The engine roared and the wheels spun to life, instantly firing up a cloud of dirt. As we burst forward I foolishly forgot to stay hidden, propped up on all fours like a dog, mesmerised by the action. As we zipped past the police car I made eye contact with Anton. His face swelled with rage, an allergic reaction to our cowardly escape. The noose we had just tied around his neck was being silently transmuted into a pact for bloodthirsty vengeance. Our eyes didn't lie. He knew without question that we were responsible for his downfall. He signed our death sentence then and there. The cops were yelling and pounding back down the steps, waving frantically for us to stop. Diego floored the gas, swallowing up their cries in a cloud of blinding dust.

# 7
# GETAWAY

Our cobalt blue Ford pickup hammered away from the crime scene. Diego was in the front seat, his body slumped forward onto the steering wheel, using it to prop himself up as he swerved erratically. The shifting of his body weight dictated the angle of our travel. The driving was fast, ugly, and desperate, like a stroke patient taking themselves to hospital. Drooling and determined, Diego's body was locked in a kind of traumatic seizure. I lay shell-shocked in the open back of the truck, half wrapped in an oily tarpaulin, my mind awash with terrifying visions.

*The Bedroom. Sammy's Face. Rigor Mortis.* I was sliding around, trying to hold myself down in a stable position, but the truck was moving too wildly. My head was propped up against the cabin, rattling on the metal, shaken into a stunned daze. I stared forlornly back into the sea of dust we kicked up. Only the rumbling of tires against soil kept me conscious. The dirt cloud was a shameful fog helping obscure our escape. I kept expecting this whirlwind of sand and filth to be punctuated by some pursuing police lamps. Red and blue flashing orbs, the beacons of law and order. But they never came. There was no pursuit. No goal existed beyond our own desperate escape from the reality of what we had just left behind. The road ahead was empty and eternal. It was a search for our freedom and the redemption of our damned souls.

We pounded over a cavernous pothole that projected me into the air. I landed back down with a thud, audible enough to grab Diego's attention. The madness in his eyes told me his mind had forgotten me, filled instead with an unsurpassable mania. Seeing me again, he cursed and ploughed the truck onward with renewed aggression. We rode more bumps. Again I was flung, as per his intention, no doubt wanting to shed his anchoring cargo.

Images of the night before replayed in my mind, the preamble of hedonistic snapshots before the whole world turned black. I remembered us driving up the same track at night. The dark palm leaves lapping the side of the truck, my mind an intoxicated jumble of ecstasy, anticipation, and mystery. I tried to recall the length of the track, whether there were contributory roads that could now become escape routes or dead ends. Rational thoughts were quickly stamped out by visions of the night preceding. The endless coke-fuelled debauchery, my midnight face laughing wildly into the night air. Back then I was in the driving seat of my own demise, gleefully slapping my hand on the dashboard, shouting for the ride to go faster. *If only I knew then where the ride would take me.*

Another hump in the road. I screamed something into the sky, a desperate cry for mercy chewed up by the dirt cloud. When we reached the end of the track, I realised I had become a mumbling, gibbering, hysterical wreck. I tapped a knuckle on the rear cabin window. Diego turned and shouted through the glass.

"Fucking stay down, Puta!"

I considered throwing myself out of the back, rolling into a bush, and letting the wildlife consume me and all my guilt. Eat me whole, leaving nothing, not a trace. I noticed we were stationary, at a T-junction. Diego scanned left and right, unsure which way to go. I considered leaping out and joining him in the front, but something told me the wheels would start moving the moment I stepped off the back of the truck. He would have simply ditched me there, leaving me to crawl into the wild and die. So instead, I just numbly waited for our next move. He eventually chose left and roared the truck onward. The tyres made a piercing screech when leaving the dirt and grabbing hold of the raw tarmac road. I wiped some drool from my lips and tried to compose my thoughts.

"Diego!" I yelled at the rear cabin window, "We gotta... we gotta go back!"

He didn't flinch, but shouted for me to "Fucking stay down!"

An ominous black speck appeared on the road ahead, an approaching car on the otherwise deserted dawn road.

I yelled again: "WE GOTTA GO BACK, MAN!"

"Fucking Puta!" he shouted back. He turned to see me again. Each sighting made him more exasperated, and forced him to reiterate his mantra: "Stay-The-Fuck-Down!"

I resigned myself to our fate, slumping back down into the trunk and allowing the helpless words I had uttered to echo through the hollows of my mind. I knew he wouldn't go back. I also knew I didn't want to go back. We were where we were, and the rest was history. I felt a burning acid taste rise in the back of my throat. I took another glance at the road ahead. The car in the distance ebbed ever closer. I had become a bystander, a mute witness watching his escape from beyond the body. A eunuch in a whore house. I slunk down to escape the view of the upcoming car, my body crumpling into a heap like a stag sucking in the rifle round. I clawed at the canvas sheet and pulled it over my face until eventually all I saw was muffled darkness. The ribbed metal surface of the truck was reassuringly cold and steely. I dreamt of being a corpse in the mortuary, Sammy's next destination, lying by her side. A blind peace took over.I simply lay breathing, next to her, wondering how long I could stay tethered to her existence.

Diego pulled the truck off the road, driving somewhere quiet and secluded. The engine cut off. I didn't move, locked into my newly anaesthetised state. Diego banged on the side of the truck to rouse me. I slowly peeled back the fabric, climbing out of a nightmarish womb of our own design, terrified of the New World we had created.

"Where are we?" I asked.

He didn't answer, opting instead to pace the length of the truck, smoking, scanning the floor for answers. We were in a clearing, surrounded by thick trees, far away from any watchful eyes. The dry forest hissed with deafening activity, insects driven wild by the feverish and unrelenting mid-morning sun.

"Diego," I tried again, croaking under the dryness of my throat. "Where are we?"

"I don't know. I think I saw a sign for Tepoztlan, you know it?"

"No! I arrived here yesterday. From England. Fucking yesterday!"

"Well, it's south of the city. Mexico City," he added sarcastically.

"Thanks. And the cops - will they be looking for us now? I mean, looking for us here?!"

"What ch'u think, man?!" he said.

I climbed out of the truck. "What the fuck happened last night?!" I said.

"I don't know, man. I don't fucking know. It's, it's…" he was desperately rubbing his temples trying to prise the answer from them. "Look, it's fucked, OK? That's it. It's fucked but that's it. We can't do nuttin' about it."

"That's it?! It's fucked and 'that's it'? Come on, Diego... Jesus. We gotta hand ourselves in. Right? We *should* hand ourselves in..." I said.

"You really wanna do that?" he said.

"Well… Maybe it's not about what we want anymore," I said again, rummaging through my conscience. *"What I want... What I want...* I mean, no, that's not what *I* want. I'm just saying..."

He raised his outstretched arms, concluding my thoughts. "Well, there ch'u go then, there ch'u go. You said it, Jack. You don't wanna go back, and neither do I."

"Look, I may not want to go back, to go... to jail. But we gotta do something." I said.

"Do what?! You go back, you go to jail. That's it." He said, brushing his hands together.

"So maybe we don't go back. But at least phone them, and explain...." I said, losing belief in my words as they formulated.

"Explain what?! Explain that we did drugs with that girl all night? That we fucked her?"

"What? No."

"Hey, hold up, you got a phone?" he said.

"No. You broke it last night. I mean, I broke it, when I saw you..."

"Let me see," he said.

"The screen's all fucked," I said, passing him my phone. He glanced briefly at it before launching it into the wilderness. "What the fuck?"

"They can track phones, you dumb shit," he said.

"But...what about you? Have you got a phone?" I asked.

"Nope. I had one, but not right now, I lost it," he said.

"So we can't phone them now anyway," I said, ruminating aloud our options. "Unless we found a payphone…"

"What the fuck you think you gonna say to them, Jack?! *'Oh hi, yes, this is the two guys who fucked that dead girl from the party. We didn't mean to do it. We are real sorry she's dead. If you need anything just give us a call back, OK?!'* "

"We didn't kill her! We can't have!" I said.

"Oh, we can't? Well, what then? She didn't look too alive to me, homes." He said.

"...But, what if we didn't kill her? I mean, what if it was just the drugs? Maybe she overdosed. It happens all the time. People overdose, and...." I said, but the words appeared to be falling on deaf ears. I tried to reiterate my point. "...It can happen."

"It don't matter if it *can* happen, dog, it matters if it *did* happen? And anyways, her fucking jaw... you saw it ese, it was hanging open," he said.

"People gurn," I said, "You know what I mean by gurn...? You can dislocate a jaw from gurning. A mate of mine-"

"Fuck your mate! You know that wasn't no drug thing! She had it broken, man, snapped."

I knew he was right. Logically, his arguments made more sense and carried more weight than mine. I was just too afraid to admit the reality. It was too horrendous to compute.

"Shit! Look, you wanna go back and explain yourself, you go back" he said, laughing ironically. "It's that way."

"Well... we'll let Justice decide our fate," I continued, in an unconvincing vein.

"Justice?! This is Mexico, dog! Ain't no justice here."

"C'mon, Diego, we have to try. We go back and say *'sorry we ran - we freaked out. But we are back now and can explain. That yes, some shit happened. Yes, we did a bunch of drugs. But that's it. That's all it is. Just a party that went a little crazy. We just met this girl, we had fun, and when we woke up – tragically - she was gone.'* " Diego was eyeing me suspiciously now, not ready to talk. I wondered if he needed clarity on my wording. "*Dead* - I mean we woke up and she was dead. We found her dead, but had nothing to do with it."

"Just like that?" he said.

"Yeah."

"How do you know 'just like that'? How do you *know* you didn't do nuttin'?" he said.

"Like what?!"

"Like strangle the bitch. Donkey punch her in the face or some shit. You were fucking high. Fucking High!" he said.

"We were both fucking high, Diego. Yes, we were both fucking high. But when I get fucking high, I don't tend to donkey punch girls to death! Fucking high... yeah, fucked, fucked up." I was saying the words but they seemed weightless, disconnected from me. They just weren't powerful enough to explain the outcome.

"Damn right we were," Diego said, mournfully, yet strangely void of a deeper level of sincerity.

"Hey, hey - are you taking this seriously?" I asked.

"Hell yeah, I'm taking this seriously! Hijo de puta!" he said, turning away from me and taking out a cigarette. He lit one with his back to me, staring into the forest.

"Her blood is on our hands, Diego," I said. He made a teeth-sucking noise. "Now, I may not remember a lot-"

Diego sucked his teeth again, and squeezed the next words out through them, "Shit, me neither."

"OK, well let's start with what you do remember. What do YOU remember, Diego?" I asked.

"Nuttin'," he said over his shoulder, bolshy, still looking away.

"OK, I'll start. I remember... I remember you giving us a lot of drugs. Coke, obviously. And... and I did a pill, I think. Yeah, yeah I remember a pill. A red one...or maybe a blue one? I guess it could be two... And your pipe. We hit that silver pipe of yours a couple of times. A *few times*, I think... What was in that thing, anyway? What was in the pipe?" I asked.

"Gringo, you don't wanna know."

"Oh, I do. I do wanna know when there's a girl-"

"It's PCP, man. Fuck." he said.

"PCP?"

"Yeah homes - Angel Dust. Makes you do freaky shit, no?" he said.

"Like kill girls?"

"Not me."

"What are you implying? Like me? Like I killed her?" I said, my obstinate confusion boiling over into anger.

"What the fuck, man," he said. "All I know is, I done it plenty before and no one wakes up dead."

A soft breeze rustled through the trees. I reached for my throat which was cinder dry. I knew we didn't have all the answers between us, not yet. Maybe they would come, but the more we delved into the night before, the less I liked what we found. I went round to the front cabin, desperately looking for water. Finding none, I checked the trunk. There was some filthy, half-brown water in a little bottle tucked behind a spare tyre, probably designed for emergency radiator top-ups. It didn't matter, my throat was too dry to care and I took a deep swig. Finally, I could swallow again. With my thirst slaked, my mind a smidge clearer, all I could think was: *PCP - What The Actual Fuck?!*

"Hey, gimme some of that," Diego said, coming over to me.

"You got a cigarette?" I asked. He offered me one, but when I reached for it I realised my body was shaking like a shitting dog. "Forget it," I said.

"Ch'u OK?" Diego asked, leaning in to see my face.

"What are we gonna do?" I said, slumping back against the truck.

"We gotta separate, dog," he said.

"What?? No, I don't wanna do that," I said.

"We gots to, man! They gonna be looking for a gringo and Mexican, how long before we stand out?"

"The police?"

"Yeah the po-lice, the fucking po-po, who'd you think?!" he said.

"But how will they know, I mean how-"

"How many people saw us, dog?" he said. Diego was saying all the things that had been circulating around my mind but had yet to form themselves into the cold hard reality of words.

"I guess a lot." I conceded.

"Exactly. Marco and Bernard, for a start," he said.

"Were they there? I mean, in the morning. Still there?" I said.

"Fuck knows. Doesn't matter, does it? They saw us the night before, saw us with her. Then there's the mariachi band..." he continued.

"Marco wouldn't talk," I said, tracing back over our candidates. "He's a coke dealer, he wouldn't talk 'cos then they'd wanna know who was giving everyone the coke." I was ashamed by my hollow self-serving, eliminating witnesses for the sake of self-preservation. But if we were going to run, and that was still a big *IF,* in my mind, I had to know what the stakes were. Knowing who might talk to the cops directly determined our chances of survival.

"Shit," Diego said. "A couple years for dealing - better than life for murder! Marco would talk, believe homes, Marco would talk. And why wouldn't he, he'd give up a gringo he ain't got no ties to, in a heartbeat."

"What about you?" I asked, "Would he give you up?"

"Hell yeah, why not? He don't owe loyalty to me. This ain't the mafia, dog. You wanna survive, you rat," he said.

He had a point. And Bernard, I knew nothing about him that suggested any loyalty, and why should it? Fuck, we'd met any number of people the night before - Felix, Edwardo, the pros. The mariachi guy I had seen eyeing me directly, that morning. *Fuck.* He had stared right at me, *I think.* For now, I concluded, he was too real a witness to mention, *I would have to keep him secret. Then again, Diego had escaped through the same room, so maybe they had seen each other too…? And then of course, there was…*

"Anton," I said, the words involuntarily leaping out.

"Anton?" Diego said.

"The host, Anton. I don't know what, he was being arrested as we left. He didn't look happy," I said. The image of Anton's face in the back of the police car was not pleasant to recall.

"Host? Anton ain't no host, man. Not his house anyway. His party, maybe. Not his house. It ain't no one's house. No one we know, anyhow."

"Someone broke in?" I said.

"Yeah, ch'u break the door, you got yourself a party. Cops always show up sooner or later.If not, people start living there and shit," he said.

"So that's why the cops came - to break up the party?" I said.

"I dunno homes, I guess so."

I hated the thought of Sammy's body lying in the bed of a strange house, lying in someone's bed that was never intended for her. I felt sorry for whoever's house it was. I felt sorry for Sammy. I couldn't understand why any of us were there. What use was this doomed fate?I was sinking off the truck onto the floor, curling up into the shape of a human turd.

"Look man, we gotta separate," Diego continued, leaning forward on his knees to try and get into my eye line. I was staring into the ground, allowing my eyes to follow the movements of any insect that passed. The ants and the beetles were just like us, insignificant little details in a vast merciless landscape.

"Let me come with you," I whispered.

"We can't!" Diego said. "You gotta think straight, Jack. We can't be riding around in this big stolen truck like the Dukes of fucking Hazard!"

"It's stolen? But it's Marco's..." I said absently.

"Well, it's stolen now, if not before."

"But he wouldn't report it stolen... would he?" I said.

"Normally? No. He could track it down himself, keep it quiet. But with cops standing there, asking questions... *'who that guy Diego? Who that Gringo? Where's your fucking truck?'* Yeah man, he's gonna have to help them. If he don't tell them that we stole it, it means he gave it to us, and then he's an accomplice. You get it?"

"I guess it doesn't matter either way," I said, my mind slowly filtering out the unnecessary elements. Adrenaline was coming and going, as was a record-breaking hangover. "I gotta come with you man!" I pleaded.

"How bro?!" he said.

"I'll go in the back like before, under the tarp."

"And what if the police check there?" he said, adding for dramatic effect: *'Oh hello sir, yes sure we'd like to let you leave, but also, we were wondering why you have a fucking gringo lying in the back of your truck?' "*

"They won't see me, Diego." I was getting desperate, I really didn't fancy being left there alone.

" *'Oh, you wouldn't perhaps be the Mexican and the gringo who just left a murder scene would you?' "*

"They won't fucking see me!" I shouted, picking myself up off the dirt and climbing into the back of the truck.

"Fuck you, gringo," Diego said. "I ain't going nowhere with you in the back."

"We're in this together," I said.

"Fuck you."

"Oh yeah, fuck me? Fuck me? How long do you think I'll last out there in the fucking jungle, you prick? I don't speak Spanish. I don't have any water. What, you think I'll just walk out through those trees and make my way home?" I said.

"Whatever man."

"I don't think so. I'd be dead in a day. It wouldn't make any sense. I'd be better off walking back up to the highway, flagging down the nearest cop, and handing myself in," I said.

"Then fucking do it, puta madre! Get the fuck out my life!"

"Fine. And when the police question me, I'll just go all doll-eyed on them. *'Sir, I was Drugged! Yes, drugged by this fucking Mexican crack smoker and he got me so high I couldn't fucking move, force feeding me PCP... And I had to watch - watch him... kill that poor girl!'*"

Diego had started moving toward me before I had even gotten close to finishing the sentence. I had overstepped the boundary and knew it. He leapt up onto the rear of the truck and dived at me, grabbing my throat and throttling me in an attempt to stop the final words from coming out. He was stronger than I had given him credit for, shorter than me, but I realised now that his forearms were powerful and his grip on my neck was clamped so tightly that I didn't even bother to try and break free. It would have been a futile exercise. Hell, maybe I wanted it there. It would certainly have been a quick solution. His eyes were ablaze with a furious blood lust. His teeth locked down hard, breathing between them and blowing out webs of spittle. I stared him down, feeling his nails pierce the skin of my jugular.

"Go on. Do it." I goaded, hoping for an easy way out.

He held on for a brief second longer, before letting go as suddenly as he had started. I dropped backward, breathing in huge gulps of air. Diego stood over me, the anger boiling in his eyes.

"Youu say that shit again, Jack, and I kill you. You got that?!"

"We're in this together," I said again. "I don't like it any more than you do. But we are in this thing together. Think about it man, if the cops find me, I'll crumble. Your best chance for survival is taking me with you…"

"Or leaving you here," he said, ominously.

"That's the choice you're gonna have to make, Diego. How much blood do you want on your hands?"

"Fuck!" he said, stepping off the back of the truck and pacing his thoughts back and forth. "OK, look… for just now, OK, but not for long ese. Once we get somewhere better than here, anywhere, we split. That's it."

"Fine," I said. "Get me somewhere good, and we split. So… which way do we go?"

"The border," he said.

"What border?"

"America, dog. America."

# 8

# COFFEE & DOUGHNUTS

We drove all morning with me lying in the back, a shocked slab of meat. Behind us lay an orgy of depravity, the motive, and accountability of which, still a veritable mystery. I had plenty of time to formulate theories about Diego, questioning his mental state, his level of criminality, and the limited shock he displayed when discovering a corpse. Then again, I was caught not knowing anything about the rules of life in Mexico. My introduction to this world was one full of drugs, hookers, and dealers. In this skewed light, how extreme *was* a dead girl? For someone like Diego with a seemingly sketchy background, he could have been exposed to gruesome scenes of that nature many times before. Perhaps that explained his numbness. Was it just my own inexperience in these affairs that displayed naivety? Was I simply getting a nightmarish glimpse behind the curtain at the savage machinery that keeps the whole sordid operation ticking along? However I phrased it or formulated it in my mind though, there was still a dead girl covered in our fingerprints. I prayed Diego had killed her in the middle of the night while I lay unconscious, rendering me somewhat innocent. The shamefulness of my own self-preservation made me want to puke, but there was nothing left in me. And besides, would it *really* make a difference? Whether it was me or him, we were both guilty now. By association and continuation, at the very least, we were guilty of fleeing the scene of an unexplained death.

It was past noon when we pulled off a road connected to a motorway service station. I stayed as covered as possible beneath the tarp, peeking out a fraction just to see what was happening through the cabin window. Diego drove us past a restaurant diner adjoining a petrol station, across a large car park, until finally positioning us at the far end of it, with the tail of the truck poking into some bushes.

"It's OK, you can come out," he said, speaking through the glass.

"Yeah?" I said, not moving.

"Yeah, yeah, just stay low. Climb out the side and come join me in the cabin."

I did so, slipping open the passenger door and sitting alongside him. It felt good to be sitting upright in the front. More human. He was wearing the look of someone that had also been doing a lot of thinking and I reasoned that he trusted me about as much as I did him. Or maybe he was just thinking of how and when he could get rid of me.

"We're not stopping for fuel?" I said.

"Nah man, gotta ditch the truck. Been driving it too long. Either by now Marco told them who we were, and the truck details. Or even if not, cops got a glance at the truck, maybe saw the plate. Same thing, tampoco - neither good," he said.

"How come the cops never chased us?" I asked.

"Dunno homes, I asked myself that too. My thinking - maybe they didn't find the girl yet-"

"-Sammy," I interjected.

"Yeah, Sammy. Maybe they didn't find her, just thought we were two ese's that didn't fancy being kicked out the party. And I moved the truck

103

pretty quick too..." he said with a cocked smile, seeking approval. I was more interested in our next move.

"What now then? How far to the border?" I asked.

"Whoa, whoa, I never said you were coming *with me* to the border. I just said that's the way we're going."

"Well, how far is it?"

"Hmm, from here... fifteen, maybe twenty hours. That's straight driving, no breaks," he said.

"We'll share the driving," I said, trying to make myself indispensable.

"That's not the point," he said.

"I can help. I'll be useful. I have cash."

"Hmm, we'll see... I gotta make a stop on the way. Chihuahua city, see a homeboy named Tito," he said.

"Just know you got one more homeboy right here, offering to help," I said. "We go to Chihuahua for now, and if I make myself handy, then all the way to the border."

"You know you're a real pain in the ass, Jack."

"You can't just leave me here at some fucking petrol station. What I am gonna do, hitchhike back to the states?" I said.

"The fuck I care what happens to you?! And what, now all of a sudden you got a hard-on for the states too?" he said.

"Well, Diego, maybe like you, I don't much fancy my chances in the Mexican justice system.Figure I *might* have a better chance explaining myself to an American cop. Someone that speaks my language at least," I said.

"Ha! Good luck with that one ese. Fucking American pigs worse than here!"

"I'll take my chances. And you? What's your hard-on for the states all about?" I said.

"I got some things there to sort out, a place I can lay low. I gotta go there…. But if I were you homes, I'd head south. Lose yourself in a gringo bar on the coast for a few weeks, wait for it all to blow over."

"I think I prefer America. My experiences here so far haven't been exactly positive," I said.

"Whatever… Or maybe you think you'll get there and no one knows about poor old Sammy. You just make up a story about losing your wallet or some shit. Wander off into the Yanky sunset?" he said.

"I guess I might just hand myself into the nearest cop shop, then hope for-"

"-For what?! That justice you keep talking 'bout? You need money for justice. A nice juicy lawyer to get you outta this mess. You got the money, you can buy your way out. Leave with a clean conscience. Well… you got that kind of cash, Jack? Do you? 'Cos if not, you're better going south. And what if they deport you back to Mexico anyway?" he said.

In truth, I hadn't truly considered what I would do if I reached America. If push came to shove, Diego's wallet theft story wasn't all that farfetched, should I decide to duck my involvement in the crime. Or maybe a hefty dose of amnesia? It all depended on how far I intended to distance myself from the events and desecrate my morality. Or the opposite, take full responsibility for my actions, but make my confession to a sympathetic ear.

"Why are you so keen for me to go South?" I asked. "Maybe hoping I get picked up somewhere and become your fall guy? Leaving you free to sneak off to the states alone?"

"Whatever," he said, his eyes keenly scanning the car park. "Hey, just make sure if you get pinched, whether it's here or the states, you keep my name out of your fucking mouth, right Jack?"

"Right," I said.

"I'm fucking serious. No talk of Chihuahua either, or I'll fucking-"

"Yeah, yeah, fucking kill me now, leave me here," I said.

"Straight up."

He stopped scanning the car park for a minute to give me a deathly serious stare. It did the job, especially with his skeletal makeup, and I looked to switch the direction of the conversation.

"C'mon, you never told me why America?" I asked again.

"I told you...I got somewhere to go..." he said, just as a long eighteen-wheeler pulled into the car park and parked between two other lorries at the rear of the restaurant. "Ah ha, Jackpot!"

"Jackpot?"

"That's our truck."

"Our truck... why that one?" I asked.

"'Cos I like it, that's why. It's a nice colour," he said.

"Diego... come on?"

"Look, see the advertising down the side? That's a big petrol firm, man. Those trucks up and down these motorways all day, so..."

"So one more truck won't make a difference? We'll blend in?" I said.

"Exactly," he said. "Plus it's a nice high cabin, so people can't see you too good from below. *Cops* can't see you too good. I may even let you ride in the front," he said.

"Wow, that's nice of you. OK, so what do we do?" I said.

"Wait, wait..." he said, whispering to himself and leaning on the wheel. "See this guy coming out? See him?"

"Yeah, the driver," I said.

"You see him?!"

"Yeah, I see him Diego, fuck! What?"

"He's our guy,"

"He's our guy?"

"Blue shirt, blue denim jeans, and that olive green waistcoat thing…" he said.

"OK, got it, he's got nice clothes. Trucker chic, lovely. What do we give a fuck? We want his truck, not his clothes, right? Let's just go and take it."

"Nope."

"Nope? Why not?" I said. "You know how to hot wire a truck, I've seen you do one today already."

"We can't do that, Jack," he said, "We steal it, he's gonna report it missing. Then it's not a great getaway truck anymore, is it? It's just as much trouble as this fucking truck."

It was demeaning having my criminal sterility waved in front of my face, but unfortunately, he was right. Although he hadn't accounted for the driver. "What about the driver then?" I said.

"That's where you come in," he said.

*Shit, he had accounted for the driver.* "OK, what about him?" I said.

"We need his keys. But we also can't leave him to tell the cops..."

"No, no, no! We can't kill the guy for a fucking truck, Diego-"

"Shit, I'm not talking about killing him! Who said anything about killing him?! Ain't you seen enough for one day?"

"What then, kidnap?" I said.

"Sort of, yo. I'm thinking we get him, tie him up somewhere, an' leave him. If they find him later, it's OK. We're gone and they can trace the truck, whatever. We just need him quiet, for about twelve hours... maybe twenty-four."

"Where are we gonna leave him?" I asked.

"I don't fucking know, Jack, I'm making this shit up as I go!"

"So this isn't any kind of master fucking plan?"

"Who said it was a master plan?! I don't do this shit every day. Jeez, you think this is what Mexicans do all day - rob trucks and sneak over borders to escape the law?" he said.

In truth, I probably did think that, a little bit, but I tried to hide this. "You're Mexican-American aren't you?" I said.

"So, what's that matter?"

"Well, you're half Mexican, half American. I just didn't want you thinking I was full of negative racial stereotypes about your-"

"-Jack, this is hardly the time, motherfucker. I'll worry about *Half* of my hurt feelings later," he said.

"OK fine," I said.

"Now go get that guy before it's too late."

"Get him?! What am I supposed to get him with?!" I said.

"I dunno, look around," Diego said, rummaging through his driver's door. "And we need something to tie him up with."

"I think I saw some string in the back. Not much, but might be enough."

"Good." Diego pulled out a short tyre iron from his door and looked pleased with his haul. "Anything in the glove box?"

I checked, "Not much - some fags, lighter..."

"Tyre iron will have to do," he said.

"Fine. But we can't go into the middle of a restaurant and just twat him with a tyre iron," I said.

"Agreed."

"Then what? Wait for him to come out? ...I guess we could hide behind the wheels there-"

"Too risky. They can still see it from the restaurant," he said.

"WHAT THEN??"

"You gonna have to lure him out..."

"Lure him out? What with, sweets?"

"Nope, even better," he said, smiling. "Violence."

"Violence? Violence?? *'Oi mate, do you wanna come outside for some violence? I've got a nice handful of violence here if you want some...'*

and then '*Whack! Get your laughing gear round that me old son.*' " I said mockingly.

"Something like that, yeah. Look, just go in there, start some shit, and get him to come outside."

I scoffed at his idea aloud, which frustrated him and made him continue in earnest. "Make sure you say you wanna fight round the back. Out of sight, you know. I'll be hiding. And then I'll hit him with the iron and we tie him up. We can lock him in the outside toilet over there, break the lock off or seal it shut somehow. Someone will find him eventually."

"And what if he doesn't want to fight?" I said.

"MAKE him want to fight," he said.

"HOW?!"

"Just be yourself. I've only known you a bit and I've already wanted to hit you several times."

"That's reassuring. But it's not the most solid plan. I don't see it working."

"It'll work," he said.

"If you're that confident in the plan then you go. *I'll* wait around the back. *You* lure him out," I said.

"I can't, Jack," he said.

"Why not??"

"Look at me! I'm wearing a fucking skeleton suit! It's hardly fucking in-cog...in-cog..."

111

"Incognito," I said. "You could get changed? Wear my clothes, we'll swap."

"No time. You see my face painted like death? Also, I don't trust you with the tyre iron. You might fuck it up. Needs to be a clear hit. Good, but not too good, if you know what I mean?" he said.

"Yeah, yeah, I know what you mean. Just don't fucking kill him, OK? We've got enough blood on our hands."

"I promise, just a tap. Now come on, you wanna pull your weight, this is it. No more fucking about, we gotta do this now, vamos!"

Reluctantly I got out of the cabin. I grabbed the coarse string bundle from the back. It looked like it could make an effective tool for a classic hogtie, provided he didn't struggle too hard to break free. The thought of some poor trucker lying motionless, not struggling at all, was a bit of a worry. When I returned to the cabin and tossed the string over to Diego, I reiterated the need for no more killing.

"Don't hit him too hard, OK?"

"Just a tap," he said, with a wry grin.

"And don't take too long either. Where you gonna be?" I said.

"Just there, by those recycle bin things," he said, pointing to some yellow bins at the rear of the restaurant block. "In fact, there's a phone there, I'll call my man Tito first. I'll be able to see you from there. And then I'll come meet you by the bins."

"OK, fine," I said, "But for the record, I don't think this is a good idea."

"Noted."

I turned to leave, but a quick shadow of doubt flickered back in my mind, "What the fuck should I say to him?"

"I told you, man," Diego said, "Just be yourself. You got stupid fucking blonde hair, so behave like a gringo - an Ignorant Fucking Gringo."

He enjoyed telling me that. I sneered at him in response and started walking off.

"...Oh and tell him *'que te follo un pez'* - *you hope he gets fucked by a fish.* Or just that you fucked his mother. Mexican guys hate that!"

"Great, thanks for the tip, Diego, really useful," I said.

It was a long, lonely march to the restaurant. Enough time to question whether I truly had the minerals required, concluding I didn't, and then wondering about beating an early retreat. I had never *knowingly* talked myself into a fight before. People just tended to punch me spontaneously. And that would mark the beginning, middle, and end of the fight. The last time I actively went in pursuit of a fight was in the school playground - a far smaller, scrappy little kid called Minky.

113

Despite his diminutive height and malnourished prisoner-of-war body shape, he had an unnerving level of accuracy when it came to blows directed at an opponent's testicles. I mournfully remembered that dull and ceaseless ache in the bollocks, and my pace naturally slowed. I rounded the parked fuel lorry with its huge gleaming bolts studded onto vast aluminium wheels. It was a worthy carriage for a border run, a sturdy juggernaut. It was the prize and the price of freedom. All I had to do was start a fight with a stranger. *Easy.*

There were a few more trucks parked in neat rows near the entrance to the roadside diner. It had a large window wall running the entirety of one side, the glass peppered with various orange stickered logos promoting coffee and doughnuts at astounding prices. Diego was right, stealing one of those trucks would have been too risky, exposed to onlookers from inside where there appeared to be a few different people scattered around eating. I had to make sure I didn't end up having the fight near the window. We needed a private spot, round the back. In truth, the place Diego had chosen was perfect for a stealthy bludgeoning. The restaurant had two full height glass swing doors. I pulled one open and a little bell rang above my head, announcing my arrival into the ring. I quickly scanned the restaurant and saw my guy, dressed in trucker chic, sitting on a stool at the counter. There was a guy sitting to his left reading a paper, and a free space to his right. I moved over and straddled that stool, making sure when doing so that I bumped shoulders with him.

"Hey, buddy, mind giving me some fucking room?!" I said, offering him an early taster of what to expect.

He had his phone in his hand, and without looking up, simply shifted slightly over to allow me more space. His nonchalant pacifism worried me. I would need to work quickly to find his pressure points. There was a waitress busily manoeuvring her way around the kitchen behind the counter. She took an order from two guys at the far end of the bar, then started pouring them coffee. I thought I would grab her attention quickly, while she had her back turned.

"Hey!" I yelled, slapping a hand down on the counter. "Hey senora, senorita... Yo, Senor! I need some coffee over here, pronto!"

One of the two guys she was serving didn't appreciate this banter, articulating this with a long eyeball. I avoided his gaze and tapped the counter restlessly. The waitress turned and approached me with muted enthusiasm, chewing her gum and raising an eyebrow for an order. She was a cute twenty-something, catching me off guard with her good looks and no-bullshit attitude.

"How about a coffee? If that's not too much trouble? A guy could die of thirst here," I said.

She rolled her eyes, and stated the price as "ten pesos." She was establishing not only the cost but also letting me know I was welcome to be passing trade.

"Sure, sure," I said, throwing down some change. The coffee was jet black and boiling hot, the steam rising off it like a New York street vent. I touched a hand to the mug but it was too hot to handle. Knowing it may scald my throat, I reluctantly grabbed it and took a big mouthful. It was even hotter than it looked, and I spat it back down onto the counter and onto my money.

"FUCK!" I shouted. "What the fuck are you trying to do, lady?! Kill me?!"

She looked genuinely shocked. I had broken through her steely veneer. "Oh mister, sorry!" she said, moping it, embarrassed but also mildly disturbed by my actions.

"You fucking believe that, pal?" I said, slapping the arm of my target. He didn't respond, but the next guy to his left stopped reading his paper in order to tut some disapproval.

"What's that, *buddy*? Hey, big man, got something to say?" I said.

I tried to remind myself not to start on everyone, being obnoxious was a necessary part of the act but I couldn't pick wars on all fronts. What

I needed was to hone in on my guy, find his hook, get him riled, and get him outside.

"Hey, you-" I said, slapping the arm of my trucker again, "Who you texting?" Still not a ruffle of interest. I was gonna have to up the ante. "Hey, Dicknose. Puta-"

"Que?!" he said, finally lured in, but confused more than angry, unsure what all the commotion was about.

"You. Fuckface. Who you texting?" I said.

"What's it to you?" he said.

His English was quite good, which told me I could get more creative with my insults. "Who you texting, your mama? Tell her you love her? Well, tell her I love her too. Tell her I miss her hairy little cunt."

He leaned away from me, looking to the other guy for support. I tried to nip this in the bud quickly. "What you looking at him for? He your boyfriend?" I said.

"Nope," the other guy said, standing out of his chair, "I'm his brother."

"OK," I said, *in for a penny, in for a pound,* "Well look, if he forgets to tell your mother tonight, maybe you can do it for me? Tell her I miss her funky little cunt. Can you do that for me? Maybe tonight, just before you go down on her?"

"Que?! Fucking what, asshole?!" the brother said. They were both out of their seats now.

"How do you work it? One at a time, or spit roast, one from each end? Spit roast, right? Pig on a stick?" I said.

In poker, they call this going all in. I had settled my odds and figured that if the calmer of the two wouldn't get involved, then I'd have to settle for both of them. Hopefully, Diego could sort it with a couple of clean strikes outside.

"Eh?! Fucking Puta!" the brother shouted, squaring up, frothing at the mouth with psychopathic verve. My intended trucker did his best to restrain the brother.

"Come on then, you fucking queers! Let's settle this outside. I'll fuck you both up! You, then him!"

"Fuck you - 'dis just between you and me, h'ok?" said the bigger brother. And he was big, over 6'3 of livid Mexican lumberjack dressed up head to toe in supermarket denim.

"Nah, nah, he comes too," I said, pointing to my target. "This mouthy little cunt had it coming, he's in this all the way. In fact, let's just you and me go outside and settle this?"

The plan had become complicated by the additional brother, he was really gonna mess up the dynamics. Even if I managed to get just one out, it wouldn't be long before the other one came out to check on progress. It would have to be a double deal, meaning two people to knock out and stow away. Complicated, but not unfeasible.

"Hector, what's going on?" shouted someone from the far end of the restaurant.

"This fucking gringo is starting shit!" shouted back Hector, the double denim brother.

The shout came from the two guys at the end of the counter who were sitting on stools, being served coffee by the waitress. They had a brief conflab with her and didn't appear to like what they heard, shaking their heads in a simmering disgust. They signalled to her that they had heard enough, pulled themselves out of their stools and started mournfully pacing towards us, latecomers to my funeral. *Shit.* This was really not ideal. There was no way I could take on four of them and no way Diego could incapacitate and hide all their bodies. *Game over.*

"What'd I ever do to you, man??" said trucker chic.

"Ah, shut up," I said absently. My mind was calculating the odds and figuring out the exit strategy. "You boys can fucking keep it," I said, shifting out of my seat and glancing over at the door.

"Where you think you going?" said Hector.

"Hey, keep him there!" shouted one of the latecomers, a nasty looking bloke with a face like roadkill. Over his shoulder, outside by the petrol

119

pumps, I could see an even more alarming sight. It was Diego, sitting in the driver's seat of a shabby old rusted farmer's truck, a 50's type wagon with a big bull-nosed bonnet and a wooden cage built into the rear tail. He was driving slowly past the far restaurant window, nervously glancing around as he did, appearing to search for the exit, rather than me. After all, he knew where I was. He was ditching me.

"OK, OK, fellas. I think there's been a misunderstanding, that's all" I said, creeping away from the bloodthirsty rabble.

"The only misunderstanding, ese, is that you think you can say that shit an' then walk outta here alive," said Hector. "No one talks about our mother!"

"Look, Hector, isn't it? I appreciate, you're probably a bit annoyed, angry even..." I said, stalling.

Out of the corner of my eye, I could see Diego's newly acquired farmyard getaway truck pulling away from the restaurant block and rounding the petrol pumps, headed for the exit. *The fucker was gonna leave me to face the music!* Meanwhile, the two backup truckers had joined the group. They were surely the most unnecessary cavalry in the history of warfare.

"...I'd be annoyed too," I continued, the fear and anxiety reaching breaking point. It was make-

or-get-broken time. "But I gotta say... she was a GREAT FUCK!"

With that, I threw the remainder of my searing coffee at them, spun 180 degrees, and bolted for the door. I hoped I would disappear like a magician in a cloud of sparkly dust. At best, however, I had bought myself a mere couple of seconds before a group of irate Mexican truckers would physically tear me to shreds. I made it to the exit, pulling it sharply open and rattling the bell above. I tried to slam it closed behind me but Hector had already made it to the door and wedged his fingers into the opening. With only a couple of inches to play with, he lacked the leverage to prise it open. I could apply more strength on my side, pulling with all my weight on the handle, crushing his fingers in the gap. The rest of the gang soon joined him, leaning around to grab bits of the metal frame and pull the door back in their favour. The little bell at the top of the door was ringing incessantly *Bing! Bing! Bing! Bing!*

"Dieggggo!!" I shouted, his truck slipping out of the petrol court.

He saw me out of his side window, and to my amazement stopped the truck. He just sat there laughing, watching me struggle to keep the door closed. Then he waved goodbye and worked his way back into first gear. I was losing the battle for the restaurant door, with each yank of it they were getting close enough to grab me, their faces twisted with seething rage. I gave up, letting go of the handle and sprinting in the direction of Diego. The four guys fell backward when the door swung open, before gathering themselves for a rapid pursuit. Diego was back into second gear now with a clear route beyond the pumps headed for the freeway entry lane, his speed gathered by the second. I ran across the petrol station forecourt without looking back, dodging a car bonnet as it circled a pump. I got in line with the rear of Diego's truck, just a few feet ahead of me. The back of the truck was fixed with a tall wooden slatted cage filled with chickens. I could see Diego's face checking the side mirror, seeing me, grinning, then moving up into third gear. There was a moment now, to run hard and get onboard before he truly embraced third gear and pulled away for good. Black fumes billowed out from the exhaust as the rusty old chicken wagon lurched forward ever faster. Behind me, four rabid Mexicans pursued. Their faces wet with scalding coffee, and thirsty for vengeance. Finally, I managed to reach the truck and clamp a hand onto the timber frame, hauling myself up and tucking my feet onto the rear rust-spotted tow bar. Diego accelerated, proving no match for the men on foot. I looked back at my would-be assailants as they gradually gave up the chase. I grabbed my nuts and praised god.

# 9

# BLACK & WHITE NIGHT

Diego fired our truck onto the freeway like a pinball launched into play. I was clinging onto the rear cabin for dear life. After a few minutes of erratic driving, it dawned on me that he had zero intention of pulling over and allowing me safely aboard. In fact, he was trying to shake me loose. My only option was to try and climb into the rear-mounted chicken pen while doing seventy miles an hour in the fast lane. The cage was filled with a thousand flustering birds all bleating out their disapproval in deafening cries. The timber-slatted framework revealed glimpses inside of the chickens thrashing wildly about, going stir-crazy with the excitement of the heist. They were contained by a six-foot high door, held in position with a lone rusty bolt that I struggled to yank loose. Diego continued to veer the truck from one side to the other, zigzagging across lanes, hampering my attempts until finally, I managed to haul the bolt free. The rear door flung open in an instant, throwing me completely off balance. I was left clinging precariously on with ever-whitening fingertips. The open cage door served as an escape chute for some of the chickens who burst free and cannonballed into the air. Any dreams they may have had for a carefree life on the open road, soon ended when they spiralled under the chassis of an eighteen-wheeler, instantly turning them into paste. News of the failed escape spread quickly amongst the chickens, ramping up their hysteria. They focused their energies on removing the invader, pecking at my exposed fingertips that remained clamped onto the timber frame. I managed to grab hold of the door as it swung back toward me, pulling myself into the coop. Once inside, I began an instant fight back against a tide of agitated squawks and incessant flapping. I had to punch and kick my way in, rampaging forward before finally pulling the door shut behind me. I was a most unwelcome guest. Birds propelled into my face through the murky darkness of the coop, a dizzying blur of feathers and gawking beaks. As the truck lurched from side to side, I stumbled, reaching out for balancing aides but finding only irate fowl. I steadied myself on my hands and knees, swatting back birds and scrabbling along the floor over mounds of gooey faeces. I was driven by a fixated urge to reach the driver's cabin. Dividing Diego and I was a grimy pane of glass, splattered up with a year's worth of chicken scuzz. Peeking inside, I could just about decipher the outline of his body, a satanic blob bouncing up and down in the driver's seat. I banged my fist on the glass to rouse him. His eyes flicked up to the mirror and when he saw my feathery shit-smeared face staring back at him, his body crumpled into an ecstasy of laughter.

"Diego! Diego, you motherfucker! Pull over!" I said.

After another bout of laughter, he finally squared himself right for talking. "Hahaha, no way ese! No talk. Just sit back and enjoy the ride. And try not to fuck any chickens!"

"Diego! I'm serious, man! Pull over!"

"Just stay back there, you can't ride in the front. I told you before, we look weird riding together," he said.

"It'll look a lot weirder if they open up the back of the truck and find a gringo sitting with all these chickens! Come on, I'll ride up front and stay under the foot well. On the floor. No one will see me."

"Nah, too risky…"

I gave up fighting him. "You fucking left me!" I said.

"What?!" he said.

I wondered if he couldn't hear me over the hum of the motorway, or the noise from my feisty neighbours. So I upped the volume, yelling: "YOU DITCHED ME, MAN!"

"Well, I see you pretty good now," he said, looking back at me and grinning.

"You left me to take an ass-kicking from those guys, you fucker!"

"One guy!" he said, holding up a solitary finger. "I told you to start a fight with *one guy*! Who the fuck were all those chicos?"

"His friends," I said. "One of them was his brother, I dunno about the other two… "

"Shit. Did you tell them that you wanted to fuck-"

"-Their mother?! Hell yeah, I told them *both* I'd fuck their mother!" I said.

He burst out laughing again, slapping the wheel with glee. "Fuck, I knew you were annoying Jack, but I didn't think you'd get four of them, homes!"

"So what was your plan? Just leave me to get roughed up? Send me in there for a beating, while you disappear off? You're cold, Diego," I said.

"I didn't take you for the sentimental type, Jack," he said.

"Nothing sentimental about not wanting your teeth kicked in by an angry mob. That's simple preservation. And some fucking plan." I said.

"You keep talking about plans like I've been planning this all week. You went in to get a guy, I waited round the back. You took so fucking long, I made my call. I waited, you didn't show. And then I saw this old boy roll in, with this here chick wagon, and I thought 'heyyyy, nice ride...' "

"And what, just chinned him? Where'd you hide him?" I asked.

"Around," he said, drifting his gaze back to a middle distance in the road ahead.

"Nice. I doubt he's doing too well. Seeing how you treat your friends, I can't imagine-"

"We're not friends, Jack." He said, loud and clear.

"Yeah, whatever. So what happened then?" I asked.

"What do you mean, '*what then?*' I took the truck. And, by the way, a little appreciation would be nice. Then I came round the front, couldn't see you, and..."

"And took off! Fuck, you knew where I was!" I said.

"I know where you are now too - always on my fucking shoulder," he said.

A chicken leapt up and floundered in my face. I grabbed it and tossed it back in with the rest. I could see arguing with Diego was futile, so I turned my sights to our destination.

"Fuck it. Where to now, then?" I said.

"As I said before Jack, Chihuahua,"

"Like the dog?"

"Yeah, like the dog. I gotta see someone," he said.

"That guy... Tito?"

"Yeah,"

"You phoned him?"

"No answer," he said.

"So how long 'til we get there?"

"Should be there by night. If I was you, I'd get comfortable."

I hunkered down and faced my new companions. Their incessant squawking had receded, replaced by suspicious curiosity. The chickens circled me, chatting amongst themselves. The bravest of the bunch tiptoed out and pecked my leg. After a little while, the sound of their clucking and garbled calls actually became soothing and I found myself drifting off into a listless sleep. A few hours passed and it was night when Diego slapped the glass, waking me and demanding my attention.

"Get up, man, we got trouble," he said.

"What? What is it?" I said drowsily.

"Dunno. Lot of people in the road up ahead, lotta flames, like... flaming tyres or some shit," he said.

"Day of the dead?"

"Nah. This is ain't no celebration."

We were stationary. Stuck in a line of traffic with a swath of people walking past us, heading in the opposite direction. Glancing past the chickens and through the slats, it appeared our two lane motorway had gone down to one, with scrubland stretching off for miles around on either side. There were no cars approaching from ahead, just the bodies walking back. It was hard to see exactly where the people had come from, but there looked to be a city outlined on the horizon. Rows of tower blocks, silhouetted by a warm orange glow. A mound of burning tyres made the twilight sky turn charcoal black.

"A crash? A big one?" I ventured, optimistically.

"But what about all these people? Hey, hey hermanos-" Diego said, winding down the window and grabbing the arm of a passing man.

They had a curt spat in Spanish, until the man walked off, slapping his hand roughly against the side of the truck.

"What did he say?" I asked.

"Said it's as far as we can go. Says the road up ahead is closed. There's a protest on, something about fuel costs. The peasants have gone crazy and shut down the city. There's no cars in or out."

"Shit, what do we do?" I asked.

Diego called out to the car ahead of ours. They had another quick chat. I overheard *"Borracho"*.

"Borracho? What's that?" I asked.

"Drunk. The peasants are drunk. They've gotten worse all day. That guy doesn't recommend we go in... he's going home."

True to his word, that driver whipped his car around in a U-turn and sped off in the opposite direction. Other cars further ahead were doing likewise. Diego was tapping the wheel, weighing up the options.

"What do you think? Can we skip it, go around?" I asked. He didn't reply, so I probed further. "What's in Chihuahua anyway? Is it really that important?"

"Yeah, it's important." He said, avoiding elaboration.

"Then what? Looks pretty bad up ahead. Flaming tyres... drunk peasants..."

"*I know, I know...*" he said, thinking.

"Just a thought," I said, "But if we did go in, you know, if we could slip in somehow... then I'm guessing the cops will be more busy dealing with protesters? They might not care about a couple of guys in some old beaten up chicken truck?"

I realised my musings could be interpreted as advice, inadvertently offering Diego a jimmy over the wall and into the lion's den. I quickly pondered the retraction of my words, but it was too late.

"Yeah, you're right," he said.

He pulled the steering wheel around and swung us into the empty adjacent lane and started speeding down it, heading for the blazing city. I fell backwards with the speed of his decision, picking myself up from a gabble of unhappy chickens that had cushioned my fall.

"Whoa, whoa! Diego, I was just talking out loud. Theorising - that's all - just ideas!" I said.

"Good ideas! I like it! We're going in!" he said.

"In?!!"

"Yeah, it's cool. I know another route, a side door!" he said.

He swerved the truck half off the road to avoid a U-turning car, showering dirt over some of the people marching away. After a little while, he spotted a tiny slip road that he had been desperately looking for in the dark. Nothing marked its existence beyond a slightly irregular clump of cacti and a little mound of weed-tangled soil, bordered by a snivelling set of tyre tracks that wisped off into a barren wasteland.

"That's it!" he shouted.

"That's it?!"

"Well… I think that's it. If it's not, then it's good enough!"

He pulled across the lane of dispersing traffic and flew off down a long-forgotten access track. Before we turned, I caught a closer glimpse of the city's boundary line. The main road was barricaded with a mountain of impenetrable objects. Twisted metal, old shopping trolleys and burning cars. The whole scene was being danced around by a group of wild protesters. In comparison, the desert road was reassuringly isolated, with the truck's soft blue headlights the only thing separating us from total darkness. After a few minutes of trundling along, Diego stopped at a small shrine on the side of the road next to a stone obelisk of the Virgin Mary, bordered by flowers. It marked a crossroad, with one side the entry point to a cemetery, which was the direction he promptly took.

"Nice, Diego. Nice." I offered.

"Not afraid of a graveyard at night are you?" he said, laughing.

A few gentle raindrops flecked the windscreen. I was standing in the back cabin, holding the cage roof to remain upright, swaying with the rocking motion of the truck. The chickens had quietened down. They looked frightened and road weary. The rain grew harder, the spits turning to spats, and the sky grumbled with a deep booming thunder.

"Whooaaaaa," Diego said up front, mocking our eerie predicament. He seemed at his happiest in situations that would for most people be their greatest cause for concern. In my mind, the situation was at least beneficial in comparison to navigating a rowdy mob of drunken peasants. I gripped firmly onto the rooster coop, bracing against the impact of our ragged driving the way a man bites down on a stick before dressing his wounds. We lurched up and over a huge sinkhole, slamming the truck cabin against the coop, rattling the bolts and twisting the framework.

"Easy, Diego!" I shouted.

His mind was occupied with grappling control over the wheel as we pitched and pounded over rolling crests and sunken valleys. The rain grew heavier, shredding diagonally through the slatted gaps. I felt like a dingy strapped to a boat, navigating stormy swells. The chickens cranked up their volatility again. They screeched bolshy throat clearings that expressed their disgruntlement at the seesaw motion. I wanted to ask Diego for an upgrade to the front cabin, but he had plenty on his plate just keeping the truck on the road.

The deeper we got into the graveyard, the thinner and more unpredictable the track became, with only the scattering of tombstones marking the route. The rain was making the clay mud slick and slippery. The wheels struggled for grip. Lightning flashed in great sparks across the sky, pinpointing the lumps of granite headstones in the black night. It became impossible to judge whether Diego was driving on the designated track anymore as he weaved between gravestones that lay semi-submerged in the melting landscape. The rain overtook the power of the wipers, obscuring practically all visibility. We were a shipwrecked vessel, desperately riding the muddy waves of a relentless sea of death. A haunted ark. Two guys with very questionable souls, and a hundred frantic chickens looking on in horror.

Suddenly, the truck slammed down the apex of a hill and pitched belly-first into the mud. Diego wrangled with the gear stick, but it had seized. He accelerated hard, without gaining any ground. The wheels span feverously, squealing in circles, over and over.

"Diego! We're stuck!" I shouted, my face sodden and plastered with mucky feathers.

"I know!" he shouted back, hammering the gears and the gas, exchanging reason and logic for the blundering of brute force. After a while, he eventually conceded.

"Puta!"

Diego climbed out of the cabin and slipped his way around the side of the truck, using it to hold himself upright. He opened the rear cage door, freeing me and a few desperate chickens that took the opportunity to break away. I felt like a prisoner released from the stocks, at the last moment spared the guillotine. It was strange seeing Diego face-to-face after hours apart, shouting at each other through a shit-stained plate of glass. His face lit up under another flash of lightning, the painted skull of death staring back at me. The rain was seemingly unable to wash off his disguise, barely even a smudge.

"The wheel!" shouted Diego into the howling night air. He was pointing to the back left tyre which was dug into its own shallow grave. We stood there for a while looking at it, shielding our eyes from the razor-sharp deluge, deciding what to do.

"Can we walk?!" I cried in a shrill, faraway voice.

He shook his head. "Too far! Don't know the way!"

"Then we gotta dig her out!" I said.

He nodded. I looked around for any object that we could use as a makeshift shovel but it was hard to see anything through the darkness and unrelenting rain. "Hands!" I shouted, dropping to the floor and scooping out lumps of mud. Diego looked mournfully down at me, before heading up to the cabin to try and start up the engine. He shouted back to me, but the words were lost in a clap of thunder. Once he started it up, I had to whip my hands out of the way to stop the wheel spin from ripping the skin off my knuckles. The truck didn't budge. He tried it again, indifferent to the mechanics of our plight and blindly making it worse. I shouted for him to stop, which finally he did. We found an old log book in the glove box and I tried to scoop out more filth, using it like a spade. The red tail lights gave off a sinister illumination to my work. Again Diego pumped the gas, the wheels of machinery spinning hellish circles in my mind. A flood of foul water came swelling around my knees. I started sinking, feeling like I was being sucked into the ground, lowered into the putrid slush. The earth was a decaying burial ground ploughed open by our actions. My feet scraped back new layers of the mire. Then bones, human bones, began puncturing the surface. More lightning strikes. Worms slithered to the surface. A small headstone toppled, sliding toward me in the mud. I tried desperately to kick it back out of sight for fear it would be inscribed with my own name. The boundary between visions and reality, fast transcending. My feet were almost completely submerged in the rank depths of festering humanity. I put my hands out to stop from falling into the abyss but the ground sucked them down into their bowels. I imagined the hands of corpses grabbing my wrists, pulling me in, shackling me to their sins. There was a demonic roar of thunder. The stars above swept across in a dynamic blur. A strobing flash illuminated Sammy's deathly face reflected upon a simmering puddle of bones. I called out to her, prayed to her, and begged her for forgiveness. She screamed an indeterminable cry of hellfire. Then everything went black, the red tail light a solitary spot in the darkness, until eventually even that, extinguished.

# 10

# RAGING CHIHUAHUA

I woke up sometime after my blackout, sitting in the passenger seat of the truck, slumped against the door with my neck contorted into a corkscrew. I yanked my chin free from my shoulder, pulling my head back around into neutral. Upon re-entry into reality I gasped for air, desperately sucking it in like a drowning man breaching the surface of an icy lake. My body was freezing and locked into a pattern of spasmodic shivers. Diego was sitting opposite me submerged in a cloud of dense, acrid smoke, the thickest pockets of which almost entirely obscured him. I was just able to make out his body position by following the motion of a cigarette cherry tip as it wafted softly through the murky grey camouflage. I could tell from the stillness of his body that he had been smoking more than just household snouts. I grabbed the window handle, winding it open, desperate to get some oxygen into my lungs.

"Relax, man," he said.

"What happened??" I replied, my head sore and my mind foggy.

"You blacked out. Mumbled some crazy shit, then fell back all twisted and locked up. I had to pull you in an' fucking place you there like a piece of wood."

The night air howled through the gap in the window, making my skin tremble. I felt stiff and uneasy, desperate for a change of scenery. I cranked my body back into shape as best as the truck's confinements would allow. I contemplated stepping out for a stretch, but another gust of wind made me think twice and I wound the window back up a notch.

"When did it stop raining?" I asked.

"Dunno," he said, his voice sounding far away, speaking from a hollow interior, calling out to me from some alternate dimension.

"How long have you been smoking?" I asked.

He didn't reply, but offered me the all-too-familiar silver pipe, his hand passing through the cloud. "No, thanks," I said, straightening myself again. I ran my hands through my hair, raking up recent images and then scrubbing them away again as quickly as they had arrived. Diego pulled the pipe back into his world.

"What time is it?" I asked, and he gently prodded the dashboard clock, which read 3.30am. "So that's how it is now? I gotta hang out with a crackhead who can't muster more than a couple of words?"

"Fuck you, ese," he said, a nasty little smile stencilled in the smoke.

"Almost a sentence. Come on, what's the plan? What are we gonna do?" I asked.

"Fuck your plans."

I wound my window down more to let the cabin clear. He yelled disapproval at this, which I ignored, asking him for a cigarette. He threw one at me, which landed in my lap. I looked down at my jeans, filthy brown with graveyard muck. My shirt was sodden from the lashing rains, my body broken and ravaged by the night. I needed food and sleep but neither were likely, so I took whatever sustenance was available, lighting the cigarette and letting the smoke warm my lungs.

"I'm cold," I said.

"Then shut the fucking window!" he replied, and duly I did.

"Looks drier," I said. I could see Diego more clearly now that a little of the smoke had cleared. I was keen to engage him while there was still a semblance of life in his eyes. "Maybe we can get the truck moving," I continued.

"Be my guest," he said.

"At least fire up the engine, eh?" I said. "Get some heating on, I'm dying here! It's OK for you, you weren't the fucker skating around out there trying to get this thing moving." He turned on the ignition, turning off the headlights as soon as they came on. "Who comes through a graveyard in the middle of the fucking night anyway?!"

"You know the score, Jack. You wanna get a taxi, go for it."

I was tired of fighting him, tired of everything. I sat back and let my mind concentrate only on the rhythm of the smoking. The rising and falling of my lungs. Outside the passenger window, there was nothing but a field of oddly-shaped tombstones sticking out of the mud. All of them leaning in their own freakish directions, like the few remaining teeth in the deranged smile of a haggard bum. I gazed up into the sky searching for some stars, some light relief, but they were obscured by a blanket of fog. There was just a dank fuzziness all around, backlit on the horizon by the soft glow from the burning city. I wondered what new disaster waited for us up ahead, what new ghoulish designs lay undiscovered. Again I contemplated getting out of the truck, to check the depths of how far we had sunk. But I was too weak and helpless to care about anything more than my next inhale. Hope was a distant bedfellow. We were in a forgotten wasteland, left to sink into the slobbering depths of our sinful demise.

"The pipe?" I said.

"Huh?" Diego replied, uncertain.

"The pipe. Let me hit it." I said.

"Eh... you sure, Jack?" he said.

"Yep."

"I mean..."

"Diego, for fuck's sake."

"Fine," he said, passing it to me.

"Remind me what to do, just light it here? Does it have a rush hole..?" I asked.

"Yeah, there, and suck here. But you sure? It wasn't all that long ago you was lying face down in the mud."

"Well, that actually sounds pretty good right now," I said.

I flicked the lighter into life and burnt up the scatty ends of whatever crap he had left in the pipe. I tried to blank out where this kind of behaviour had taken us before, but soon I didn't have to try. The chemical scent of the PCP opened my airwaves and cast me backward into a sinking sponge of blissful indifference. I could feel my breath rising and sinking. The crashing waves of nihilism swelling softly down until they settled into a surging sea of hallowed tranquillity. My facial muscles twitched as if connected to puppet strings. Strings pulled by some higher force. My body neither sank nor rose, but floated aimlessly along without direction. A strange kind of frank levity took possession of my fears. I passed the pipe back to Diego. We both sat there for a long silent moment, cocooned in our own cosmic hibernations. Eventually, a voice spoke through me from my resummoned soul, across a vast peaty wasteland, until it reached his soul, which was neither present nor recognisable in Earthly form.

"Why Chihuahua?" I asked, my voice softened, free from accusation or anxiety.

"Gotta see Tito," he replied, his tone equally translucent.

"Who's Tito?" I asked.

"Tito's my boy. I mean, not 'my boy', but Ma Boy, you know?" he said, with a deep, far away chuckle.

"Got it, but why…" I said, rubbing my face to recall my own question, "Why are we going to see him?"

" 'Cos he's the only one who knows... Who can warn Marianna,"he said.

"Warn Marianna? Who's Marianna??"

"That's his cousin. Marianna. She's also my girl. Well, she was my girl, anyway..." he said.

"OK, now I see... I didn't know there was a lady involved, you sly old dog. Wait a minute... I still don't get it, why does she need to be warned?"

Diego went from chuckling in the background to stony silent. The mood in the truck shifted, and I had an uneasy feeling that I wouldn't want to be privy to the forthcoming revelations.

"Shit man, shit," he said, putting his head in his hands.

"What? What is it? Why do you need to warn her? What did you do?" I asked.

"It's not what *I* did, it's what *we* did man!" he said.

"Us?! What the fuck did I do??"

"Don't you get it? It's what we did back there... what happened back at the party," he said.

"No, I don't get it. Why don't you try enlightening me," I said, and with each passing moment I felt myself being pulled back up from the depths of the ocean floor and meeting face-to-face with the reality of the broken world we had so recently left behind.

"The phone call I tried to make earlier, at the gas station?" he said.

"Yeah, I remember."

"I called Tito. 'Cos I ain't got Marianna's number, si? So I couldn't call her direct? So I called Tito..."

"How come you don't have her number?" I asked.

"I got it on my mobile. But I ain't got that, right? It's at the party somewhere."

"The house party?!"

"Yeah," he said.

"Fuck Diego, you said you lost it! So your phone is in *that* house?"

"Yeah, I lost it at the party. What difference does it make?" he said.

"Where in the house is it? In Sammy's room?" I said.

"I dunno."

"If someone finds it in there…"

"Then it could be a big fucking problem for me, OK? Only me. It don't make no fucking odds to you, Jack. You're in the shit already. And as I said before, you're welcome to make your own way out of it."

"Fine, fine. Forget it," I said.

"So look, me and Tito do a little business, so his number is the only one I fucking know by

146

heart. So I figured I'd call him, lay things out, and get him to phone Marianna..." he said.

"Wait, Marianna is your lady?"

"She used to be, yeah," he said.

"Used to be. So why…?"

"We got a kid," he said.

"A kid?" I repeated, the alarm bells slowly dragging me out of my sleepy recoil.

"Yeah, what the fuck you think I'm saying?!"

"OK, I just don't see what one thing has got to do with the other. And where does Tito fit in? She's with him now?" I said.

"No, man, Tito is her cousin. So we gotta get to Tito, to get to Marianna. To warn her and my boy, you see now?"

"Warn them about what?!" I said, exasperated, the words ricocheting sharply from my mouth like rifle rounds rattling in a tin can.

"Warn them about Anton," he said.

"Anton?!"

"You remember the freaky Mexican Sasquatch from the party?"

A dark cloud was looming in my frontal cortex. Aside from trying to block out the harrowing flashbacks of Sammy's swollen face distorted through rigor mortis, I had also been wrangling with the occasional pop-ups from the big angry Mexican I had last seen getting bundled into the back of a police car while we made our hasty escape.

"But the police…" I hesitantly began, before Diego cut me short with words I truly didn't want to hear.

"The police aren't our biggest problem, Jack."

"Anton? Anton is a bigger problem than the police?!" I said.

"About the size of it."

"But he should be in jail now? At least for twenty-four or forty-eight hours? I dunno how you work it here, but they either charge him or…"

"Maybe for now he's locked up, doesn't matter," he said.

"Doesn't matter? What, he's got the power to reach us even from inside?" I said.

"What you think I'm telling you - he's a big fish.. We stepped in something real big back there, dog. Real Big." Diego said, pulling out his cigarettes and lighting one up.

"Shit. How long would they keep him locked up for? I mean, if there's witnesses, maybe some people will come forward and say he was with Sammy that night. People that can put them at the party together…" I said.

"Yeah, they can be connected at the party, pretty easy. But that don't matter," he said.

"Right. I guess if he's powerful then he could just lean on people, or pay them to say that he had nothing to do with her..?"

"No, not that easy. You see, Sammy was his girl," he said.

"His girl?!"

"Well, one of them. He has a lot of girls," he said.

"A prostitute?"

"Nah, not really. Not like that… well, sort of, I guess. When you move big blow like Anton, you just have girls. Comes with the role. You know like a king or some shit always has his servants an' jesters? Some are for your amusement, and some you lend out."

"So, let me get this straight. We either directly, or indirectly, were involved with the killing of one of Anton's working girls?"

"Don't say '*killed*' man!" he said.

"Insert whatever word feels good for you, but that's about the size of it?" I said.

"Yeah."

"And the cops would know that Sammy was one of his girls? Would know his entourage?"

"Yeah, man, that's my worry. Even if they ain't got no hard evidence like fingerprints, DNA, or whatever. What they do got is-"

"Circumstantial."

"Exactly. They know he threw the party. They know she's one of his girls. And they know she's dead. It's enough, man, it's enough," he said.

"OK, OK, isn't that kind of a good thing? I mean, that he's locked up? At least for now, they can't release the guy if all fingers point in his direction?" I said.

"I told you, Jack, that don't fucking matter! He's got fucking guys everywhere. If you get pinched, it don't stop you. You have systems in place for sorting this shit out whether you locked up or not. All it means is he's pissed off, and trust me, the word is out."

"Fuck. FUCK! So not only do we have to worry about the police, now we got some big time fucking crime lord who wants our blood?!" I said, my body turning back to ice cold.

"Pretty much. But that's why I gotta get to Tito - he can help us out. He has money and he can phone Marianna. We can check she's safe, and my boy Santi. I gotta know he's OK, homes, I gotta know he's OK!"

Diego's eyes were filled with panic, he sat upright, his hands grabbing the keys in the ignition, even though the engine was already running.

"You really think Anton would go after your family? Does he even know where they live?" I asked tentatively.

"No, no, I don't think so, they've been in America for years. But I gotta check - I gotta check - my fuckin' head's been doing cartwheels. I gotta check Anton hasn't got to them," he said.

"Yeah, yeah. Sure thing, Diego. I guess that explains why we're heading to the states," I said.

"And Tito's place is on the way. So I can warn them first, then I'll go to America and see if I can move her - get her and Santi someplace safe. Then that's it for me, I'm out. I ain't coming back. Fuck Mexico man, there's nothing here for me now, nothing but pain. All I got to show for this place is bad dreams," he said.

"But what are you gonna do in America?" I asked.

"I dunno. Marianna and me, we didn't exactly end on the best of terms, you know? I seem to fuck up anything good that comes into my life. But, it's the boy - I need to go for the boy. I run over the border a couple times a year and visit him. But it's been a while now. Seems like everything I do nowadays is here. I guess recently I've been thinking about all that. About him growing up with no papa, you know? An' then all this shit, with Sammy... it made me realise it's time to get out, before I wind up..."

"Yeah, I get that," I said.

"Oh, you do?" he said, unconvinced.

"The getting out bit anyway, for sure," I said.

"Look, Jack, I can't go to prison. Not for what happened with Sammy. 'Cos if I do, and my boy grows up with no pappy, it'll be history repeating itself. Just like me. And then what? Drugs, gangs, tatts and slang?"

Diego had worked himself up into a sombre mood of remorse, lost in a cycle of blame. I had until then mostly written him off as the harbinger of doom and the architect of my downfall, but now I felt a little compassion toward his circumstances, even if I found it hard to wholly believe his boy Santi would be any better off with Diego's presence in his life, rather than out.

"OK, OK," I said, placing a hand on his shoulder. "It's a lot to take in. But how about this - we put the crack pipe away and get this truck out of the mud? We make our way to Tito's and make sure all's good on the home front. Sound like a plan?"

"Yeah, Jack. Yeah, let's do it," he said, climbing out of his door and bracing against the swirling night wind.

I felt like a corpse hoisted out of the grave, allowed to grace the goodly soil once more. I pulled my door open and stepped out onto the sloppy clay. I had to steady myself against the door to stop from falling over, clambering round the truck to meet Diego at the rear. He was on all fours, digging around the wheel with his bare hands. I joined him, pulling out handfuls of mud and bone, tossing them over my shoulder. The fossils of loved ones hoicked out and discarded, their spirits climbing back down below to linger forever more in their forgotten realms. After exposing a couple inches of tyre, we leapt up and got back into the truck. Diego, motivated by the recent thoughts of his family, bound forward with renewed vigour. He eased the truck slowly out of the hole and then we were off, slipping back into the groove of old tyre tracks, sticking more easily now to recognised thoroughfares. We didn't speak again unless it was to warn of an upcoming divot or headstone to avoid.

Half an hour later we wriggled free from the grieving maze, exiting the graveyard under a large stone passageway that led directly out onto the shanty outskirts of Chihuahua. The road ran parallel to some garages, all facing directly opposite to the cemetery. We looked for a way in, but each opening was blocked off with rubbish stacked too high to pass. Eventually, we reached an entry point that was completely free from obstruction. We took this route, finally driving inward, heading for the city centre. All subsidiary roads leading from this main artery were also blocked off with more mounds of rubble and upturned paving slabs.

"Do you get the feeling we're being funnelled in? Like someone *wants* us to come this way?" I ventured.

Diego didn't answer, which did little to quell my fears. He had not only become silent but was curb crawling, apprehensively passing each new block of garages. Tito's place was downtown, but to get there would mean sneaking past the protesters who had made it known that entry and exit was prohibited. Behind the rows of garages and temporary homes came a misty amber glow from the city's fires. We reached a T-junction. To our left was clear but Diego turned right, failing to spot a loitering mob in the distance until it was too late. He paused the truck. The group looked roughly two dozen in number, a flailing mass of arms and placards silhouetted by a string of burning cars.

"Diego..." I said.

"Yep," he said, grabbing the gear stick and pulling it backwards, struggling to find the reverse.

The mob spotted us and there was a brief moment of hesitation before they heard the clanking of gears and realised we were prey. Then they started waving their sticks and banners, breaking forward into a charge like medieval soldiers on the battlefield.

"Diego!!" I shouted, desperate for him to find the gears, helplessly watching him struggle.

"Fuck! Fuck, it's stuck!" he screamed, yanking on the gear lever.

The mob grabbed rocks from around themselves and started hurling them. The tink of stone on metal. Again. Tink. Tink. Gradually more and more projectiles hit the roof and bonnet, until eventually, one crashed through the windscreen in the top right corner, showering us with fine fragments of glass.

"Come on! Fuck!" I shouted, slamming the dash with my hand.

Diego was mumbling his persuasions, preaching to the gear stick until finally it slipped into position and he was able to reverse back for a 5-point turn. My passenger side window looked directly onto the ensuing hoard. Their ambling charge turned into a sprint. I saw a man at the back of the group hunched over a tequila bottle, shoving a rag into the opening.

"Let's go, man, let's fucking go!" I shouted.

The scene turned to slow motion, the man lighting the dripping rag, a flutter of fire illuminating his half-masked face, his menacing intent glimmering in the darkness. He arched his back, cocking the Molotov in final preparation for his Hail Mary javelin throw.

"Go! Go!" I screamed.

Diego spotted it too, yet hesitated, momentarily mesmerised by the beauty of the flaming bottle licking through the night sky. The tequila comet provided the final impetus for Diego to find the right gear. He slammed the truck against some bins before finally lumbering away from the pursuing rioters. We struggled for speed in the entry-level gears, unable to outrun the Molotov. It exploded onto the roof of our cabin. A burst of 40% proof liquid fire came showering over the vehicle, dripping down the windows and engulfing the chicken cage. Diego lurched the truck away to the sounds of cheers and jeers from the jubilant protesters who eventually gave up the chase, dissolving into nothing more than angry shadows in our side view mirrors. The faster we drove, the more fuel we gave to the fire. The flames spread across the entirety of the rear coop. The chickens found a new level of berserk, screaming as they cooked alive. The truck was billowing out thick black barrels of smoke in our wake, a caustic tunnel of burnt flesh and feathers.

"Fuck, man! We're on fire!" Diego bellowed.

I looked through the rear cabin window which had darkened with soot and the smearing of charred wings cindered by the bright naked flames. The birds were frantically flying about, wild with the heat, desperate to escape. Their deafening cries sent shivers down my already taut spine. We had become a mobile crematorium, a satanic rotisserie truck with the devil at the wheel. When one bird slapped its tortured, half-cooked face against the glass, I turned to Diego, ashen, and suggested it was time we dump the truck.

"Where?" he said.

"Anywhere. But we can't carry on like this, my mind can't take it," I said, the words creeping out of my mouth, slow and jumbled. I recalled our recent graveyard PCP hit. Whilst knowing little about the intricacies of the drug, I made the assumption that some kind of safe zone was imminently required to avoid falling long and hard into an inescapable hole.

"Fuck it, we'll have to go on foot. I think I know the way from here anyway," he said.

One of the rear tyres burst just as Diego was pulling over toward the curb. We both leapt eagerly out of the cabin, rife with the fear of an imminent explosion. We were parked under a motorway flyover which Diego said we could follow on foot to reach downtown.

"Do we need anything from the truck?" I asked.

"Maybe, yeah. Let's check, quickly," he said.

"Will it blow?" I asked.

"Not yet… but if you want we can hang on and get some flame-grilled chicken!" he said, chuckling and opening the side door to salvage anything of value.

I checked my door, plus the glove box. "Nothing much here," I said, pulling out a tea towel that was woven with a 'FRESH EGGS' logo above an idyllic farmyard scene.

"Take it," Diego said.

"Huh?"

"You can use it as a disguise, wrap it around your face like a bandito. Might help us get into the city if you don't look like so much of a gringo."

It was a fair point, and I tied it quickly around my lower face. It tasted oily.

"The chickens?" I said, my voice slightly muffled by the tea towel rag. Diego looked at me confused, so I jabbed a thumb over my shoulder in reference to the rear.

"What about 'em?" he said.

"You got the tyre iron?" I said.

He nodded and came round to hand it to me, shaking his head. The tyre iron was still red with blood and had some matted hair on one end, both belonging to the farmer whose livelihood we had hijacked and now torched.

"It might be nice to try and at least balance out the scales on all the bad shit we've done," I said.

"You're crazy, man, they're gone."

A wing flapped through the charred cage side. I moved round to the rear, but the heat was so intense that it made me take a couple of steps back and shield my eyes. I made another approach, this time staying low until the last moment, then popping up and whacking the lock with a hefty swing. On the second attempt, it broke free. The door dropped on its hinges, hanging for a brief moment, then collapsed onto the tarmac. I jumped back as dozens of flaming chickens burst out from the cage, their wings laced with tequila, their bodies black and burnt. Firebirds, flying up into the night sky.

"Happy now?" Diego asked.

I passed him the iron and in doing so realised the bloody end had left a smear inside my palm. Acknowledging that my blonde hair was still a gringo calling card, I ran my blood and soot-stained fingers through my hair, slicking it back with bloodied filth.

"Happy." I said.

# 11

# TITO'S TACOS

We followed the freeway into the city, doing our best to blend in with the mobs by waving two placards that we had found discarded in the gutter. Mine was a 3ft square board on the end of a 2x4 timber plank sporting a poster of a suited politician with his eyes scrubbed out. There was a slogan written in scrawled red paint that I quickly rehearsed. Diego said it was about not believing the lying eyes of politicians and so whenever we passed a rabble of protestors we would wave our placards and shout our slogans. Having circumnavigated the city's closed-off main arteries we met no further resistance on the streets, the assumption being that we were fully-fledged members of the riot.

"How much further?" I whispered as we cantered past another mob.

"Almost there," he said.

We stayed close to the freeway underpass, scampering between its vast concrete legs. All businesses and buildings were closed, the lights blackened as if turning their backs on the crimes being metered out below. There was the occasional cry of faraway looting. The distant sound of shop windows and government offices being ransacked. Hoards of discontented peasants rising up to batter the face of buildings that represented authority, bureaucracy, and the cathedrals of the West. Capitalism was being clubbed to death by stick-wielding paupers. Their territorial rage was a shifting battleground of flashpoints, a rampage against a society that no longer valued the even keel of fairness. As the Powers That Be sought to close off the doors of opportunity, the people set about kicking them in. The citizens of this city had snapped. A petrol tax levied to save five percent for the one percenters had brought this place to its knees. We could feel the city under attack but it also felt strangely far off. Thrashing sounds of shattered glass were a faint howl that filled the mysteriously quiet void of silence. We were pop-up ballerinas in a haunted jewellery box dancing to the mesmerising tune of civil unrest. The Great Unwatched Pot of Civilisation, allowed to boil over into anarchy. In between the cracks of this fractured city, slipped two devious souls with blood on their hands and the cremated remains of incinerated fowl emblazoned upon their brows.

The metropolitan grid spat us out at a residential cross-section. Apartment blocks towered over every corner bar one, which was instead levelled to the ground. A mound of pounded rubble lay waiting in anticipation of future redevelopment. The site was closed off by an interlocked diamond patterned chain link fence where homeless people had set up camp. They had dragged in a battered sofa, a car bonnet, a TV set, and two mangled shopping trolleys filled with miscellaneous detritus. All of it neatly encircled a flaming oil drum. Everything was arranged with a strangely accomplished kind of vagrant feng shui. Diego was leading the way to Tito's but had stopped short at the metal fencing surrounding the tramp site. He looked through the fence across to the road on the opposite side.

"What is it?" I asked.

"The building, through there. See? That's Titos," he said.

Diego crouched down, creeping behind some bins for cover. I did likewise, spotting only one tramp asleep on the sofa in the compound, lord of his domain.

"Shit, see that car?" Diego said.

Parked on the opposite side of Tito's block of flats was a mauve Cadillac convertible with a white trim hood. There were only one or two other cars on the entire street so it stood out distinctly with its auspicious paint job and glistening wheels.

"Very bling," I said.

"Yeah, I don't like it. It don't feel right. I mean, for the street. It really don't fit in, you know?"

"Yeah, if you had a car like that, would you really leave it parked on a street like this, tonight?" I queried.

"Hmm, I don't like it," he repeated, turning suspicion into a mantra.

"Is there anyone inside?" I asked, anxiously peeking over Diego's shoulder.

"Can't see. Fuck... Let's find another way," he said.

We found a section of the chain fence that had curled open, a gap in the mesh curtain wide enough to squeeze through with only minor scratches from the frayed ends of wire. We ran across the far side of the hobo yard sticking close to a wall that kept us away from the sight line of the Cadillac. From the rear of the apartment block, we were able to count down a couple of buildings until Diego was satisfied that we were in line with Tito's place. There were no signs of life in the alleyway, just a few closed garage doors and an eight-foot high breeze block wall decorated with broken glass.

"We'll have to go over," Diego said, looking around, expecting company at any moment.

I didn't like the alleyway much, but the main streets were not great either. I nodded ruefully and offered him my palms bridged upward for a booster. He climbed up my body, stepping off my shoulder and onto the wall, kicking away some of the larger slices of anti-intruder glass. Then he pulled me up and I did my best not to slice open a hand or foot before we lowered each other down the opposite side.

"Looks pretty quiet," I mused while dusting myself off.

The rear of the block was dark. Not a single warm glow from any window except a top floor apartment that had the harsh strobe flicker typical of a TV hypnotising its viewer to sleep. Tito's place was on the third floor, about halfway up, shrouded in darkness. A fire escape snaked its way up the entire rear of the block. I offered Diego another boost and he reached up and pulled down the access ladder. Every movement we made was slow and deliberate, using hand signals where possible and cursing each other if we disturbed a bin lid or a loose piece of rubbish.

"You wanna come up, or keep look-out down there?" he whispered.

"I'm coming up! There's no fucking way I'm staying-"

"Shhhh. OK, let's go," he said, hurrying up the fire escape.

We crept off the ladder when we reached the third floor, staying cautiously low as we approached Tito's windows. The curtains were pulled back, allowing us an unobstructed view into the lifeless living room. All that we could see were dark blobs of furniture staring back at us, everything bathed in a pale yellow glow coming from the streetlamp as it shone through the front windows. Beyond the two large sash lounge windows at the rear, there was another to our adjacent left, where the building dog-legged out. That room was also quiet and dark, hidden mostly by the veil of a lace curtain. I gestured quizzically to Diego.

"Kitchen," he hissed.

Diego opted instead to prise open a lounge sash. I stayed low, hunkered. The alley behind us was quiet, worryingly devoid of life. Diego crept into the lounge slowly, one leg at a time. After hearing no disasters, I followed. Inside we tried to navigate as best as possible in the dark. Diego reached the window facing out to the front and hid behind a half-open gap in the curtain.

"Shit," he said.

I joined him, allowed a fraction of an inch through which he directed my gaze to the Cadillac below. From this angle, it was clear there were two men sitting in the front of the car, casually smoking. Before waiting for me to pontificate, Diego turned and made his way down the hall. By the time I caught up with him he was pulling closed a bedroom door, shaking his head; empty. We both gravitated to the only remaining door at the end of the hall, leading to the kitchen. Diego pressed it open, then lurched backward when startled by his glimpse inside. I stopped him falling, then turned on my heels, ready to beat a hasty retreat.

"No, fuck, no..." he said, tiptoeing slowly back towards the room.

From my cowering safety spot, now several feet further down the hall, I could see a kitchen table sitting at which was the silhouette of a man, motionless, upright, as if ready to begin his evening meal. His shoulders, head, and upper body were a clear stencil outline against the cream kitchen units behind, like a shadow puppet against a silk screen. I edged closer, my eyes locked onto the imaginary eye line of the black figure. The room smelt of death. Not old and decayed, but young and sickly. I realised from Diego's gentle sobbing that this was Tito, and that it was dinner for two - him and the reaper.

"Ah, Tito, man!" Diego said, standing alongside the body at the table, resting his hand on Tito's shoulder.

Tears fell from Diego, little pearls of light falling softly in the darkness. I moved around to the other side of the room feeling the eyes of the faceless man watching my every move. I opened the door of a tall freestanding fridge which sent a shard of golden light beaming onto the face of Tito. His head was tilted slightly back and his throat had been slit from ear to ear. Beneath the thick gaping wound, he wore a chunky metal necklace that glistened with the overspill of blood. He had short, black, curly hair, bleached artic white on the tips. Tattoos covered his neck and shoulders. Sharp swirls of ink scythed across his body, partially hidden beneath a crimson-soaked vest. His hands were laid out in front of him, palms down, pinned to the table by broad kitchen knives. There was a garish symmetry to the scene, an orchestrated kind of mayhem. This was the work of more than one man. Perhaps two holding him down and one driving in the daggers. The meticulous nature of their work contrasted by a ferocious lack of mercy. A great swell of gut-wrenching queasiness started to curdle in my bowels, a nauseous paranoia that made my temples pulsate wildly. There was some great, unseen, maligned force out there, hunting us down and littering our destinations with corpses. It foreshadowed our movements with an unnerving sense of righteous comeuppance. It was a heady mix of sorrow and fate, one we had been surviving on since discovering Sammy's body almost exactly twenty-four hours previously. Death was not simply following us, it had *become* us.

"We need to leave," I murmured.

Standing there staring at Tito's hands impaled to the table with twelve-inch kitchen knives, I was able to fully understand what Diego meant when he had said "fear Anton, not the police". After all, the police rarely crucify you to a dining table and slash your throat from ear to ear.

"We need to leave," I reiterated.

"I heard you," Diego replied, not moving.

I knelt down and looked under the table to where the knife tips protruded, coated in thick, congealed blood. They must have been swung down with great force. The pain inflicted would have been unbearable. Diego went into a kind of autopilot, leaving the room with a thousand-yard stare and heading back into the lounge. I stood there staring blankly at Tito until eventually Diego returned holding a shiny silver AK-47 rifle.

"What the fuck is that?" I asked.

"Bong," he replied.

It was indeed a life-sized chrome AK-47 bong with a pencil-thin pipe protruding from the side next to the trigger. Diego placed it on the kitchen side counter next to me and threw down a handful of skunk buds alongside. Then he made his way over to the fridge and leaned in.

"Cerveza?" Diego asked, in a tone very much composed for someone who had just discovered the mutilated body of his close friend.

"What?! No. Diego, we need to get the fuck out of here," I said.

"Oh sweet, tacos!" Diego exclaimed, pulling out foil-wrapped trays and placing them on the table. I looked on at him wondering if he had gone into some kind of shock, as he casually laid out plates of food and sauces.

"Really? You can eat?" I asked.

"We can't do nuttin' for him," he said, gesturing to Tito, "He's gone now. Don't mean I don't care, and don't mean I gotta like it. But that's it. Besides, Tito makes the best tacos."

"That's it?" I said.

"Don't go getting all self-righteous on me, Jack," he said, opening a bottle of Quilmes and passing me one.

"I don't think it's self-righteous to maybe, I dunno... to warrant more... feeling of loss," I said, placing the beer he had given me next to the bong on the counter.

"Loss? That's his loss, man. His loss. And it don't mean I don't care about him either. Tito was my boy! But getting upset about it ain't gonna help. We need to keep our emotions in check right now. Trust me, you don't want me getting emotional," he said, gulping his beer.

"Fine, whatever,"

"Whatever? Yeah, whatever. And what do you know about it? What do you know about death? Because you seen one dead girl? How you handling that loss? Huh?"

"I dunno, but I'm handling it," I said.

"Yeah? Well me too," Diego said, putting the final dish on the table and closing the fridge door just enough for us to see around the room. "You gotta relax Jack."

"Relax?! I'm standing next to a guy with two throats and knives sticking out his hands. How am I supposed to fucking relax?!" I said.

"Ah Tito, man. I love you brother," Diego said, raising his beer to him.

"How did they get here?" I asked, thinking out loud.

Diego was building his taco with various layers of dips, sauces, and spreads. He was deeply occupied with the taco construction, so I had to press him again to get a response.

"Diego, we led them here, right? Those fuckers outside. Tito is dead because..."

"Jack, don't. Don't finish that fucking sentence. I'm gonna sit here and finish my tacos, and you gotta respect that, man. This is my farewell, OK? You don't like that, then take yourself, and that funky little bong, into the lounge, OK?"

"I don't wanna fucking smoke. In case you had forgotten, Anton is nearby, so therefore I would much rather just get the fuck out of here." I said.

"I'm eating," he said, between mouthfuls. "He ain't near, they just some goons."

"OK, well I have a question, just how capable is Anton? I mean, he's reached as far as here, right?" I said.

"Right."

"Well, something occurred to me earlier... I left my passport at my hotel. So if someone was able to track down where I stayed, the cops, or Anton... well then they'd get my passport. And get my address back home."

"How would they get your hotel?" he said.

"I dunno, maybe just phone around a few in the city, see if any gringos didn't show up for breakfast, that sort of thing."

"How many nights were you checked in?"

"Three. The first night was, well, last night, the night of the party," I said and began pacing around the room as these buried fears began to surface.

"So then tonight is night two? Means you got one more night before the guy at the hotel expects you to check out...? Unless he's some paranoid type that would notice you not coming and going. So I'd say you got one more night before you need to worry. And as for Anton's guys, I can't see them checking all the hotels. Same with the cops. You're not the only gringo in Mexico City, dog." Diego said.

They might not phone the hotels checking for me, as Diego predicted, but I also remembered phoning Angel from my hotel room. Assuming he worked for Anton, which seemed an almost certainty, then he might tell Anton that he dropped me off at the La Casa Roca. I hadn't seen Angel again after the drop off so maybe I would get lucky, maybe he had punched his final meth ticket. The more I added it up, the more I realised Anton's guys had the better chance of finding out who I was. They had a chain of contacts. The greater motivation. And a brutal taste for retribution.

"Would they come to England, Anton's guys? If they found my passport, my stuff, would they come to England?!" I said, my mind starting to simmer.

"Chill, homes. He's a big cat but he ain't Pablo fucking Escobar," he said, calming my nerves slightly. "What's waiting for you in England? Who you worried about?" Diego enquired.

"Me? No one, really... No wife, no kids." I picked up the beer from the side and took a long hard slug. "Mum died when I was young. After that, a few years after, my dad bailed too," I said.

"Where'd he go, your pops?" Diego said, showing flickers of genuine concern.

"You tell me. He's out there somewhere. He was a big businessman. Super successful, had it all, you know... I used to think he was a God. All I wanted to be was like him. But when my mum died, he just couldn't take it. He lost the plot. Didn't feel like there was any justice in the world. He went into self-destruct, started hard on the bottle. Shit, I found out later that most of his talk was bullshit anyway, all the businesses, they'd been in debt for years..."

"We don't get to choose our parents, Jack, you ain't your father, ese. None of us are," he said.

"Yours?"

"Never met him. Spent most of his life in prison, died there. A bum fight over a bunk bed, you believe that shit?"

"So who raised you?" I said.

Diego pulled his ruffled tuxedo shirt up to reveal his torso littered with tattoos, various names and tags scrawled over his skin. Latin font type, heavy on the ink, a patchwork of gangland identity.

"This is my family Jack. This is where I learnt my right and wrong."

"Oh right - code of the street and all that shit?"

"Damn straight, kid. Shit, I don't know nuttin' else, but I gotta try, right? Only one way outta this life," he said, pointing to Tito. "So, you wanna try one of Tito's tacos? Taste the good life?"

"I don't have the stomach for it, any of it. All this," I said, gesturing around the room, "it's not me. And all this getting to know you shit, it's all well and good but we have to leave Diego, we have to leave, right now."

Staring at Tito again, I wondered how long he had held out and whether he had given up Marianna's address. If so, then they might already be on their way there. The thought must have occurred to Diego. I decided to keep this assumption to myself, really no need to labour the point. As I stared at the knives poking out the back of Tito's hands, I experienced another sinking realisation. It occurred to me that if I had been in his shoes, I would have given up every last morsel of information they required. I wouldn't have been able to get the words out fast enough. I wondered if Diego might also suspect my cowardice under interrogation. And if he drew the same conclusion as me, he might reason that I was a walking liability. A loose end that needed tying off. I tried to bury this fear, partly to hide the realisation from Diego, and partly because I just had too many overlapping fears that I couldn't contend with them all vying for top spot. But deep down I knew that if I was Diego, I would definitely cut me loose soon. Or worse even. It was time to stick or twist. And if we were sticking, then it was imperative that I knew we were on the same team.

"Look, Diego, I'm a fish outta water here man, and I do appreciate what you've done for me so far, and I thank you," I said.

"Oh, you do?! For bringing you here?" he said sarcastically, opening his arms out wide to the sad glories of the room.

"Well, OK, no, I'm not overjoyed at sitting here, having dinner with corpses, driving through graveyards, or waking up next to dead girls. If I'm honest then I'd say there's very little about hanging out with you that I do like," I countered.

"Ah, and we were getting on so well Jack!" he said ironically. "What you really mean is, *thanks for getting me out of that hell hole, and please let me ride with you to America.*"

"Whatever, yes I guess so, and I've never made any bones about needing your help. But Diego, we gotta leave this place. If we stay here, we die."

"Jesus Jack, fine. But we can't leave yet, we need to find Tito's mobile." Diego slapped his taco down and leant over Tito's body and started searching his clothes. "Shit, no phone, but...ha! We got keys!"

Diego tossed a set of Kawasaki keys down on the table, then went over to the drawers and started searching through them.

"I'll check the lounge," I said.

"Look for a phone, Jack, or anything with Marianna's name and number on it. Can't leave that shit lying around. And cash, you know, anything that's got some value," he said.

I went into the lounge and began prodding around the room, sliding my hand under sofa cushions and lifting magazines off the floor. The room's darkness began ceding ground to the rising sun as it peaked through the lounge windows, heralding a new dawn and with it hopefully a reversal of our fortunes. I knocked a lamp over into the curtains and blindly kicked a whiskey bottle across the room with an inadvertent toe poke. I was doing more damage than good so gave up the hunt and returned to Diego in the kitchen.

He had removed the oven door and was taking the casing off the internal sides.

"What are you doing?" I said.

"Tito used to keep a stash here, rainy day money. But, fuck it, there's nothing there," he said.

"You think someone got to it first? Anton's guys?"

"Nah, if they took it, then why put the thing back together again?"

"Maybe it wasn't Anton's guys then," I said, gesturing to Tito, "Maybe someone else did that, like a rival?"

"A coincidence? Possible. But I don't buy it. You find anything?" he said.

"Nope."

"Fuck! That's weird, no? Where's his fucking phone? Everyone keeps their phone in their pocket right? Unless they took it?" he said.

"Why would they take it?"

"In case I phoned it. Or to call me from it…try and negotiate," he said.

"Get you to come back to Mexico City to face the music?" I said.

"Maybe. Maybe they'd want us both to come back... you think about that? They might not just stop with me. But you can't negotiate with these fucks, Jack. You can't reason with a dog when

LA LUNA

he's starving hungry, when he tastes blood," he said.

"And what about Marianna? You don't know anybody else who can warn her?"

"Don't know any numbers. All in my phone which is either with the Po-Po, or sitting in the lap of Anton's guys. Fuck! We gotta warn her in person," he said.

"You know where she lives?"

"Yeah, I told you, I set her up there... but it's in the States. Fuck, that could take a day or two from here. What about the bedroom, did you check the bedroom?" he said.

"No, you just said the lounge, so-"

Just then there was a clash of metal outside, from the rear, a dustbin lid being knocked over. Diego and I looked at each other, gripped with panic.

"Fuck, fuck - close the fridge!" he said.

I pushed it shut, while Diego crept up to the kitchen window and pulled a little of the lace netting to one side.

"Fuck! I can see movement!" he said.

I darted back into the lounge, booting the whiskey bottle again. I sneaked a glimpse out of the window and saw the purple Caddy still parked outside. There was only one guy visible this time. I ran back to give Diego the news.

"Just one guy, driver's side," I said.

178

"How many earlier?!"

"Dunno, we saw two at least, didn't we? Could have been a third in the back seat too, I guess," I said.

"So we got one coming round the back for sure. And maybe one or two coming up the front. Fuck, fuck, fuck." he said.

"What are we gonna do?!"

"Grab something, anything," he said, reaching around and arming himself with a saucepan.

"Fuck this," I said, turning out of the room and not looking back.

End of the line for me. Time to operate a little self-preservation. The idea of hosting a standoff against Anton's henchmen with nothing but kitchenware was futile. If Diego wanted to stay then that was his suicide pact. He made no attempt to stop me. His silence I took to be the agreement that from here on out, we were better off separate. I went directly to the flat door, opened it, and peeked out into the communal corridor which was barely lit. The corridor had the feel of a Victorian library, the walls embossed with an olive green Fleur-de-lis paper and a staircase made from mahogany balustrades. Everything was old, leathery, and sinister. A large sash window at the end of the landing allowed a pale dawn light to shine across the glossy wallpaper.

I decided I would take the stairs up and hide out until Anton's men had entered the apartment, then escape when the coast was clear. As I say, it was not a plan born from bravery in the face of defeat, but perhaps this was my price for freedom. I stayed hidden on the next landing up, the idea being that I would need to move rapidly past the flat door when the time came. It also enabled me to hear the footsteps rising up the staircase. I left the flat door ajar. I heard footsteps approach it, then the door creaked gently open, meaning the assailant must have now made his stealthy approach. I tiptoed back down the staircase and across the hall. I paused briefly at Tito's flat door listening for any sounds of confrontation, but there was only silence. I moved a few paces more, glancing down the staircase, my passage to safety. But I paused, something was stopping me from going any further. An uneasy feeling, like guilt. This was a fine time for my conscience to show up. However, I couldn't stop the feeling, that niggle, speaking to me about future shame and regret. *Was I feeding Diego to the wolves?* Probably. *Did he deserve it?* As yet unknown. They wouldn't seek answers or clarity of motivation, they would just pin his hands to the table opposite Tito. I couldn't just let that happen. That didn't feel like the closure Sammy deserved.

Cursing myself for a delayed sense of morality, I made my way back to Tito's flat door. It was still ajar so I eased it open, slinking back into the apartment. There was nothing inside but darkness and silence. I went further, wanting to whisper out Diego's name, to warm him, to find him. Yet silence was the only thing keeping me alive and the only sound I was able to make. I saw nothing in the lounge so headed to the kitchen. It looked identical to when I had left it, except the window was now open with the net curtain fluttering in the wind. It dawned on me that Diego must have made his own escape out the back. This was not good. I had needlessly walked back into the lion's den. I scanned around the kitchen and spotted the chrome AK-47 bong rifle. I grabbed this, clinging onto it as my lifeline. I moved toward the window until I was halted by a sound from behind, it was the kitchen door opening again. Looking back over my shoulder I saw the doorway now occupied by one of Anton's men standing there holding an Uzi 9mm automatic pistol, pointed squarely at my head.

"Hola chico!" he said.

I lowered my arms by my side and in doing so unwittingly pointed the barrel of my silver Bong-47 directly at the man. His eyes flashed with intent, his grip tightened on the pistol. If I hadn't been so rooted to the spot with fear, I would have thrown the bong down in surrender. Yet I couldn't move. He hesitated from the confusion of the standoff, calculating why I was holding a chromatic rifle with diamonte studs on the ammo clip. When I recognised his doubts, I tried to hold the gun with a little more authority. Unfortunately though, as I angled it more deliberately, the bud pipe fell out and it started leaking bong water all over my crotch.

"Haha. Hey chico, your gun is leaking," he said, creeping into the room."Now, why don't you tell me where your friend is, eh? Where's that little piece of shit, Diego?"

Appearing in the shadow behind the man came the ghostly apparition of Diego, as if summoned from the grave. Diego had the saucepan raised to ceiling height, before swinging it venomously down onto the back of the man's head. The guy crumpled into a heap and Diego stood over him, reintroducing the saucepan to the man's head, again and again, relentlessly. With his blood lust finally satiated, he switched from attack to interrogation.

"Hey, puta, you hear me? How many more of you?" Diego said.

"Fuck you!" the man replied, which was more than I expected from him, given that blood was pouring out of every hole in his face.

"What'd Tito tell you? What did he tell you?!" Diego said, trailing off his English and continuing in Spanish.

I couldn't understand much of it, but the gist was that Diego would ask something, the guy would tell him to fuck himself and spit some blood on the floor, then Diego would reacquaint his face with the frying pan. Eventually, the handle snapped clean off and Diego started looking around for something made of strengthened steel.

"Ah, what a stupid fuck I am, the knives!" Diego said.

"What?" I said.

"The knives!" he said, gesturing to Tito.

"What about them?" I said.

"Pass me one!"

"Diego… Look, I'm not too keen, you know, to get my fingerprints..."

"Jack, shut the fuck up and get me one of those fucking blades, it's time we taught this bastard some fucking respect," Diego said.

I walked over to the table and grabbed the handle of a kitchen knife. It was smeared in blood making it difficult to gain any purchase. It was also buried well into the table, so I had to use my knee as leverage against Tito's wrist, yanking the blade slowly out through the shattered bones in his hand. I passed it over to Diego, before looking for something to clean myself up with.

"Right, fucker, you see this, you see this?" Diego said, waving the blade under the eyes of the man. "I'm gonna do to you, what you done to my boy Tito. And you gonna tell me all I wanna know…"

At that moment, I noticed some movement in the shadow outside the kitchen window where the lace curtain was still flapping in the breeze. I realised that the open window had been a ruse designed by Diego to create the impression that he had escaped. His plan had worked, but alarmingly there was something else now in its place, one of Anton's men standing there with a shotgun aimed at me. I barely had time to recognise the sight of him before the trigger was pulled and the window exploded. A vast invisible force grabbed hold of my body and hurtled me through the air, slamming me into the kitchen units.

As I lay wounded on the floor staring into the vinyl tiling, wondering what in God's name had just happened, I looked up and saw the man stepping off the balcony and entering the room through the window he had just obliterated. He had the shotgun pointed at me, not noticing Diego crouched on the opposite side of the room, his view obscured by Tito's corpse. Diego sprang up and without a moment's hesitation threw the knife he was holding across the room. It spun in a swirl of luscious blood-splattering cartwheels, before ploughing directly into the man's head, plum between his eyes. The guy dropped to his knees, dropped his gun, and collapsed into a sorry mess on the floor.

"Fuck me! Who the fuck are you, Diego?!" I said.

"Not bad, eh? I was in the circus for a couple years. I learnt that one from Shiva and his Wheel of Daggers."

"Oh shit, I'm shot," I said.

My shoulder had taken the impact, a cluster of black holes in my shirt marked the entry point for a blast of pellets. Diego came over, glancing at me without major concern. He stopped next to the man's shotgun, picked it up, and pumped the chamber. *Fuck, could this be it, if he just takes me out now, it's just one more body for forensics and one less loose end.*

Attention, however, returned to the guy whose face had been used as a testing ground for frying pan durability. He had pulled a little pussy-shooter out from his sock, every bit as shiny silver as my Bong-47, but arguably able to do a little more damage. He was pointing it at Diego but with the languid strength in his arm of a man who'd been beaten nearly senseless by Teflon. Diego spotted him and swung the shotgun round to face him, firing a round into the man at close range and shredding his torso open. The force of the round slammed the man back against the cupboard units, the blast continuing through him and ripping apart the wooden doors and their casing. The number of dead bodies in the room now outweighed the living.

"I think maybe it's time to go," I said, steadying myself against the kitchen sink.

"Yeah," Diego said, helping me up. "Oh, wait..."

He went over to the guy he had just Jackson Pollark'ed, picking up the Uzi from the floor and a spare clip from the man's jacket. Diego continued his search, opening the man's wallet and pulling out some notes. He encouraged me to do likewise, but I was too busy prodding my new shotgun shoulder injury.

"Fuck, no more shells for the pump," he said, checking the other body, "But... ha!" He pulled a card out of the dead man's wallet and slipped it into his back pocket. I was too exhausted to enquire what it was.

"Which way?" I asked.

"Rear - we don't know if they still got a guy at the front.. Oh shit, the keys," he said, grabbing Tito's Kawasaki set off the table.

We made our way down the fire escape and back down to ground level, my dismount off the ladder made ungainly by the restricted movement I was feeling in my shoulder blade.

"Fuck, I dunno if I can get back over that garden wall," I said.

"Don't worry, don't have to. Look, the garage door," he said, waving the keys.

A quick, fumbled examination of the garage door revealed a lock that did not match any of our keys. Then we had a bigger problem – a third goon, up above, on the fire escape. He must have come late into the apartment, assessed the massacre, then poked his chops out of the kitchen window and seen our getaway. He was armed with a pistol, making his presence known by firing off a round that whizzed a couple of feet above our heads and tore through the garage roof. We jumped backward, hugging the wall of the apartment block. He fired two more shots which ricocheted off the myriad layers of fire escape.

"Where the fuck did he come from?!" I said.

"Dunno, but we can't stay here. Hang on!" Diego said, grinning inanely, brought alive by the mania.

He got up and ran full pelt toward the garage door slamming his shoulder into it, crashing clean through to the other side. More pistol rounds went off, the garage floor puffing up as the goon shot through the newly opened doorway. Diego stood inside the garage door and spurted off a few rounds from the Uzi. This provided me enough cover to dash over and join him. Inside the garage, I saw no sign of our getaway vehicle.

"Fuck, where is it?!" I said.

"Tranquillo, tranquillo," Diego said, reloading the gun.

He went over to the side wall and pulled back a large dust sheet covering an old Kawasaki KLX230R dirt bike, painted lime green with 'Renegade' written on the petrol tank.

"Me and Tito used to ride the dunes. You can ride?" he said.

"Yeah.. ish. I hired a scooter once in Thailand," I said.

"Well, it's ride or shoot?"

"I'll ride. I'll try, anyway. You're better on the gun... Just show me how it works, OK?"

"Kick starter, pedal, gears, twist throttle to go faster. Now kick that metal bar there, kick that down while I get the door," he said.

I did as instructed but it wouldn't start. I kicked it again, nothing. Diego opened the main sliding garage door which led straight into the alleyway. He looked out either side, seeing nobody. I kicked the pedal again and when it fired up, he jumped on the back.

"Now when we get out there, don't fuck about, OK? We fucking go - got it?" he said.

"Yeah, let's go!"

I eased the accelerator on but it lurched faster than expected, scraping us along the garage wall before bursting us out into the alleyway.

"Easy!" he shouted in my ear, grabbing hold of me for support.

Once steady, I was able to open up the throttle, turn left at the end of the block, and head up toward the main junction.

"Easy, easy…" Diego said.

The junction ran parallel with the entrance to the flats and the hobo yard. There were a couple of parked cars on our nearside that provided us with cover. Just visible beyond them was the elongated nose of the purple Caddy. One man was still sitting in the driver's seat.

"OK, just creep out, then as soon as you can, floor it to the right. The Caddy's facing down the street so by the time he sees us - on this thing, we'll be long gone, cool?"

"Cool," I said.

The main communal door to Tito's apartment block sprang open and the guy who had been shooting at us from the fire escape appeared waving his gun and shouting to the guy in the car. He then spotted us sitting on the idling bike and immediately began firing in our direction. I ripped back the throttle, propelling us out into the road. I tried to turn right but my mangled shoulder froze and locked in position. I lost control of the bike, sending us both flying off the back while it skated out from under our legs and across the road. The guy in the driver's seat of the caddy started to get out. He was fat and bald, his size working against him, forcing him to grab hold of the door frame and roof lining to hoist himself slowly out. By the time he was on his feet, Diego had taken a few steps out into the road and was firing his Uzi into the car, shattering the side window and peppering the paintwork with nasty little holes. Then Diego switched targets to the guy in the apartment block doorway, forcing him to dive behind parked cars for cover.

"Bike!" Diego shouted.

I got up and ran over to the bike, pulling it upright by using all the strength I had in my good shoulder. The engine had died so I had to kick-start it back into life. On the third attempt, it worked.

"We're good, let's go!" I shouted.

Diego stood in the middle of the desolate street, dressed in a skeleton bone tuxedo and spraying Uzi rounds as carefree as a man watering his garden. He was back lit by the rising sun, a new dawn waking up to the familiar sounds of chaos and gunfire. Diego jumped onto the back of the bike and I yanked down on the rasping accelerator of the Kawasaki while he unloaded the chamber of his gun until the final *click*.

# 12

# RIDERS ON THE STORM

We drove the Kawasaki clean out of the city with no eyes over our shoulders and no fear of pursuit. Diego was confident he had tagged a wheel on the Caddy during his liberal hosing down with the Uzi. If true, they would never catch up with the Renegade. I had just about managed to handle the 230cc engine that gurgled away between my thighs and rasped out of the exhaust. It was a handy mode of transport, allowing us to weave between the remnants of the looted city. The protesters had mostly deserted, hiding from the coming sun that revealed the full extent of their ransacked metropolis. Thankfully, therefore, our dawn exit was met with no resistance. The roads in and out still had piles of rubble and burnt-out cars blocking off the main routes but the Kawasaki nimbly threaded its way through. Getting clear of the city felt good, the concrete apocalypse soon dissolving into a soothing expanse of undulating desert. The road opened out, stretching long and straight, blanketed with swirls of sand blown across in drifting, mesmerising patterns. It became a lunar landscape of molten rock formations bubbling up through the scorched earth. Upturned stalagmites seemed to rupture through the land, like driving through an unfurled cave. The tarmac stretched with infinite needle-like precision, pointing us toward the horizon under the steady gaze of the rising sun. The bike kicked up a tunnel of dust as we rode, the angle of the soft morning light creating a fuzzy halo around our shadowy forms.

"Is that your gun in my back?" I shouted over my wounded shoulder to Diego.

"Or am I just pleased to see you?" he said.

"Can you put it somewhere else?"

"Where? I ain't got nowhere else. It won't fit in my pockets, I can only tuck it in here."

"Why do we need it? It's empty now...?" I inquired.

"Could come in handy. I'd rather have it and not need it..."

"OK, OK. So, how far are we going?" I asked.

"Another couple hours. How's the fuel?"

"Quarter tank," I said.

"Should be OK. How's the shoulder?"

"Hurts like fuck."

"Want me to drive?" Diego said.

"Might be an idea... might also need to get it looked at. I suppose a hospital trip is out?" I said.

"You suppose right, Jack. But I'll check it for you when we next stop, OK?"

"Oh, so you're a doctor now? They teach you that in the circus too?" I said.

"I seen a few gunshot wounds in my time," he said and started examining the back of my shoulder blade, fingering the exit holes in my shirt.

"Ah! Fuck! Stop, that hurts man - you'll make me crash," I said.

"Again? Please don't. My fucking leg is all ripped up the side from the last time."

"Boo hoo. Gunshot wound - trumps it."

"Well, it looks like most of the bullets come out the back. You lucky Jack. I can see exit holes," he said.

"Great, I got holes in my back?! Fuck me... weird thing is though, it doesn't actually hurt *that* much," I said.

"Hmm, maybe hit some nerves? And yeah, you still wanna check it proper, make sure there's no bits left in there. You know, that's what causes problems," he said.

"Is it bleeding much?"

"Nah, it can wait 'til the next stop. Sure you don't want me to drive...?"

"Nah, fuck it, I'm in a position where it can rest, so I kind of just wanna leave it. Let's just get there. Where is there, anyway?" I asked.

Diego reached into his pocket and pulled out the card he had taken from the shotgun wielder responsible for my shoulder injury. He leant round and held it up in front of my face. It was a laminated business card with a simple cartoonish picture of a man with the lower body of a horse. The horse-man was reared up on his hind legs and holding a hamburger proudly in his hand, raising it to the sky, with a lightning bolt striking the centre of the patty. The logo was embossed in gold: "Centaur Burgers".

"What the fuck, you got worms or something? You had tacos, like, two hours ago!" I said.

"It's not a burger joint, it's a processing place - they make the burger meat," he said.

"A burger factory... you mean, a slaughterhouse?"

"Exactly."

"Cute. And why would we wanna go there? Because if you feel you need to add any more stops onto this vacation, for my benefit - you really don't. I mean honestly, Diego, have you ever thought about a job in tourism? I'm sure the Mexican government would love to have you."

"Ha, ha. I'll have you know they make a fucking tasty burger. But that's not all they make, if you get me?" he said.

"Sausages?"

"Jesus Jack,"

"Enlighten me,"

"It's a cover. The burgers are cover for the real business. Opioids," he said nonchalantly.

"Opioids?!"

"Used to be fields and fields of weed back in the day, a jungle of the finest bud you ever smoked. But there's no money in it anymore, 'cos our biggest market, America, legalised it, right? So we gotta diversify. Didn't take long to realise that after the weed market went, the next best thing to go into was the opioids. Plus steroids, all that shit. And the only fucking thing Americans love more than their hooky fucking opioids is burgers, man! So this way we get to do both under one roof! I tell you, Anton's a fucking genius!"

"Whoa-whoa-whoa, Anton?! This is Anton's place?!"

"Where you think I got the card from? It was in Gini's pocket. That's the big fella who shot your ass," he said.

"Anton's place?!" I repeated, flabbergasted.

"I used to work there back in the day. Few years ago. I totally forgot until I saw the card again. But then I realised the factory is practically on the way, just a little diversion. When I worked there we had the bud crop, then it all changed over to meat and 'special cheese', the tootsies, sobos, Apaches, all that shit. I only ended up going back there for the odd truck run. Anton likes to move his people around, work in different sectors, find out where you operate best. And that was fine with me. You know, that's what I'm saying - the game has changed just in my time, an' I preferred the old style. I like to deal in stuff you can smoke, sniff or fuck. That way there's always something you can skim off the top, you know? Hey, you aight?"

"I'm just waiting for you to tell me why the fuck we would wanna go to Anton's place?!"

"Don't worry Jack, he ain't gonna be there. He's in prison back in Mexico City, or did you forget?"

"We *think* he's back there, but we don't know for sure. Why take the risk? What's the point?"

"Because we need money. Or I need money, anyhow. If this is me getting out of the game, for good, then I gotta have some cash to get myself set up," he said.

"Money?"

"Yeah, we gonna rob the motherfucker!" he said, slapping my good shoulder jubilantly.

"You wanna rob Anton? Have you got a death wish?!"

"You think we can piss him off anymore than we already have?! We killed one of his girls-"

"Hey, hey, we agreed, don't say *killed*," I said.

"Well, what then?"

"I dunno, just not that."

"OK, so we accidentally *discovered* one of his girls dead..."

"Ugh. OK, that'll do for now," I said.

"He gets wrongfully arrested," he said.

"We think. We think wrongfully arrested."

"We steal the truck of one of his foot soldiers, kill two of his men at Tito's place, and shoot up their car. So really, we ain't on the Christmas list no more. So I say we do one final job on him, one big one, and then out," he said.

"*'You killed'* at Tito's place. Not me. *'You killed'*," I said.

"Whatever. But *we* are gonna take his place down. *We* are gonna do that, together," he said.

"And if I say no?"

"Try it. Then what's your plan? Drive this thing 'til it's empty and hitchhike back to the states? We need a new set of wheels anyway, so this is the way I see it: we drive there, scope the place out, see if we get a good feeling,"

"And if we don't? If we don't get a good feeling at the drug-cum-slaughterhouse, then we bail?"

"Sure, what you think I'm saying? But it should be ok. It's really just a factory, like any other. At least, that's how it's gotta look to the outside world, you know? There's no guard turrets or shit. The last time I went there, there wasn't even no security. Just staff packing burgers in the front and lab boys packing powders in the back. So we get in, get out, real quick. And we take whatever we can. Plus, we take someone's car, and that gets us the final way to the border. Then - boom - we're done."

"I feel pretty uneasy about that plan,"

"Which bit?"

"All of it. And do I need to remind you that I've been shot? I've literally got blood pouring out my shoulder and sticking to the inside of my shirt."

"Stop being such a pussy, Jack. It's a little shotgun wound, he barely clipped you."

"I just dunno how I feel about robbing a known psychopathic dealer. I haven't been a criminal for as long as you, Diego. It's only a day for me, so I'm still coming to terms with all of it. And I'm just not sure I'm ready for that kind of escalation."

"Then let me put your mind at ease by telling you that you ain't got a fucking choice. We're doing it. You won't have to be selling the shit in America, I'll be handling all that. And, by the way, keeping all the money. 'Cos when we get to the States, we're splittin'. That's also non-negotiable."

"No money, gotcha. This just keeps getting better."

"Jack, one minute you don't want in 'cos you're worried about your moral fucking collapse, the next minute you're arguing 'cos you want a bigger cut?!"

"I don't want a bigger cut, Diego - I don't want any part of it at all! But you're right on one thing - as soon as we cross that borderline, as soon as I know I'm in America - we split. Just get me there. Preferably in one piece."

"I will," he said, "but this is the price. You want out, then this is the price."

# 13

# ARMADILLO
# DESERT

We got to the burger factory at lunchtime. Perfect if it had been an all-singing, all-dancing hamburger joint, with chicks on roller skates wheeling out frothy milkshakes in metal cups coated with sensual condensation. Not so perfect if it was an abattoir on the edge of a desolate landscape in the middle of the Mexican desert, operated by a drug kingpin, whom you intended to rob. The site was set over endless acres of shabby grazing land. Dry, cracked earth, lying barren and devoid of all nutrients. Dirty scrubland populated by sad gangs of malnourished beasts standing dormant under the fierce midday sun. The centre point of this farming armageddon was a cluster of windowless air hangers, vast steel domes with ribbed exteriors. Their metallic sheen long lost under the layers of rust spreading over their surface like an infectious, wildly irritant rash. The buildings acted as an oasis to the seemingly infinite fields of neglected pasture land. Any hope of refuge would prove to be dangerously misplaced under the shells of these gargantuan meat-processing armadillos. The buildings simmered and throbbed under the relentless pounding they received from the sun. I stared into the sky, wincing at the fiery burning ring that shone ever brighter and more expansive with each new weary gaze. We turned off the main highway past endless acres of these forgotten wastelands. Eventually, we stumbled upon a mangled dirt track with a surface scarred by potholes and craters. The larger craters had dark liquid pooled up inside them. These were drain-off points from the buildings that oozed a foul pus-like substance from fractured pipe work. Fissures in the failing construction, ejecting their effluence like a series of lanced boils. We splashed through some of these stagnant pools, through filthy water that seemed unable to dry, opting instead to slowly evaporate in the form of rank odorous vapours.

"Well, this is nice," I said.

"I hear that. Pull up here, we can ditch the bike, fuel's out anyway. This is the last of the animal houses, we gotta go on foot from here."

We dumped the Kawasaki behind a silage pit. I felt a little mournful leaving it there, in light of how well it had facilitated our escape from the ravaged city of Chihuahua. In truth, my uneasy feeling was more deeply rooted in the uncertainty of what we were about to attempt, coupled with the lack of available transport in the event of things turning sour. We moved rapidly on foot, keeping our backs pressed against the cow sheds, with Diego leading the charge. The main centre point of these buildings was the processing factory which sat in front of a large empty courtyard. At the front of the building, there was a "Centaur Burgers" sign, replete with the matching horseman logo and a few steps leading up to the main door. We decided a pincer move was wise, ducking inside an adjacent barn to mask our approach. Prising open a doorway to this barn revealed a mass of caged animals, horses on one side and cows on the other. They were all feeding furiously, their eager heads poking through metal grills, gobbling up grain from scabby troughs. We tiptoed along, reaching a door at the far end.

Entering, we discovered a small office with a window facing onto the main courtyard and factory frontage. From this vantage point, we peeked out, noting one side of the factory lined with parked cars. There were no people about and few signs of life.

"Take your pick," Diego said.

"I'll take any. The red one, there. Where is everyone?" I said.

"Must be all inside. Perfect," he said.

"Hmm, this doesn't feel right to me... how many people do you think are inside? I count at least ten cars. That's a lot of man-management Diego." I cautioned.

"Will you stop worrying?"

"Fine, but I need a gun. You've got the Uzi, but what about me?" I said.

"It's not even fucking loaded!" he retorted.

"Well at least it's something," I said, looking around the office. I spotted a fire extinguisher on the opposite wall. Above it was a mounted glass case housing a ruby red fire axe. "Oh, hang on!" I clipped the case open and took out the axe, weighing it from handle to end. I tossed it from hand to hand, getting accustomed to its dynamics and swiping the air with a few choice practice swings.

"It suits you. Now, pull your mask back over your face. The less gringo they see, the more scared they're gonna be," he said.

"Done," I said, speaking muffled through my Fresh Eggs bandito tea towel. "What now?"

"The main door there, under the Centaur sign; there's cameras above it on both corners. So let's run across, quick as possible so that even if they see us on camera they ain't got time to react," he said, speaking excitedly.

"Wait, I thought you said there wasn't any security here? That it was just gonna be a few old ladies packing burgers?!"

"Yeah, hopefully. But we go prepared like they got someone, si? Also, last time I was here, they didn't have no cameras. That's new. Maybe they changed some things. Anyway, we go straight in the door. Anyone we see, we take down. OK? You gotta be aggressive, Jack. Don't show them any weakness. Then you got two main areas inside: the meat packing facility at the front, and then a back room where there's a door leading underground. And that's where they make the shit, right? That's what we're after."

"Not the burgers?" I said sarcastically.

"Jack, serio."

"Joking. Come on, you're always telling me to go with the flow, and I am... I'm trying to stay relaxed about the whole thing. Even though I think it's a fucking stupid idea and we should just take one of those cars right there and split."

"We're not taking any cars until we got some green and some gear. I ain't heading back to America to see my old girl with just my dick in my hand. I turn up with some yayo or some dollar, then I can get her out and set her up someplace new. You got that, ese?"

I disapprovingly nodded my approval and stroked my axe tip for one last rush of reassurance. Diego nodded back, his eyes alight with pre-fight adrenaline. He grabbed the handle and swung open the door to our office. We burst out and sprinted low and hard across the courtyard. When we reached the main door, Diego yanked the handle down, but it was locked.

"Now what?!" I pleaded.

"The axe!"

Diego stood back to leave me an unobstructed swing at the door. I cast him a doubtful look, the steely sheen of the door creating the impression of an impenetrable foe.

"Aim for the lock - here," he said, pointing at the gap between the door and frame.

I shot Diego another pessimistic look, before resigning myself to at least give it one decent whack. I pulled the axe head up high over my shoulder, ready to strike, when all of a sudden Diego frantically gestured for me to stop. He was training his ear down one side of the building. I heard it too; footsteps. Diego pushed into me and we batted a rapid retreat back across the courtyard to our original starting point, re-entering the mini office. Once in, we checked the success of our stealthiness by peeping again out of the little window. A man in well-worn gaucho denim and a plaid shirt appeared from around the corner and approached the main factory door. I cowered behind Diego, the two of us studying the man's movements. I gripped Diego's shoulder, hoping to convey that this could be an opportunity, if the man opened the main door then we could rush him. With that grip Diego nodded firmly, asserting that he had drawn the same conclusion. Diego reached a hand up to our office door ready to swing it open. However, the cowboy stopped walking, instead choosing to pat down his pockets in search of keys. When he found the set he was looking for he changed direction, abandoning the factory, instead striding gayly toward our office.

"Fuck, he's coming here!" I said, as we both instinctively ducked down from our spy hole.

"Shit, shit, shit," Diego said, lurching back into me.

We darted across the little office, toward the rear door that opened back into the barn. Without discussion, we opened the door and slipped out. I took one last glance around the office to see if the man would notice any disturbance. We were leaving it as we had found it, except the fire case that was now missing an axe. We scurried back into the recesses of the barn, finding a spot to engage in hushed whispers without any danger of being overheard.

"What the fuck are we doing?" I said.

"I dunno, I dunno," Diego said, his mind a scatter, his disposition exposing the fragility of his haphazard plan.

"Let's wait until he comes into the office. Then we'll swing in, grab him, and grab the keys?" I said.

"What keys?" Diego said.

"The keys to the factory!"

"We don't know he even got those! We know he has *some* keys, but what if they're not the *right* keys?" he said.

"Fine time for you to turn pessimistic! They *must* be the right keys," I said.

"Why?"

"How else would he get into the factory?"

"I dunno, a buzzer? They could buzz him in," Diego said.

"So now that door's a buzzer door?!" I said.

"Yeah.."

"There wasn't even supposed to be a fucking camera there." I bemoaned.

"I know."

"Now there's cameras and a buzzer door. The place is like Fort Knox! And you thought I could just smash through it with my axe?!"

"I don't know, I don't know!" Diego said, his voice shrill with uncertainty.

The door to the office opened so Diego pushed me further back into the shadows, behind a large plastic water tank.

"This is a bungle, Diego, an absolute fucking bungle. We should just grab someone's car and split," I said, defiantly.

The cowboy entered the barn and began unlocking padlocks. He hoisted free great lengths of clanking chains that dangled mournfully above the animal pens like bunting at a funeral. He walked over to a metal roller door and began coiling it open by yanking heartily on some rusted chains. He pulled his weight into each tug, the way a sailor raises a mainsail. The newly opened doorway poured light into the barn which made the animals antsy under the blinding glare of the sun. The man then pulled out a series of metal barriers in a concertina, creating a gangway from the barn to the factory. He walked up to the factory end and hit a couple of switches that activated a wall-mounted red warning bulb. The horses in the barn began stomping their hooves in a frenzied state of agitation.

"What the…?"

"Shhh, this is it," Diego said.

The man opened a gate to allow the animals access to his temporary corridor, but none of them took the bait. The first in line was a clapped-out bunch of horses, but they backed away from the light of the outside world, opting instead to remain in the relative safety of their continual darkness. The man hopped in amongst them, waving a cattle prod and jabbing it into their rear ends. The technique worked and the mangy old mules started clambering over each other in the direction of the new doorway. The shuttered corridor had a funnelling effect, reducing their numbers to a single file that led directly to the abattoir entrance. The denim rustler returned to the wall-mounted switches and readied himself. He was almost out of sight from where we stood huddled at the back of the barn, yet we could see enough to make out the shuttered door opening into the factory. The first horse entered through the doorway, becoming instantly more agitated when sighting the new slaughtering abode. Then the steel door whipped closed.

"Perfect," Diego said.

"What?!"

"Let's go!"

Before I could mount a defence, Diego was low-running across the damp hay-strewn barn and over to the newly erected causeway. Instinctively,

I scuttled along in tow. He jumped over the railing and I did likewise. We were inside the horse alley and staring at each other from across a floundering horse's ass.

"What now?" I said.

"Creep. Stay low. Once we get to the door we'll grab that guy and force our way in," he said.

I gave Diego a sarcastic thumbs up and followed his lead, scampering on all fours. The horses were stamping, pounding, and scraping back their metal shoes against the stone-cobbled floor. Our presence inside the murder corridor did little to quell their fears. As they rallied around I had to curl myself into a ball to avoid being trampled. Horse dung was dropping by the suitcase load and as I looked across for Diego, all I could see was a massive purple horse cock swinging gamely between us. A meaty metronome counting down the seconds of our ensuing demise. I made a dash for it, past the Trojan dong and over to Diego's side of the channel.

"We can't stay here - the horses are backing up!" I said.

"Just wait. And stay low, as long as we're in this tunnel the cameras can't see us!" he said.

The cowboy noticed the backlog and left his post to walk down the line and prod the relevant horses back into the correct direction. Then he returned to the factory door, hitting the switch so that the giant steel mouth could swallow up another horse, and we all moved up the line.

"OK, now!" Diego said, hurriedly moving forward in hunchback.

I followed, ambivalent now to all the hooves, swinging horse cocks, and oceans of shit. Once at the end, Diego popped up alongside the lead horse and pointed his Uzi in the face of the gaucho.

"Tranquillo, tranquillo, ese. Take it easy. Now, gimme the stick." Diego said.

The man was caught by surprise but calmly handed Diego the cattle prod.

"Jack, you ready?" he said.

"Yep," I said, positioning myself next to the shutters of the factory door.

"Ok, amigo," Diego said to the man, "you gonna climb into this side of the fence, then lean over and press that button, ok? You don't shout, you don't do nothin' stupid, and everyone goes home safe, comprender?"

"Si, si," the man replied nervously, before carrying out his instructions.

He climbed inside with us then reached over the railing and pressed the button, sliding open the shutter and revealing to us the true nature of the slaughtering pen in all its hellish barbarism. There was a short ramp that sloped down to a bucket cage with a barred floor where the animals were stunned, then sent sliding down to a chopping

211

table for dissection. There were two men working in a sea of blood, hacking up a horse into multiple sections. The blood ran off through a series of grills on the floor. One man was holding an ankle, hacking away at the thigh with a meat cleaver. The other man walked away from him, with a bucket sloshing at his side full of pink goo and swollen organs. Across the floor were a scattering of body parts and severed horse heads wearing terrified expressions.

"OK, which button closes the door?" Diego said.

"This one-" the man said, leaning over to press a yellow button.

Before he could reach it, Diego took the cattle prod and fired full voltage into the back of the man's head. He flew forward in a swan dive, his body limp, face-planting down the chute and into the final holding cage. The man who was chopping off the horse leg looked across in disbelief, then up to where we were standing in the doorway.

"Go, Jack!" Diego shouted.

I hesitated for what felt like minutes, locked in the horror of the chop shop, trying to calculate my role in all this madness. The momentum arrived with adrenaline. I leapt forward with my axe raised, slid down the ramp, and bellowed out a war cry.

"Don't fucking move! Don't fucking move! Don't fucking move!" I said, using the incapacitated gaucho as a stepping aid to climb out of the first holding pen.

Diego was half in the doorway, with his Uzi trained on the two butchers. He leaned an arm back around the doorframe to the yellow switch and pressed it, bringing the shutter down closed behind him.

"That's right, that's right, don't chu move, stay right there," Diego said.

The man with the bucket of horse slop released his grip on the handle. It crashed to the floor and showered his rubber boots and overalls in equine slurry. The man who had been carving off legs dropped his knife down and raised his arms in surrender. I ran up to the men with my axe raised, telling them to get down on the floor. I looked up and saw a blinking red light on a CCTV camera mounted in the corner. Noticing it, I glanced straight at Diego. He nodded, jumping over a railing and joining me on the chop floor.

"OK, eses, you do as we say and no one gets hurt," Diego said.

The two men hesitated, looking over at their recently electrocuted friend in the trough, they seemed unconvinced.

"Forget him, he'll be fine. Who else works here?" Diego said.

They remained silent. Diego rewarded this withholding of information by pistol-whipping the nearest one across the bridge of his nose. I raised my axe menacingly and the one who wasn't clasping hold of newly-fractured nose cartilage soon spoke.

"Just Juan and Ernesto, back there.." he said, gesturing a thumb, "and the girls, on the packing floor."

"OK, take us to them. And the lab?" Diego said.

"The lab?!" the man said, playing dumb.

Diego dangled the cattle prod in his eye line. "I swear ese, you wanna play it tough, I do what I did to your friend there, 'cept I use it on your balls, comprender?"

"Si, si! I show you, OK, tranquillo," he said.

"Good. You and you, start walking," Deigo said, pushing them together in line.

The guy with the broken nose was not responding well to our harassment and kept shirking back his arms when pushed. There was a side of me that wanted to softly, gently, persuade him to cooperate for his own safety and to avoid any more broken bones. But there was another side erupting out of me that wanted him to disobey the orders so that I could experience the thrill of smashing his already broken nose with the butt handle of my fire axe. I was mildly perturbed by these Jekyll and Hyde emotions, swallowing them down inside myself and justifying them as nothing more than a man finding joy in his work.

"OK, this is it? Who's in there, both of them?" Diego said, halting our posse at a walk-in fridge door.

"Should be. I mean, I don't know, they normally are together, but could be…" the talkative one was saying, but then his friend cut him off.

"Fuckin' stop it, man! Don't tell these arseholes anything!"

"Hey, ese," I said, adopting a faux Mexi-gangster voice that bubbled up subconsciously out of my newly found Jekyll state, "I advise you to keep your mouth shut, or I'll take my axe here and start making my own fucking burgers! You got that, Sanchez?!"

He mumbled through blood-curdled nostrils that he understood. Diego ducked into the freezer section, coming back a moment later with another butcher boy dressed in white garments and a little plastic face screen designed to stop bits of horse meat from being inhaled.

"Who's he?" I said.

"That's Ernesto. So we gotta find Juan," Diego said.

"Hi Ernesto," I said to our newest recruit, "you do as we say and nobody gets fucking hurt, capiche?"

"Si," he replied.

"Get in a line, like a conga. We're gonna march ahead onto the shop floor, OK? No one do nuttin' fucking stupid," Diego said.

"Hey, D-" I said, cutting myself short and gesturing over to the man he had cattle prodded who lay motionless in the meat gutter.

"Nah, he's out, leave him there. Let's get going. And the second you see the next guy you take him, OK?" Diego said.

"Capiche," my alter ego said, and I made a mental note to drop the "capiche" from then on, or I was at serious risk of undermining my armed robber gravitas.

We opened two double fire doors by slamming into the crash bars that connected them, swinging open onto the shop floor. This was the packaging phase of the operation and consisted of two long tables facing opposite each other with several women working alongside one another. In front of them was a conveyor belt with a steady stream of burger patties moving past them. Some fiddled the meats into position and others added grease-proof paper, before stacking the burgers into boxes. Around them was a variety of clunking machinery that mostly drowned out the sound of our arrival, although one or two had spotted us out of their peripheral vision.

"Down, down!" Diego said to the three men we had escorted into the room, and they promptly dropped to their knees.

Next to us on the left was a small office cubicle, out of which a rather shocked butcher dressed in matching white overalls and holding a clipboard, came walking out to meet us.

"Juan?" I asked.

"Si," he replied.

"Get down on the fucking floor."

"Si, si, OK," he said, joining the others.

"Diego!" I said, tipping my chin in the direction of the far side of the room. This was the reverse of the main door we had initially intended for entry. Behind the door was a bank of CCTV monitors and a man visible through a large glass window, his feet up on the desk, appearing to be asleep.

"OK, OK!" Diego said, running toward the security cubicle.

As the women became aware of our presence, they yelped in acknowledgment. I kicked my guys in their backs, reminding them to lie face down. My eyes were fixed on Diego. If he didn't make it to the security booth quickly then things had the potential to turn ugly. The security guard woke up and rose from his seat but before he could fully

217

comprehend the scene displayed before him, Diego was upon him with his Uzi raised. He pointed it at the man's head. I think the sight of his terrified staff being held at axe point, plus a man dressed as a Mexican Baron Samedi wielding an automatic pistol in front of his face, rendered any possible thoughts of resistance as futile. He lumbered out of his glass station. His shoulders hung low and remorseful, not saying a word. He took a few more paces toward Diego, who congratulated him with a fierce striking backhand of the pistol butt, plum on the centre of his nose. I admired the effectiveness of Diego's technique, amazed at how nobody saw it coming. The noise of more broken bones and agonising reactions made the packaging girls scream and some of them started to rise from their seats.

"Stop! Down, down, comprender? Just stay where you are. Stay seated. Put your heads down on the table, OK?" I shouted, taking over the role of crowd control.

"Si, si, heads down!" Diego said, marching his guy up to join me.

The women did as told, dropping their heads down but unable to fully rest them on the table as it was a moving conveyor belt. Instead, they had to just hover their heads an inch off the surface, watching at point-blank range as a series of horse meat patties cycled past their faces. Diego reunited with me and the guys at the back, pushing the security guard down to the floor alongside the others.

"Just Juan and Ernesto, eh? You forget about this fucker here?!" Diego said to the guy who had seemingly been our onboard informant.

I kicked this guy up the arsehole for his treachery, and then looked at Diego for the next planned move.

"The lab??" Diego said to the men on the floor.

There was no reaction, so Diego passed me the cattle prod and gave me a look that was self-explanatory. I knelt over the guy I had just anus-kicked.He was moaning from the last hit but I didn't hesitate, swinging the prod between his legs and sending a bolt of lightning up his colon. His scream curdled, his eyeballs inflated, then he passed clean out. I looked up to see the shocked expressions of the bent-over patty women. One of them raised an arm, pointing toward the back of the room where some plastic drums were positioned. Diego saw this and started moving the drums away to reveal a trap door, barely visible, with a sunken latch that he managed to hook his finger into, before pulling it open. A staircase disappeared down below floor level.

"You watch them," he said.

Diego passed me the Uzi, upgrading himself with a shiny, round-barrelled six-shooter he had confiscated off the security guard. Then he climbed down the hatch and out of sight. It was only once he had left that I suddenly felt all alone and well out of my depth. As heists go though, things had gone without a hitch.

# 14

# THE HITCH

With Diego in the basement, I was left standing alone on the factory floor watching over the four men in butcher's overalls. They were lying on their bellies and behaving themselves (which internally I gave them credit for, even if one man's stillness was the involuntary result of colonic electrocution). I had half a fear that I could have killed him, but I swallowed down this anxiety, a trade of late that I had begun to master. I had a vaguely uneasy feeling about the first cowboy that Diego had stunned directly to his skull, lying back in the dissecting trough of the chop room. I reasoned, however, that he was unlikely to pose any imminent threat. He was probably in a similarly stunned condition as the man planked in front of me with the smouldering loins. The dozen or so female hostages were also doing a fantastic job of remaining heads-down over their conveyor belt of burgers. The noise of the operation slowly whirred away in the background. The patties at the business end of the table, no longer being packaged, started piling into one another and creating an ungainly mush, a towering turd-shaped pyramid of raw horse meat. As well as the four butcher boys (one rectally incapacitated), there was also the security guard, the final piggy in the row. He was ominously silent; fully obedient and yet I felt his mind plotting against me. I sensed him mulling over his options, weighing up attack versus apathy and the eventual wrath of Anton when he found out his business had been crippled by a gringo and an ex-employee wearing fancy dress. The guy who had won first place in the broken nose competition started to get lively again. He murmured some unpleasantries at me in Spanish. Next to him, the guard lifted his head up off the deck, his assessment continual.

"Down! Down, you fucker! Heads DOWN!" I said, with as much gravelly toned menace as I could muster through my breakfast tea towel.

I marched along the line, the Uzi in one hand and the axe swinging loosely in the other. The hope was that the sight of either of these weapons would be enough to quell any rational thoughts of resistance. If they had known the gun was empty, they would of course have rushed me in a heartbeat. I glanced nervously over at the trap door. It was eerily silent down there. I wanted to call out to Diego for a progress report. I bit my lip, not wanting to show any signs of wavering faith in our actions. But then two things happened, neither of them welcome. I heard car tyres pulling up to a skid alongside the warehouse. They were as clean and unmistakable as the tyre sounds that had greeted us on the morning of Sammy's death. A pang of remembrance and impending doom zigzagged through my nervous system. The second unwelcome sound came from the basement, that of raised, frantic voices.

"Diego? Diego?!" I called out. No response.

The muffled, agitated sounds from the underground lab grew ever more urgent and demanding of my attention. Four of the five little piggies in front of me lifted their chins off the floor, with the guard brandishing a sinister grin. The scene was turning foul, and fast. I darted down to the front security booth, with my gun trained back on the hostages. When I reached the CCTV monitors, I scanned until I saw the collaborating 6"x 6" black and white screen. It showed a side view of the factory and an all-too-familiar bullet-riddled soft top Cadillac parking alongside the workers' cars. Stepping out of the Caddy were the two surviving men from our recent dawn encounter at Tito's place. I ran back, eager to share my discovery with Diego, but I was stopped in my tracks by a muffled gunshot from beneath floor level. Then a second shot, followed by a scream. And finally, silence.

"Diego...??" I said, tip-toeing back toward the trap door.

Suddenly, a Mexican jack-in-the-box popped head and shoulders out from the trap door sunken on the floor. He had long greasy hair, wide lips, and a crazed look in his eyes. He must have been the chemist as he wore an industrial-style face mask displaced around his neck. Both it and his face were flecked in powder and blood. The blood, I reasoned, belonged to Diego.

Instinctively I began retreating, edging backwards with an awkward nonchalance. The Mex-in-a-Box assessed the scene. He scanned his eyes around the various parties, which provided me with an extra couple of free reverse tiptoes. When he finally had it all figured out he raised his pistol at me and opened fire. By the time realisation was apparent in the man's frown, I had already turned and bolted for the exit. He was wild with his shots and accompanied them with a warcry, sending bullets ricocheting off the various meat-mashing machinery. The women packers were perilously in the line of fire and more so the closer I ran past them. They launched themselves out of their seats, unintentionally obstructing my escape as they dove for cover. I reached the security booth and glanced back over my shoulder at the factory floor. The women were sprinting in the same direction as me. This, I found foolish - *did they not realise I was the target?!* All the men were now on their feet and the little trapdoor Mexican was almost fully out of his hole. The black barrel of his gun was now the centre of my universe. *BANG!* The glass of the security booth window next to me exploded. I threw down my unloaded Uzi and reached for the exit door handle, freedom bound. I pulled it open to reveal Anton's two henchmen standing there blocking out almost every inch of sunlight. Through the chinks of light I just managed to make out some movement. Arms raised skyward, a swift transformation in the shadows of a distant object being brought rapidly into the foreground. It was the butt of a shotgun. At first out of focus, then momentarily in focus in the middle distance, and then blurred again as it reached its final resting place between my eyes. Needless to say, the only decipherable memories from there were of an interminable blackness cloaking out the living world.

When I awoke, my body began an immediate conflab with my brain. The two of them were eager to establish a damage report. The initial memo was vague and troubling: EXTREME PAIN, OVERWHELMING DANGER. These were followed up with a status update from my slowly creaking open eyelids: MEAT HOOK, HANGING.

I vigorously shook my head from side to side, trying to erase the horrifying imagery like shaking out a doodle discovered on Joseph Fritzl's etch-a-sketch. It didn't work. Instead, I merely flicked my face with hair wet, sticky from a congealing stream of blood. A thick strand of gooey hair stabbed into the corner of my eye. This required yet more head shaking to set it free. In doing so I felt my whole body sway. I was weightless, like a pendulum dangling above an abyss. My eyes hadn't lied. I was indeed hoisted up with my wrists wrapped in chains and coiled around a vast meat hook. Two more sensations rushed in, latecomers to the pain party: FREEZING COLD, SHOULDER AGONY.

I was in a walk-in freezer with arctic dry, refrigerated air. My lips were as steely as a playground swing in winter. My teeth began an instant chatter. As I craned my head back once more to assess the height from which I hung, I felt the bones in the back of my neck crunching into position. *How long have I been hanging here?* My shoulder, I noticed, bare and exposed, with four malevolent little black shotgun holes perforating the skin. The sharp fiery pain of the pellets going in seemed a lifetime ago. In retrospect, a somehow joyful experience when compared to the deep and unrelenting coldness that had since permeated my core. The freezing had at least stopped the wound from getting any worse. There was no blood coming out of the holes. They just sat there, sooty dots that had torn through me like paper tears on a gun range target practice. I moaned and looked down at the rest of my body. They had taken off my shirt, but left my jeans and shoes on. *Why did criminals always do that? Was there a handbook somewhere that said any man being strung up must also have his nipples exposed?*

I spun a half-turn to my left, pirouetting on my manacles. There I saw, to neither surprise nor delight, Diego hanging in much the same fashion as I. His gut blobbed out over his trousers like a side profile dado rail.

"D- D-....." I tried, words hanging heavy in the cold vapours.

He moaned something, and I tried again. "Dee... Diego…"

"What?" he said, his spunk all removed.

I couldn't actually think of anything to say, so I just spun another half-turn back on myself. I guess I just wanted to check he was alive, yet the confirmation of that brought little comfort. After all, it felt like it would be distinctively short lived.

"How you doing?" I mustered.

"Where… are we?" he said, slowly revolving.

"I think a freezer," I said.

"No shit," he said, choking out something that had the semblance of ironic laughter.

I looked around again. The freezer was about the size of an office meeting room and no less depressing. The floor had crystalised pools of cherry-red blood with ice running up the walls and over a large window, almost obscuring it, semi-submerged in the frost. Hanging up alongside us for company were rows of stallion carcasses split right down the middle. Great, burst-open cavities. Rib cages of yellowing bone and darkening meat. I think I made a confused promise to myself to never again eat an animal. *Why couldn't we have been captured by a vegan drug cartel? Our situation wouldn't seem so dire if we were surrounded by crates of peaches and Granny Smiths.*

"What are you laughing about?" Diego said.

I hadn't realised I was but confided, "Apples. I'm thinking of becoming vegetarian."

"Good, it's a.. good idea. If we get out of here, maybe I'll join you. Hey, you think they'll make us into burgers?" he said.

"Fuck. I hadn't considered that. But now you mention it, I'd say there's a distinct possibility... How many quarter-pounders do you think we'll make?" I said, the conversation slowly bringing us back to life. Talking, for now at least, meant living.

"I don't know, Jack. I... I just hope I taste good. That would be something, wouldn't it?" he said.

"Yeah, that would be something. Hey, maybe they'll mush us together into one huge burger?"

"Ah, fuck no. I hope not," he said.

"Why?"

"I just wanna be my own burger, you know?"

"Suit yourself,"

"And it sounds kinda... I just don't like the idea of you being in - me..." he said.

"Do you think... really I mean... Do you think we're gonna die?" I asked.

"Honestly, I'm in too much pain to even consider it. What do you think?"

"The thought had occurred," I said.

"Oh, it had?"

"To tell you the truth, I really can't see any scenario where we don't die," I said.

"That would make you pessi-mistic, dog. You gotta look on the bright side of life," Diego said, smiling at me with menace.

I noticed a dark red streak running down Diego's leg, his black tuxedo trousers couldn't hide the blood or impact spot.

"What happened?" I asked.

"Fucker shot me. I didn't see it, but he had another gun... Should'a known," he said.

"How was it? Not getting shot, I mean - down there, the lab, how-"

"Fucking beautiful, Jack."

"Yeah??"

"Yeah, man, fucking beautiful. Tables and tables of the shit. And money, so much money. I had it, man - I fucking had it! All bagged up into this little baggy-type thing. I fucking had it!"

"Maybe next time, eh? Maybe next time..." I said.

"Jack?"

"Yeah?"

"I'm... sorry," he said.

"Yeah, me too."

"I really fucked it up, didn't I?" he said.

"I guess we both fucked it up. You know, I was just thinking, maybe this is our punishment, like... like some kind of retribution."

"For Sammy?"

"Yeah. This is our... comeuppance, right? You believe in that? Fate? Karma?" I asked.

"Startin' to," he said.

"Well, here we are - paying for our sins. Retribution. Plus maybe a dollop more. You know, all my life, as far back as I really, truly remember at least, I've always feared death... And now-"

"-Most people fear death, Jack," he said.

"Yeah, but there's a difference to fearing death as some strange, shape-shifting thing that you don't know where it is, or what it is... to fearing death and actually knowing what it is. Like now I can almost see it, smell it, feel it moving around us. I guess that sounds weird. But I watched the cancer for years, my mum, slowly losing the fight. One taking over the other. Like a sun gradually setting. Each passing moment the darkness grows stronger, even if barely perceptible. Just tiny changes, every day, a little more death, a little less mum. Until in the end...she was gone, and all that remained was death," I said.

"You're not lightening the mood, Jack," Diego said.

"The way I see it, when death hangs around long enough, it's like he never leaves. The guest who never leaves the party. Even when it's all over, everything is packed away and everyone else has gone home. And there he is, just sitting on your sofa, eating all the leftover hummus."

"Fuck Death."

"I just wish he would get on with it. Shit, or get off the pot. But instead, he just lingers. A storm on the horizon that never makes land, never actually rains, just rumbles and lurks, and hangs around, waiting..."

"Jack, when you do even half the shit I done... That motherfucker you call Death, well he's been with me my whole life. But I see him different to you. He's more like a friend, you know? Someone you take with you, 'cos you in it together. You need him. To keep you sharp, t'keep you focused, 'cos you fuck up out there and believe me, you'll be seein' a lot more of the guy then."

"A friend...?" I said.

"It's true. I swear, best keep the motherfucker close."

"He always was, that's what I'm saying. He was always there. But I feared him then... and I guess I still do."

"Even now?" he said.

"Especially now. How could you not? It's a plague, a headache that won't go away. I don't think it's anything you can master. I've just come to accept him being always there, hanging in my shadow."

"Nothing to fear, man. Nothing to fear. You can change all that," Diego said, sighing heavily and struggling with his restraints. "Death's really just the end of the pain. The end of the suffering. Shit, right now, that sounds pretty good to me."

"Unless, of course, you go to hell, Diego. In which case, the suffering is really just beginning," I said.

"Ha! You really believe all that heaven and hell shit? Nah man, this is it. This is as real as it's ever gonna get. Shit, I seen plenty of guys, looked them right in the eyes, just beggin' me to kill 'em. I consider them like, mercy killings or some shit," he said.

"But beggin' you because the fate they'll suffer at your hands is gonna be worse than death, right?"

"Maybe..."

"Not wanting to be tortured is not the same as wanting to die. Semantics, I guess."

"It's honour," he said.

"Honour?"

"Yeah, honour. 'Cos either he dies, or tells us what he knows. Or we kill his wife, his sister, his child, his whole family. It's better just to go, don't make no fuss. Just take it like a man and die." He said.

"Is that what's gonna happen to us? Are they gonna torture us?" I said.

"The thought had occurred," he said, echoing my earlier phrase.

"And you? Shouldn't you just lay down your life then, for honour..."

"I'm different," he said.

"Ah fuck... Maybe it's just this place," I mused, "Hanging here.. could really get a man down."

"True dat," he said.

"I never really thought it would end like this, me being hung up in some Mexican horse meat freezer."

"You might be right, though. This might not be the end. It *might* be just the beginning. A new life after this one," he said.

"Hell?"

"Nope. Reincarnation," he said.

"Reincarnation??"

"Burgers."

"Oh yeah, I forgot, even better," I said sardonically.

"Get this, we get turned into some big ass, juicy ass burgers. We get sizzled, we get eaten, and then our essence, our DNA, goes into the DNA of the person who ate us. So yeah, we get reincarnated."

"Reincarnation, with a side of onion rings."

"Yeah, bro! Two fat, rosy-red fucking burger patties, chucked down on that red hot flat grill, sizzling and sizzling," he said.

"Little sprinkle of salt and pepper?"

"Damn straight. Lightly browned on each side. A quarter-pounder of heavenly, juicy fucking man-made meat," he said.

"That sounds good. A nice hot grill, smoking hot. The meat - my meat - sticking to it... Fuck, I'm hungry now," I said.

"Me too. Shit, I'm thinking of myself minced into burger meat and it still makes me hungry," he said.

"It's the grill man, can't you feel it?" I said, desperately taking our minds off the inescapable, bastard cold.

"Yeah, yeah, I can feel it. Damn, it's hot!"

"OK, flip me, I'm done this side," I said. We were both giggling and delirious.

"Szzzz, Szzzz, we cookin' now! Slap me in a bun, daddy! Get some bacon on my back, it's time to chow!" he said.

"Table 6, pick up!" I said.

"Mmm, I hope they're sexy, Jack..."

"Table 6? Dutch lesbians, my friend. Lips like cola, legs like french fries."

"Eat me, baby, eat me! We live, Jack, we live again!" he shouted.

At that moment, the freezer door clunked open. Both Diego and I shut off our laughter in an instant. Standing in the doorway was a squat man with broad shoulders. His short, fat frame packed tightly into an electric blue satin suit with shoulder pads like slabs of concrete. He was carrying a slim cane by his side, tilted at the hip for dramatic effect. He looked Mexican but with a gaunt face. Pale, malnourished blobs of flesh clung desperately to a squished pygmy skull. His skin was the colour of a discarded condom. I couldn't understand how someone could be so fat and yet devoid of colour. He looked in worse condition than us, it just happened to be that there was more of him. He had ghoulish, bruised eye holes. Ghastly, sunken, rat-black sockets. His beady little pupils flicked back and forth like windscreen wipers as he switched his gaze between Diego and I, choosing his prey. He stepped into the freezer, his black polished brogues crackling across the frost-caked floor. He stood for a moment, staring at me. Then stepped in front of Diego, tossed his cane with silver skull decoration up into a mid-height grip, and started wrapping it against Diego's ribs. His strokes were gentle, tapping them the way a doctor tests for broken bones. He glanced back across at the door opening, which was occupied by the driver of the Caddy - the bald-headed guy sporting an NFL sports vest whom we had sent diving to the floor earlier that day.

"I think we'll start with this one," said the blue-suited freak show.

"Wait, wait, hang on!" Diego protested, but the man simply grinned back at him. The discussion was over.

"Hola eses," said the guy in the football vest, grinning at us. "We meet again."

"We should'a fucking killed you this morning!" Diego said.

"But you didn't, did you?" the man said, stepping into the fridge to join us.

"Sir, there's been a terrible misunderstanding-" I attempted, but my words were met with a swift gut punch from the quarterback that made my spine snap and my bowels evacuate. I was left coughing out my final protestations, gulping desperately to get air back into my lungs.

"OK, you can start with that sack of shit right there. But we gotta save one for Carlos, he'll be here soon. We need to save one of them for him, he don't wanna miss all the fun," NFL said.

"Good, good. But this one can watch," the suited gimp replied, glancing at me. I was to bare witness to Diego's torture and execution. He turned to leave, unbuttoning his jacket as he did, preparing himself for his duties.

"Carlos?" I mustered, unsure why I was speaking and praying it wasn't met with the previous reply.

"Si, Carlos, you know him, you piece of shit? He's really keen to see you boys," NFL said.

I remembered Carlos as the handlebar moustache guy I had bought the coke off back in bar La Luna. If only I could take back that chance encounter, all of it, as far back as which taxi to choose at the airport.

"Yes, Carlos. I need to talk to him, it's important... I need to talk to him, before you do *anything* to us. I have some important information I need to share with him..." I said, my believability quashed under the weight of my desperation.

"Sure, man, sure, that's good. I like that," NFL said.

"I'm serious!" I cried.

"Would you like to see *me* serious?" He said.

My balls evaporated.

"Hey, Cooch. Hey, man, it's all a big misunderstanding. You got the wrong guys!" Diego said.

"Aw, Diego, not you too? Come on, you talking to me like I just got fucking started in this game. Boy, you done really fucked up this time, hermano. What was you even thinking?" The guy in the NFL shirt, Cooch, said.

"I swear, man!" Diego said.

"So how do I explain that to Gini? Last I saw, he had a fucking knife sticking between his eyes. So how do I explain that one to him?? And Paco, he's lying there with fifty holes in his chest. How'd you explain that one, Diego?" Cooch said, pulling a large hunting knife out from a sheaf that was tucked into the rear of his jean belt. He held the tip out in front of Diego, stroking his skin with it. "And Sammy? Poor little Sammy. That fine ass bitch. You know she was one of Anton's favourites..." he said, grinning and tickling the blade end across Diego's chest.

"Look man, Gini and Paco drew on us - what were we supposed to do? My guy there got some shotgun lead in his shoulder as a take-home, man," Diego said.

"And you?" Cooch said, scanning for injuries. "You ain't got no hits? So what, this gringo here done killed our two boys, that's what you saying?"

"No, no. I did, Cooch, I did. But 'cos we didn't have no fucking choice!" Diego said.

"Oh look, you did get hit, here in the leg. 'Cept that weren't in Tito's place was it? That was here, when you tried to fucking bust this place!" Cooch said, taking his knife tip and poking it into Diego's leg wound.

"Ah! Fuck! I swear, I swear we didn't start this!" Diego said.

"Who then?! This little gringo faggot here? He done everything?"

"No. I mean, look, yeah, we done this, but we didn't start it. And Sammy, we never done that. You gotta believe me, Cooch. You know I could never hurt her!" Diego said.

"Oh, I 'gotta believe you'?! Shit, it don't matter if you did or didn't do it no more. It don't matter," Cooch said.

I interjected, "Hey, erm, Cooch, is it?"

"Yeah. And you're Jack Marden, right?"

My blood ran another degree colder with the revelation that he knew my name but I had to stay on target. "Diego's right, we didn't do anything. We just woke up at that party - wrong place, wrong time. Everything since has been self defence-" but before I could finish, Cooch slowly tutted me into silence.

"My guy, enough of this foreplay, eh? Not that I'm not enjoying it, but come on, we know you did it," he said.

"You don't know! You think, but you don't know. Do you even care, really, about what happened to her?" I said.

"Ha! Not really, no. He's got me. I'm starting to like this gringo! Maybe we should start with him first?" Cooch said.

"Fuck you, Cooch," Diego said, "if you're just gonna kill us anyway, then get the fuck on with it."

"Not so quick, ladies. We wanna have some fun first," Cooch said.

"OK, Coochy, fine. You know what, I'll confess and you can fucking kill me. Blitz me up, do whatever you want, but you don't need the gringo. You can let him go. I got him caught up in all this, and he ain't got no place here," Diego said.

"And why would I do that? You boys are also forgetting something - this ain't my motherfucking show. So even if I could let you go – and why the fuck would I - Anton would have my balls. Besides, it's gonna be far more fun to watch you get gutted. A little payback for Gini and Paco. Who knows, maybe we'll do you quick. Maybe not. I just hope you last longer than that pussy Tito," Cooch said, laughing.

"You motherfucker!" Diego screamed, writhing in his shackles.

"Whoa, whoa, easy Diego. Man, you should'a seen the look on his face," Cooch said.

"Fuck you!" Diego said.

"Bitch sang like a bird. And cried like one too. He gave it all up - all about your lady in the States, about your boy. Fuck man, where you think we're heading next?? Same place you were heading, 'cept we ain't gonna be so friendly when we get there... Or who knows, maybe we'll be *real* friendly..." Cooch said.

"Fuck you! Fuck you, puta madre!" Diego said, head down and lost in the misery of envisaging his only surviving family being tortured and killed.

"How'd you end up rolling with this piece of shit?" Cooch said, directing his words at me being lumbered with Diego.

"We just met at the party... It was a total fucking accident, I don't know this guy. And the girl, Sammy- I danced with her at the party, but that's it. The next thing I know, I just... I woke up in the same room as her and Diego, and she was gone. I mean, dead.... and that's all I know," I said.

"He's right," Diego said, "He didn't have nothing to do with this. It was all me, Cooch."

"How could you fuck it up so badly, Diego?! Couldn't you just gut punch her or some shit? Push her down the stairs. Just get her fucked up, or I dunno, spike her drink with some shit?" Cooch said.

"What? What's he talking about, Diego? What does he mean, 'you fucked it up'? What did you fuck up? What's he talking about??" I said.

"It's... Look, Jack, it's not that simple," Diego said.

242

"What's not simple? What's he talking about? It's starting to sound pretty fucking simple. You did something, didn't you? If not, then what is he fucking talking about?!" I yelled, exasperated.

"Ohh, this is sweet!" Cooch said.

"The girl, Sammy, she was…." Diego said, his head hung low.

"Was what?!" I demanded.

"Was what, Diego? What was she, Diego?!" Cooch chimed in, gleeful to the point of ecstasy.

"Please, Cooch, please. I'm begging you to stop. Diego, Diego what *was* she?" I said.

"Pregnant," Diego mumbled.

"Yeah, and with this fuck's baby! Pow!" Cooch said, clapping his hands together.

"What?! Oh fuck... Diego, look at me! Look at me! Tell me that's not true. Say something else, man, say something else," I said.

Diego didn't answer.

"Shiiit," Cooch said, sucking his teeth, "So you see now, there ain't no way you boys getting outta this. Someone's gotta pay!"

"I swear. I swear I didn't..." Diego said.

"Swear what, you punk motherfucker. Anton said get rid of the baby. Take care of business. That's it. Not kill the fucking girl! What's wrong with you?!" Cooch said.

I had a horrible sinking feeling and if it wasn't for the chains around my wrists, I would have crumpled onto the floor and fallen into a pit of despair. *Pregnant?? A baby; inside her. While we had sex? When Diego killed her? She had been doing drugs all night, she must have known ...unless she wanted to get rid of the baby too? She might not have had a choice, or even needed our help. And Anton? I could only suppose the way he saw it. A girl of his gets pregnant - that's an asset with no value for nine months of the year. And then what, a single mother on the books? Doubtful. Was this how he kept everything in check? Diego gets her pregnant, so therefore Diego is told to tidy up the situation? What kind of sordid milieu was I drowning in?*

In a way, my conscience cleared some, the guilt changing shape from a murder suspect to someone unwittingly involved in a double homicide. Knowing Diego was the killer should have been a relief, but it came with way too much baggage.

"Diego? Diego, say it ain't true… Come on, it ain't true... say it!" I said.

"Honestly, Jack, I don't remember… I don't remember..." Diego said, shaking his head, his mind lost in a remorseful fog.

"Bullshit, you do remember! You fucking killed her, you useless fuck," Cooch said.

"I'm sorry, Jack. I didn't mean for you to get involved in any of this.." Diego said.

"Hey, look at me, Diego. This guy Cooch doesn't know what he's talking about. We still don't know anything for sure... so you didn't do it, Diego, you hear, you didn't do it," I said.

Honestly, I couldn't tell at that point whether Diego was sincere or not when he denied any memory of the events. Whether it was seeing him broken by the interrogation or the thoughts of his family suffering retribution, I made a decision to try and help Diego. I wanted to clear his conscience before his inevitable demise. Because if he was innocent, in my mind at least, then I could be innocent too. *Unless him being innocent meant I was guilty?* But it didn't wash. No matter how fucked up I had gotten on drugs, that seemed a step beyond the realm of reality, especially under the weight of the revelations about pregnancy. *No, it could only be Diego that was guilty, and me also by association. Or he was innocent, and therefore I was innocent too. But did it even matter now? I mean, what the hell, it was clear at this juncture that they weren't just about to untie us and let us go.*

"You're a stinking piece of shit, Diego," Cooch said.

"I don't know, I don't know. Fuck! We just got so fucked up at that party that it all became a blur... it still is. I don't remember half the shit I done in my life, least of all the bad stuff... Look

Cooch, fuck... OK, I did do it, I did it, I fucking did it... So you can let the gringo go, feed me into the fucking machine and just end it, OK? But Jack didn't have nuttin' to do with it. I fucked up getting him involved…"

"You fucked up everything you ever touched, ese," Cooch said.

Diego knew he would be killed. It was almost admirable to watch him try and save me. Even though I suspected he was really trying to salvage one last remaining fragment of his long departed soul. In my heart of hearts, it was becoming clearer that he must have killed Sammy. He had motive, coupled with form. But there was still a bit of me that hoped it wasn't true, that we were both somehow innocent. That we had been chewed up by the cogs of some shape-shifting, evil being. A great, unwieldy mechanical warhorse fed on the blood of men. We were both victims and always would be. Maybe we made love with Sammy, but someone else killed her. We were guilty of being men, nothing more than men.

"Let him walk, just let him walk," Diego said.

Cooch laughed. "Are you really fucking serious?! Haha! What you been eatin' for breakfast son, retard sandwiches? It's over, forget it. And you, blondie, too bad for you. Looks like you picked the wrong party to crash. Carlos has got a real hard-on for seeing you boys... One of you is gonna be leaving in a burger box. But the other needs to go with him back to the city, you see? Someone's gotta switch seats with Anton, do time for that girl. So I guess it looks like it'll be you after all, gringo. You'll be a real hit with the inmates of El Hongo."

Diego screamed a cry of anguish, but for my part, silence. Something in me had died. Then the blue dwarf reappeared at the doorway dressed in butcher's overalls. He stared solemnly at us, and then across to Cooch.

"I'm ready."

# 15

# ORGY OF VIOLENCE

An hour hanging upright in a horse freezer can really play menace with the mind. My hands had turned white, the circulation cut off at the wrists where the metal chains remained coiled in an ever-tightening knot. My arms were locked at the elbow, as upright as goalposts. My head hung back, occasionally slumping forward, involuntarily, and it felt like all the blood in my body had sunken into my swollen toes. All I had for company were the carcasses of animals and Diego's screams wafting in through the open door. The blue meanie was going about his work in the adjacent room with fiendish pride. He had insisted to Cooch that Diego be taken off the hook and carried next door onto some kind of human-sized wooden chopping board. It took two of them to lift Diego up and off his hook, with help coming from the second of Anton's henchmen, a bald and burly man with jagged facial features, deep craggy cheekbones, and a nose like the summit of K2. He had a goatee beard and a scar running from eyebrow to chin, with eyes as black as a shark. His face was made of aggregate and his name was apparently Casanova, or Casa, for short. After carrying Diego next door, the blue man returned to make sure I would be getting a decent view from the large window that ran the length of the wall opposite where I hung.

"Ah, this won't do. This won't do at all," he said, rubbing his finger against the frosted glass.

"It's OK, I'll use my imagination," I said.

"No, no, but I want you to see! Casa!"

Casa appeared and was told to get a portable heater and place it between myself and the window, to defrost the glass, and to "warm the gringo".

"Very kind of you," I said.

"I don't want you to freeze," the blue meanie said, "It makes it so much harder to get the implements into frozen skin."

Casa brought in the heater and set it up as instructed. There was little solace to be taken from the raising of my body temperature when the objective was to facilitate the ease of my dissection. As the heat increased, gradually, inch by inch, the ice on the window began melting. Soon the true brutality of the scene next door was revealed, one defrosted dribble at a time. I couldn't see exactly what they were doing, but Diego was splayed out in an X. His hands and wrists were bound into steel clamps, while the blue man jiggled some forceps between his legs. Each new twist brought an agonising scream. I would have settled for the cold, to have the glass cloud over and my organs shut down as painlessly as possible. Instead, I started to thaw, with droplets of water falling off me and fizzling onto the amber coils of the heater below. The other horse halves started to melt, great lengths of rib cage softened in the moist air releasing pestilent rotting smells that summoned up an involuntary gag reflex.

What I couldn't work out in all of this, what I failed to grasp, was what they hoped to gain from it all. Other than the feeding of some vaguely latent psychotic impulse? I mean, *what did they expect Diego to tell them?* He had already confessed to murdering Sammy, more or less. Albeit under some duress, but a confession nonetheless. After all, they knew it was either him, me, or the two of us combined, so what good did it do to torture us? *Unless it wasn't supposed to do us any good?*

As far as I could tell, Diego had been honest when claiming amnesia regarding Sammy's final moments, the truth being that we were both so wasted we couldn't fully remember, *God knows I had tried.* Even amongst all the madness that had followed it since, barely a minute had passed where I hadn't tried to summon up the exact memories from that first night, but each time I drew a blank. Maybe that was the result of dabbling in PCP, or any of the other miscellaneous substances, but I came up blank every time. I could only assume it was the same process for Diego. The only difference for him was that he knew in advance about Sammy's baby and Anton's instructions to deal with the situation. This gave him a motive. But then again, her carrying his child was also surely a motive *not* to kill.

It started with a lie. He knew that night, going to that party, who Sammy was and that she had his baby inside her. He knew of Anton's instructions. *What he knew, I now also knew.* So we were back to square one, just on different timelines. We were both culpable, both guilty in some way or another, and both going to pay the ultimate price.

I pondered on the morals and working methods of a woman on the game. *Is there a chance the baby wasn't Diego's?* Assuming she was actively employed, could it open up a world of potential sires? *Had Diego thought the same, killed her in a wild and chaotic frenzy of jealousy? Or was it love? A sweet, but hidden love, that meant he could never harm her. Or at least not while in a correct state of mind.* I realised I didn't have all the answers. Even Diego might not. And it was moot now anyway, as he lay next door being tortured from the genitals upward.

*What good would come from this?* We deserved to die, for our sins. We could deny all we liked, but we both had murky souls. I had shovelled up whatever drugs I could get hold of, leaping over them like hurdles, pounding toward the finish line of bedding a pregnant Mexican prostitute. I had dallied with the foolish notion of her being an angel, willfully romanticising her as a goddess, but in reality, I hoped she had loose enough morals to warrant first encounter action. And maybe she knew too. Used me as a pawn to tease out a response from Diego, or Anton, or both. *Damn it!* A pawn...another pawn, if not me then someone else. Diego, Sammy, and I, just lowly chess pieces reacting to the changing whimsy of a higher order. Under those terms, maybe we were all the victims. Or was that just another phoney post-murder rationalisation? *A few Hail Mary's and I would be clean.* It's hard to reason, to find justice in the dark, and take responsibility for your actions when you don't know the whole picture. Even harder when the blood has drained from your brain into your toes. My body now hung like an anaemic sheet of flesh, a blank canvas ready for the next Francis Bacon masterpiece.

Swinging there, I could think of no better justice than a quick unsavoury exit from this cruel and tormented world. *If there is any higher realm, then let me be judged there, by those worthy of the act, rather than here, in a cartel's abattoir, my fate determined by the souls of the damned.*

*Maybe I do deserve to die, and to be tortured... Diego might even have the shorter straw - he would see death sooner than I. Whereas I would get an extended period of playful mutilation, then spared death at the last moment, in exchange for a lifetime of imprisonment.*

*Fine then, so be it. Slice me up, carve out this guilt at the very least, and maybe, maybe I'll have a chance in the next life. After all, Diego was right, there's nothing to fear in death. The fear is this - hanging in uncertainty. Morality, or my lack of, is simply a construct that's learnt. A system of rules passed down. Only our circumstances can dictate our viewpoint. We can only be as morally pure as the waters in which we swim. Right now, right here, I feel no more guilty than the rest of them. To be human is in itself, vice.*

*So whose fault is it? Can I blame society for my sinful appetite? Is it society's fault that Sammy did what she did, working for Anton? Why Diego moved his gear? Why I went to Mexico? Society's fault? Or are these human modes of behaviour simply taking on a modern form? Heinous tales repeated through time. A morph expression of mankind's eternal lust.*

*Capitalism and Cartels. Governments with wars on drugs, on people, on humanity. All in the guise of trickle-down economics. But by the time the trickle reaches us at the bottom, it's picked up so much filth along the way it makes you retch. The Great Pyramid of Life, a drum beat sounded by the Mayans. At least then they knew the score, knew their masters. Lived without the illusion of any self-worth. Now it's Mexican factories making American drugs, destroying lives on both sides of the border, and making vast wealth for the impure fiends that dance gleefully in the flames of their creation.*

*The greed of man is our incurable condition. To never be satisfied, to always want more. Our eyes trained over the neighbour's fence, envying his lawn, lusting over his wife. This is our primal calling. An everlasting lust. To renounce these sins is to deny my human form. What I did was human, born from excessive love. It's done to whatever extremes we see fit, on a daily basis across the globe. So I denounce your newfound morals as fateful lies. I am human, and if I'm going to die as a human then let me die as one now. When we reach the gates of heaven or hell, I'll consider my forgiveness then, not before. Morality is man-made. Everything else is life or death. In a world where cancer exists, how can there be divine justice other than the one we make for ourselves? I'll show these fuckers. I'll take every last one of them with me. They are nothing more than cancers. Human-sized tumours walking the earth. They need to be removed, rooted out like weeds, and cornered like vermin. This is not an anecdote, but a calling. I see it now! The hubris of man be damned - give power to my hand and I'll show you a divine reckoning!*

And then something strange happened.

My wrists had become moistened by the heat of the fire and with the blood all but gone from the surface of the skin they had shrunk and shrivelled like a pair of leather gloves left out in the rain. They slipped clean through the confines of the cuffs and my body dropped to the floor as if thrown from the sky. Cast out from heaven and sent plummeting back to earth. I landed balls first on the heater. The weight of my body followed suit and I splattered over it like a globule of coughed out phlegm. My legs rested limply on the heater and I could smell my skin starting to burn. My body was so weak from its suspension that I simply couldn't move. It took long skin-smouldering seconds before I was able to jerk myself off the damn thing and slump into a heap alongside. My face pressed down onto the floor, breathing in the misty red air tinted with microscopic blood droplets from the defrosting carcasses.

I was Free. From all of it. The guilt, the shackles.

Free from morality. Free from humanity.

*Free.*

And now it was time for revenge.

A bloodthirsty, carnal revenge.

I lay on the floor awhile, elated and exhausted. It was not for me to question why I had been set free, instead, my mind set about an automated process of emotionless retribution. It seems strange upon reflection, but it was like a calling. Not from God, but from a realm non-personified, if such a realm exists. *Perhaps it was all just in my head.* But I had a purpose now, perhaps for the first time in my life. I knew what I would do next and I would do it without question.

My wrists were tender and frost burnt where the cold skin had rubbed against the freezing metal and there were deep sunken imprints left from the compression. I tried to massage life back into my hands, then my legs, which felt numb and lifeless. I wanted to move quickly, fearing that the torturers would notice me missing from the fridge window. Eventually, I was strong enough to pick myself up by sliding my body weight up against the wall. I was Bambi on ice, holding myself in place as I got my first glance back into the torture room, and saw the pattern of behaviour unchanged. Diego was still screaming, while the blue meanie jiggled items of silverware between his legs. Over his shoulder stood Cooch talking on a mobile phone. I couldn't see Casa, the man-mountain with a head carved from stone. He was a concern due to his size but I had unwavering confidence in myself, like a divine messenger, *I would not fail.* I would just move quickly from one to the next. *But I was still mortal.* I would need a weapon to overcome them. Then I saw The Bright Red Fire Axe. It was lying on a table on the left hand side of the room. This would be my first stop. I held my hands in front of the heater again for a final pang of warmth, shaking out the blood and making open-air grabbing gestures to ensure they were working properly. They were. I shook out each leg, steadied myself, and cranked my spine up into vertical. *It was time.*

I left the fridge and began walking slowly down the short corridor toward the main chopping room. I moved like a lion stalking its prey, upping my pace as the corridor opened out to the room. The sight of my approach risked losing the element of surprise. I reached the table without detection. The blue-suited pygmy was squatting between Diego's legs, lost in his work. It was only once I had the axe in both hands and the head of it scraped loose off the table, that he noticed me and started to recoil aghast. In a dainty few steps, I had waltzed within a metre of him with the axe primed. As I stepped into his comfort zone he dropped his surgical tongs. He whimpered, raising both arms horizontally in front of his face for protection, thus tendering free access to the crocodile's soft underside. I swung the axe in a voluptuous underarm arc, the head soaring through the air with a gentle 3-wood swish. The axe head buried squarely into his netherregion, decimating his plums and harris. It finally lodged itself somewhere deep inside his bowels. His inside leg measurement was now raised a few inches on either side. He collapsed backward, releasing a fowl haunting cry. Cooch stood behind him, slowly turning around to witness the horrors of the scene. The phone held to his ear instinctively pulled away from his head like each was made of opposing magnets. His free hand reached inside his jacket where I could see a holstered gun. I scanned the table around Diego's splayed-out body for weaponry. I tried to avoid Diego's gaze, although I saw from my peripheral vision that he was watching me intently, awestruck. And then I saw it. Next to the scalpel, and above the assortment of razors and long pointed knives, was a giant meat cleaver. As large as a man's thigh. I grabbed it and in one continual motion, I swung toward Cooch. He had removed his pistol as I came flailing through the air with a backhanded sweep. The blade must have been sharpened by the Devil himself because it tore clean through his wrist without any loss of momentum. Cooch and I watched in amazement, united by the splendour of this wicked science in motion. His severed hand maintained its grip on the gun butt, spiralling through the air. His face contorted with pain and unbridled fear. Rightly so, as I was halfway into the second swing, my thirst for blood unquenchable. This time, the cleaver landed on his neck. The soft blubbery flesh was no match for it and it went deep into the windpipe. He dropped to his knees in front of me. I was able to hook the blade out, then made another swing. Then again. The same spot each time. *Thwack!*

*Thwack! Thwack!* On the fourth swing, his head came clean off and bobbled across the floor like a dam-busting bomb. Gravity took care of the rest, his body collapsing inward, droopy and lifeless, while his neck squirted fluids like a fractured faucet. The whole series of events had taken on an abstract otherworldly quality that I didn't recognise. A postmodern reorganisation of the human form. A satanic canvas of truly radiant beauty started to emerge. It was hard not to admire, hard not to feel the hand of God, his gaze averted but his fists clenched.

A serene peace washed over me. I turned to Diego and began untying his shackles. I felt no need for words. Each hand I unclipped drew instinctively back into his body, each leg curling back into the foetal. It was only when I stood in front of his bruised naked body that I truly saw him, and the set of implements he had protruding from his piss hole.

"Hey... you need any help?" I said.

"No!" he yelled, crumpled and emasculated.

I walked across the room to retrieve the gun from Cooch's severed hand. It had flown several feet and the knowledge of such and the recent memory of it made logical reason a distant bedfellow. I glanced back at Diego as he pulled a series of thin silver needles out of his penis. Each one tinkled to the floor under a sprinkle of fresh blood. I even saw him pulling something out of his anus, something I hadn't initially spotted, meaning it must have been well submerged. Once he had removed all the utensils, he collapsed into a sorry heap on the floor. His torturer was lying on his back screaming with pain, the axehead still wedged between his legs. The blue meanie was drawing attention with his walling and in many ways sealed his own fate. Diego's resolve seemed to galvanise under these screams. He used them to summon up the strength to stand, hobble over to the man, grab hold of the axe handle wedged between his legs, and yank it free like the mythical sword removed from the stone. The blue meanie writhed in agony but before he could pass out, or pass on, Diego had one final treat in store for him. He leant over and retrieved the item that had been rectally housed inside himself until just a moment ago. Diego held it skyward; an Olympic torch of sodomy. It was thick and weighty like a Catholic church candle holder, full of intricate nobbly details, shining proudly in brass beneath the streaks of shit and blood. Diego climbed onto the chest of the man and began prising his teeth open with the anal intruder, forcing it into his mouth. The man deep-throated this evil metallic dildo, gargling on a backwash of faeces and black colonic matter. His throat swelled under its full length and his eyes bulged to the point of popping.

Diego finally pulled himself off the body, sitting alongside it and ruefully admiring his work. The man lay dead on his back with the used dildo rammed in his mouth, and the gentle nodding of his head told me Diego felt significant retribution had been served.

*Then a noise.*

There was a stainless steel door on the far side of the room with a large mounted handle, the type found on fifties-style refrigerators. It started to open. My money was on Casa standing on the opposite side of it, attracted by all the commotion. The severed-hand-gripping-pistol that formerly belonged to Cooch, had been flung to the opposite side of the room. Too far away to be useful. Instead, I ran toward the door as it opened but the distance also appeared too far to reach in time. Another yard of hasty dash would equal an inch more of the door opening. Another inch for him, another yard for me. A quick calculation later and I realised the door would be almost fully open about the same time I had reached Cooch's decapitated head in the middle of the room. The distance from head to door was roughly the same as a penalty spot to a football goal. As such, I decided to use my head, or more precisely, Cooch's head. I summoned the penalty taking prowess of the idols from my boyhood. This was my World Cup moment. My Mexico '86.

Casa opened the door, the landscape of horrors momentarily gluing him to the spot.

*My final swing, the stadium a cacophony of giddy anticipation.*

Cooch's dead eyes twitched as my boot swung inward.

My foot swooped an inch off the floor, somewhere near his chin, ideal for projection.

Then connection, *Shlap!*

The head spun in even circles, east to west, his scalp pointing up to the ceiling, his neck oozing out a flickering trail of blood that spiralled like a demonic catherine wheel. On each half turn, Cooch's dead eyes locked onto mine. He stared back at me in astonishment, while his tongue flapped limply out the side of his mouth. Casa was rooted to the spot, wrong footed and mesmerised. Their heads collided with a hollow cracking sound that echoed around the room, a queasy belly-churning noise of bone-on-bone. Casa and Cooch had come eye-to-eye in that final moment and Casa's legs turned to jelly on impact. I wasted no time and paced back to free Cooch's pistol from his dismembered hand. There was a problem though - the fingers had locked onto the gun with some kind of early rigor mortis. I tried desperately to free them, biting at the fingers and thumb with little success while Casa gradually shook himself free from his temporary concussion. I abandoned freeing the hand from the gun, opting instead to bundle the mess of blood, flesh, and metal into my two scooped hands. I strode back over to the doorway where Casa lay slumped with Cooch's head resting in his lap. Casa fiddled with a holstered gun inside his jacket but I was already standing over him. I examined the mechanics of the gun I held and found a technique that would work. My right hand cupped over the severed wrist, acting as the supporting grip, with my left hand pinching between thumb and forefinger, Cooch's fingertip as it curled around the trigger. I aimed at Casa and pulled back and forth on the fingertip. Short, sharp movements like a coin rubbed against a lottery card.

*Bang! Bang! Bang! Bang! Bang!* All into his chest.

Then I returned to Diego, neither of us feeling the need to articulate reason into these scenes. Shame and torment averted our gaze. We were lost in the ether of barbarism, an orgy of violence that was still in the infancy of its evolution. I picked up Diego's clothes from the floor and threw them in his general direction. He mumbled thanks, before turning his attention to his newly acquired wounds. I caught half a glance at these injuries which looked raw, savage, penis related. I felt suddenly grateful to be sporting a mere few pellet holes in my shoulder. I examined them quickly but they looked unchanged. A mess of black and purple dots, the skin fading to yellow between the blood blisters, creating a garish kind of pointillism.

"How's your... leg?" I said, starting up the motor of normal conversation and dodging the mention of his more severe-looking injuries.

"Bad," he said.

Diego pulled his trousers back on with a few anguished motions, scorning my half-hearted offers of assistance. He took his white tuxedo shirt and wrapped it over his trousers, tying a tourniquet over the bullet wound which had been teased open more fully by the knife-wielding manipulations of Cooch.

"Think you'll be able to walk?" I said.

I was speaking in reference to the immediate wound he had bandaged. However, my mind was probably more troubled by the various implements that had, until recently, been Kerplunked in his rectum. I thought it best not to reiterate.

"Yeah, I'm fine," he said, rising to his feet in a less than convincing manner.

"Here," I said, passing him his tuxedo jacket, which he pulled over his bare chest.

"Gun?" he said.

I held up Cooch's pistol with the hand still attached. Diego smirked, "Could come in handy."

"Oh, and Casanova over there, he's got one," I said.

Diego went over to retrieve it, while I took a small meat cleaver and began hacking Cooch's fingertips off his pistol. Diego stood up from Casa's body holding a giant hand cannon.

"Smith and Wesson .357 Magnum... the most powerful handgun in the world," Diego said, elated. "What you got?"

"I dunno," I said, and had to turn it on its side to read the make, "says, 'Desert Eagle'."

"Nice. So, you wanna finish this?"

"Let's do it," I said.

Diego staggered to his feet and slung an arm over my shoulder to shift some of the weight off his bad leg. We left the room without hesitation, keen to put the recent horrors behind us. We entered a long corridor with plastic car wash type walk-through flaps at the far end. Several office doors ran down the length of the hallway. A door opened, occupied by one of the earlier butcher boys, nonchalantly walking through while taking notes on his clipboard. Diego raised his magnum to eye level and pulled the trigger. The man's head exploded like a firework. Without time to ponder, another of the men in white overalls came striding through the plastic curtain flaps at the end of the corridor. I had my gun primed. I fired once into his hip, followed by a cannonball round from

Diego that propelled the man backward through the flaps.

"Who was that, Ernesto and Juan?" I said.

"Does it matter?"

"Guess not."

We went through the operating room flaps and came out in a room used to separate cows into various subcategories. Dismembered body parts decorated the walls like nightmarish wallpaper. The lighting was dull, blue, with modern fluorescence. We gravitated to a double door in the opposite corner of the room. It had two little viewing windows, each about the size of a magazine. I popped my head up and saw through the glass that it was the main cutting room that we had first entered the building through earlier that day. Standing over the chopping trough were the two other workers. We kicked open the doors and came in shooting. Diego was still holding an arm around my neck to prop himself up. He fired a round into the back of one of them, square between the shoulder blades. We were close range and the man should have flown twenty feet across the room but his trajectory was blocked by the skinless carcass of a horse that he had been standing over in mid-dissection. His body crumpled against it the way a crash dummy folds upon impact with an immovable object. I raised my gun at the other man. He turned to face us and

I saw he was the one with the broken nose, an earlier gift from Diego.

"What are you waiting for?" Diego asked.

"Hang on, hang on…" I said.

"What for?"

"How many are there? I mean, how many left? We've killed Juan, Ernesto, that one," I said, gesturing to Diego's recent kill.

The nose-bandaged man spoke up to correct me, "That's Ernesto there."

"OK, whatever," I said, "So that leaves just the security guard, and the chemist, right?"

"Right. And that fucker is mine," Diego said.

"And the cowboy guy you cattle prodded first, where's he?"

"He… you killed 'im," the butcher said.

"Sweet."

The man gulped, visibly uneasy at the discussion being had about his felled companions, "Hey amigo. Please, I have a family…" he said.

"You ever wanna see them again you do what we say, OK?" I said.

Nearby was a waist-high trolly-dolly on wheels. Two stainless steel shelves filled with horse bits. Hooves on the bottom shelf, heads on the top. I reasoned with Diego that if we were gonna go next for the security guard, we needed a disguise or distraction to get us close. We then convinced the butcher with the broken nose that if

268

he cooperated with the plan, we would release him later. This was of course a total lie, and in all likelihood, he knew that, but for now it was the only one of two options that didn't result in his immediate demise. We set about decorating the trolley with horse skins, which were in plentiful supply. We draped them over the tabletop so that they hung over the sides, creating a miniature Trojan horse on wheels. Diego climbed into the body of it, sitting on the lower shelf. The instructions we gave were unequivocal. Push the trolley along the factory floor, until you reach the guard's booth. Don't attempt to give him any signal and you'll walk free.

"I mean it now, no signals. I'll be watching from behind and if I notice anything funny I'll come out firing. You'll have slugs in your back in an instant, got it?!" I said, unsure of why I used the term 'slugs' and wishing I could retract it for something less 1930's.

"We're fucking serious, ese, don't do nuttin' stupid. You wanna see your family again, you do exactly as we say," Diego reiterated.

The trap was set. Diego climbed in and was hidden by the folds of horse skin dangling along every side. He prised back the odd flap so he could see where he was going. Our hostage pushed the trolley in front of himself, while I marched behind him with a gun nestled in the small of his spine. Once we got to the door, I halted him. I took a peek through the little window into the meat packing room. All quiet, all calm, and no women. They had evidently been sent home after the first shooting. There was initially no sign of the security guard either, which was a worry. A few anxious seconds passed until he came walking in through the main entrance. This hopefully meant he had been absent long enough from the CCTV monitors to miss any of the recent snuff scenes that had enabled our escape thus far. Less than ideal, however, was the fact he was now carrying a sawn-off pump-action shotgun. It was essential to get in there and get across the room before he had a chance to look at the monitors, which now displayed a veritable house of horrors on every screen.

"Let's go, let's go, let's go!" I said, shoving my guy in the back, prompting him to enter the room while I stayed hidden behind the door.

The guard was closing the main door, about to get comfortable at his wall of TVs, when the sound of our plan came wheeling into earshot. He turned to see our guy nonchalantly pushing along a trolley loaded with flayed skin and giblets. He cocked his head slightly and came out of his booth to approach the delivery. His body language was suspicious. I wondered if our guy was leading us down a trap of his own making, maybe distorting his facial features in a manner that expressed alarm. If he behaved weirdly enough, he might be able to subtly convey panic. I juggled my desert eagle between my hands, unsure how many rounds, if any, I had left. If the game was up, I would need to be Billy the Kid when I broke from cover. I watched anxiously as the two men crossed the room to meet in the centre. The trolley squeaked to a halt. The guard spoke but our hostage made no reply. *Something was up.* He spoke again and got no answer, nothing decipherable from where I was, at least. *Was he shaking his head slowly?* I was too far away to be certain but I saw clearly when the guard took hold of his pump action with a second hand. Unbeknownst to him though, through a slit in the horse skin curtain, a five-inch long silver barrel came poking its ugly head out, aimed at the man's balls.

*Oh, it is on!*

*Boom!* Diego fired the magnum into the man's crotch from point-blank range, his manhood instantly disintegrating and splattering up the adjacent wall. I came pouncing out from cover as Diego climbed out from the trolley to assess his work. The guard was dead with a basketball-sized hole in the area previously housing his groin. Our hostage turned white with fear.

"C-Can I... can I go now?" he said, in my mind, optimistically.

"Not yet, sonny," I said, glancing back over at the trap door leading down to the lab.

There were no sounds coming from down there, but we knew enough to not trust that wily little jack-in-the-box who had surprised us earlier. Diego had a score to settle, to get even for his leg. He picked up the security guard's pump-action and held it in one hand, the magnum in the other. He was about to march over to the hole when I stopped him.

"Easy Diego, he would have heard the shot. He'll be waiting for you," I said.

"Good," he said.

"How about we send in an advance party?" I said, gesturing to our hostage.

"Hey, you said..." he began in protest, but Diego was quick to point the pump action at his balls. The man glanced down at the guard and realised he held little clout in the proceedings.

"Unless you want your balls turned into putty, you'll go down there and tell that piece of shit to come out. If he doesn't, we'll kill you both. If he does, you have my word, we will let you live," Diego said.

The man scoffed at Diego's word, rightly.

"Or we just blow your balls off right now?" Diego said.

Reluctantly the man accepted his fate and started toward the trap door.

"Not so quick," I said, "We need an element of surprise. Something to make him think twice, to make him realise we mean business." I picked up a severed horse head from the table. "Wear this."

"W-what??" he said.

"Do it," said Diego, quickly on board with the mania.

"B-But it's... I can't get it on, there's no room!"

"Then scoop some shit out - you do this all day," Diego said.

The man began pulling out lengths of throat, tongue, and cartilage. He was sobbing now and a little far away light came on in my mind. A late-dawning realisation that maybe what we were doing wasn't divine reckoning, but simply a sadistic massacre? I didn't have long to dwell on this because Diego had become impatient and started screaming at the man to pull the horse head over his own, finally getting it stuck about halfway down his face. Diego came over and used the butt of the shotgun to bash the bestial hood down and into position. Completed, it was a gloriously horrific costume. Diego grabbed his shirt and spun him back in the direction of the trap door, marching him over there. Once at the top of the steps, the man hesitated.

273

"Go!" said Diego, shoving the shotgun into the man's back.

Tentatively, he took the first step, craning his horse head down to see further inside. There was no sound from below but we guessed the chemist would have a gun trained on the staircase as it was the only way in or out. The man took two more steps. His hands were opened palms-outward to show possession of no weaponry. He looked to be struggling to breathe and started clawing at his horse mouth to make some space for air. He looked back at us, desperate for retreat, but Diego showed him the twin barrels and the man descended a further run of steps. Diego moved round to the side of the trap door, the deep end of the staircase, lying on his belly. The man reached the final step of his descent. There was a moment of prolonged silence broken by a sudden flurry of wild Latino chatter.

"No, no, no, argh!!" screamed the horse head, but it was too late, a bucket load of ammunition went pulsing into his body, fired upon by the chemist.

Diego swung the upper half of his torso through the trap door and fired a shotgun round into the room. He was firing upside down and God only knows how accurately. His legs started to lift up, his weight cantilevered. He was about to fall headfirst into the hole so I ran over to him and leapt onto the back of his legs. Anchored now, Diego fired again. This shot was followed by a yelp, then the noise of gas quickly escaping, like a gasket blowing.

"Pull me up, pull me up!" Diego said.

I grabbed the back of his jacket and hauled him out. "Get him?" I asked.

"Yep!"

"Thank fuck."

"We got a situation though."

"What situation?" I said.

Diego moved swiftly over to the staircase and ran below. I followed, stopping at the base of the steps next to the horse-head guy, who lay in a shredded heap. The sight of him unlocked a sudden grievance that caught me off guard. I pictured his family's loss, the suffering, and the funeral. There was no time to ponder, to reason, but a brief head-wind of consciousness momentarily tugged back at the seemingly unstoppable locomotion of our murderous retribution. I stepped over his body and looked down into the lab. I soon realised what the "situation" was: the place was a raging inferno.

"What the fuck?!" I cried.

"I hit some of the bottles when I fired at this fucker," Diego said, kicking the body of the greasy-haired chemist.

Several bubbling test tubes of liquid popped and exploded, showering their flammable contents over table tops. Flames licked over every surface. A fire was rapidly spreading out of control.

"Let's get the fuck out of here!" I bellowed.

"Not yet," Diego said, creeping deeper into the burning lab, rummaging around and chortling to himself with childlike enthusiasm. "Te-he! Fuck man, we got enough shit here to blow up Iran!"

"What the fuck are you doing?!" I yelled, climbing steps, not wanting to be part of a narco meth lab as it reached atomic levels.

"The bag, the bag!" he shouted back.

"There!" I said, pointing at a green sports duffel bag. "Now come on!"

"Nice, Jack!" he said, grabbing the bag. The room behind him was blasting with balls of fire. It was like being in the gully of a Napoleonic warship getting torn to shreds by thunderous artillery.

"Diego, COME ON!!"

"Almost there!" he said, leaping over a table before stopping to scoop a mound of powders off the surface, shovelling it into his open duffel bag.

"Let's go!!"

I helped him up the final steps, just as a backdraft fireball blew out of the underground hole. All the factory lights went off, followed by a deafening fire alarm. Diego still couldn't run so I had his arm over my shoulder again. We shuffled as quickly as possible toward the exit. There were some pounding explosions sounding off under the floor beneath our feet. Great belting rumbles, like volcanic eruptions from the shifting of tectonic plates. We swung open the door and ran out into the courtyard.

"We need a car!" Diego said.

We glanced down the side and all the previously parked cars were gone, save for one rusted Chevy and the purple Caddy. They were parked below floor level, near vents that would access the basement. In an instant fireballs came bursting out from these vents, spitting out a flammable liquid that raged all over the cars.

"Forget it!" I shouted.

We ran a few more paces away from the building before the inferno exploded with such vigour and magnitude that we were catapulted into the air. We soared upward into the clear blue sky, temporarily defying all natural laws of existence. A pair of phoenixes, rising from the flames.

# 16

# THE WHITE HORSE

Ommmmmmmm.

That's the primordial sound of the universe. It's been resonating since the last Big Bang. It was also the only sound I could hear after our narco-abattoir lab explosion, aka Big Bang 2. We were launched into the air by the force of an ever-expanding jet propulsion. Two spacemen whose shuttle never left the takeoff pad, destined not to reach the outer limits of mankind's ceiling. Instead, we found ourselves cast back down to earth with a disgusted indifference. Perhaps punishment for overreaching the boundaries of our mortal relevance. This was the new dawn of a new kind of sapien, one covered in blood and barbiturates. We landed on our backs, staring in awe as the old world ceased and the new one formed in front of our very eyes. A rapidly expanding dust cloud was punctured by massive chunks of rubble cascading down around us within a shower of reinforced steel and concrete meteorites. Hunks of raw meat flew down, slapping onto the ground around us with moist thuds. A blizzard of chargrilled hinds and hooves pounded heavily onto the surrounding corrugated rooftops. A cindered tail swirled through the air wafting us with a nauseating, gut-wrenching, aroma. And finally, a flaming horse cock pierced the sky with the pinpoint accuracy of an Olympic javelin, spearing itself helmet-first into the blackened soil between our legs. Diego pulled out his cigarettes, chuckling, and we smoked.

"Well, that didn't go exactly according to plan," I said.

"Eh, seen worse."

We giggled nervously, two men pleased as punch to be given one more shot at life. The factory was nothing more than a twisted set of metal legs and broken brick walls. The roof was ripped off leaving only a smouldering ruin that housed the worst of our sins. Great plumes of black smoke billowed out of the gaping window openings, covering us in a murky charcoal haze that restricted visibility to within just a few feet. The stables and surrounding cow sheds had also been destroyed. Their gated communes were obliterated and their beasts set free. Through the grey soot clouds came horses, newly released, cantering rhythmically through the wasteland of our 21st-century apocalypse. The soil beneath them was sodden with the blood of their brethren, trembling under the pounding of their escaping hooves. No saddles, no chains. No cages, no malice. Just the fading remnants of human captivity and a thousand miles of raw empty desert in every direction. And so they ran.

"How far is it?" I asked.

"To the border?"

"Yep."

"Ten kilometres. Maybe twenty," Diego said.

"Think you can make it?"

"Do I have a choice?" he said.

"I guess not," I conceded.

"Then I'll make it."

"Dude, I hate to bring the positivity down, but you're not exactly in showroom condition."

As if to prove my point, he collapsed into a coughing fit and threw away the remainder of his cigarette. His condition concerned me because without him as a guide I would struggle to make it even halfway. There was also a new and deeper realisation forming in my mind. Namely that our fates were somehow inextricably entwined. That if he didn't make it, then some higher force had predetermined that I wouldn't make it either. Diego zipped open the green sports bag tucked underneath his arm. His shoulder turned away from me while he rummaged inside. This was followed by a loud sniffing and snorting. He turned back around grinning, his face caked in a mask of white crusty powder.

"What the fuck is that?" I said.

"Horse power."

"Horse power?"

"Well, it's whatever they make down there. Mostly steroids," he said.

"Can you even snort steroids??"

"I think I just did. Plus whatever else they make. They used to do all sorts: coke, pills, opioids... I grabbed a handful off each table."

"How is it?" I said.

He pushed his hand out in front of me and it was full of nasty white powder speckled with pink and blue flecks. Potent odds and sods, mashed together and gradually darkening on the surface with the falling flakes of ash. A heartbeat later and my face was submerged in Diego's hand mound. My nose ploughed so deep that the powder reached up over my cheeks and smudged into my eyebrows.

"RAAAARRRRRRRRR!" I cried when my head whiplashed back into neutral.

"Good, huh?" he said.

"Wait a second... wait a second... You're a genius!" I exclaimed.

"I know, good right," he said, burying his face back into his hand for another burst.

"No, no, think about it: horsepower. *HORSE... POWER!* It's just what we need!" I said, leaping up and searching the fog, looking for a suitable stead. "We'll take horses to get to the border!"

"Can you ride?" he said.

"No, not at all. But it's been a day of firsts. You?"

"Jesus, no… and anyway, I can't be sittin' on no saddle, Jack."

"They don't have saddles, Diego. They're beautiful, naked beasts…"

"Yeah, but what about my fucking balls and shit?" he said.

I remembered his recent testicular rearrangements and ceded that we were not about to go riding off into the sunset. "Not much we can do about your balls. But if I can get us a strong horse, we can use it to carry you. I'll bring the finest mule in the land…"

He was about to protest the logic but I was jacked out of my mind on a bizarre concoction of powdery marvellous medicine. This stuff could give a horse a heart attack. Blood was surging through my veins like lightning strikes pulsing through an electrical storm. I disappeared into the fog unsure of when I would return. What happened there was dreamlike. The memory of it, like all dreams, will never be wholly accurate in its recreation. The level of visceral absurdity remains forever locked in the fantasy of that moment. From what I *can* recall the journey began with some tentative footsteps finding my way around the newly-ruptured surface of the world. Hellfire and damnation roared in defeat, not ceasing to exist, but allowing me free trespass. Death was in the wind, palpable and indignant. It flowed through me and I through it, walking tall, seeking my answers. I wasn't visited by any spectres or ghosts. The visions of family and loved ones remained hidden, but I felt their presence. I felt the hand of my mother guiding me, leading me through the steely forest of destruction. Everything went quiet except the wind. The rustling wind, like a voice, soft and elevated. I took a few more steps, deeper and deeper until I saw the head of a white horse. Blurry at first, until closer and next to mine. I found myself staring at a fine, ethereal beauty. I reached my hand under her chin. I held it there for what felt like hours, time forever lost as we shared the eternity of each other's gaze.

As I say, a dream can be lost in translation, but my next conscious thought was knowing I could find my way back without any trouble. I arrived next to Diego, leading the horse with my hand on the back of her neck, my fingers bonded with her mane.

"You found one!" Diego said.

"This is Marilyn," I said.

"You named it?"

"Hop on."

Diego slung his body over the back of the horse, riding it like a saddle bag. He complained about the comfort but accepted it was better than walking. He was worried about what would happen if it bolted. I assured him it wouldn't. I found it odd that Diego did not fear death - in fact, by contrast, he seemed giddy in the face of it - but here on horseback, carried to safety by an equine prophet, he looked truly ill at ease.

"Do you know which way?" I said.

"Pretty much," he replied. "We'll head out of the farm, up over that hill there. Then it's pretty much west after that. We just gotta follow the sun, hermano, follow the sun. There is a road, but I think it's better we go cross-country, eh?"

It was late afternoon which made for easy navigation. The sun was low enough in the sky for it to serve as our compass. Diego felt we could make the border by nightfall and then either press on through the night or sleep rough. If we had the minerals by that point then I preferred the notion of pressing on. Mainly because we had nothing in the way of camping gear and the desert would be freezing at night. It felt good to get some distance between us and the farm. I cast one mournful look back at the smoking remains of the annihilated factory. A tangle of destruction left in our wake, with animals fleeing into the endless expanse of undiscovered land.

Skirting the hill was a treeline of dry bushes with long bare arms and needle-thin foliage. Nothing was blowing through the wood. No wind, no insects, no birth of nature affected its shape. It had the feel of a graveyard, one locked in immortal poignancy, where only the changing shape of shadows could affirm the existence of time. It was hot, dry walking. At times we stopped to drink-in the silence. We climbed toward the summit of the hill, picking up a trail. It was easier under foot, although its narrow width meant we no longer walked side-by-side. Diego had turned sleepy. Occasionally I would make conversation just to keep his mind active and stop him from slipping away into some further, less savoury realm. When we reached the crest of the hill we stopped briefly, taking shade under a chalice-shaped pine tree. It afforded us some welcome respite from the sun. Laid out before us was a vast, sweeping panorama of dust-ravaged plains. The lands folded out to eternity. Rolling hills with sandy contours and crevices, a crumpled blanket of arid perfection.

"Fucking dead, huh?" Diego said.

"Actually, I was just thinking it was rather beautiful," I said.

"Beautiful? It's fuckin' harsh out here, man. Nothin' but cactus and rattlesnakes living here. Seems nice to you, but trust me, this place can be a bitch. We always lose a few on border runs. Go ask them if they think it's beautiful."

"How do you lose them?" I said.

"Usual shit. Unprepared. Not enough water, or not fit enough. An' some of them set off in better condition than us. Shit, a *lot* better!"

"But we have a horse," I said, affectionately patting her brow.

"This old mangy thing? And water... we're out of water."

"Shit, if you'd have said, maybe back there we could have got…"

"I'm supposed to remind you to bring water into the desert? Christ. And by the way, I've been shot, and tortured," he said.

"I've been shot too."

"Whoopty-do.A memento to t-take home with y-you.." he said, his sentences starting to stutter like an engine about to stall.

286

"You alright?" I asked, coming round the side of the horse and leaning toward his face.

"Bueno,"

"What about the water? What do we do?"

"S'OK, we'll be aight for tonight/ It's tomorrow I'm worried 'bout. Walking in the midday sun. But I think I got it figured out - we gonna walk down that valley there. You see that?" he said, pointing to a sloping hillside that divided itself off into five parallel finger valleys.

"I see," I said.

"We'll follow the valleys. Should be a river there, we can drink from that. Then we follow the river,"

"Good," I said.

"It's longer," he warned, "but not much. And it means we got water next to us the whole way. After a couple miles along the river, we gotta turn back inland, go past an old mining village..."

"Mining village?"

"Kinda like a gold rush town. But not gold: oil. It's empty now, don't worry. The people all left years ago. Shit ran out, I guess... It's a ghost town."

"Sounds about right," I said.

"It's OK. I like it, anyway. All these old timber houses with nobody in 'em. Peaceful," he said, his voice drifting again.

287

"Could we get there tonight? That way we could sleep in one of the houses. Keep us warm for the night, surely?"

"Maybe. We'll see if we have time. I don't usually like to sleep there. It's too obvious, you know. You could be in the radar of patrols an' that shit. But there is a water well. Right in the fucking centre of the town. That's the only reason we ever go there nowadays - a water run."

A hawk shrieked in the sky above, circling us.

"That fucker's been following us since the farm," Diego said.

"Maybe waiting for us to cark it. Pick on our bones."

"He'll eat my fucking magnum before he eats me."

We headed down into the valley where the trees gave way to sporadic clumps of cacti. This meant longer periods of time exposed to the final warmth of the sun. I took my Fresh Eggs tea towel and draped it over the top of my head for cover. The sand kicked up puffs of dust with each step. My blue jeans were now beige from the knee down. I got a taste of the heat we would experience the next day and it started to play on my mind that we might be walking into a desert from which we would not re-emerge. I tried instead to focus on the undulating majesty of the hills. Carpets of slate grey rock and pale green cacti, woven together in a hessian weave, washed out by the burning sun as it bade us farewell.

"You hear that?" Diego said.

"A river?"

"Yes! Fucking yes! Ha ha!" he said, leaning up.

"Which way?" I said, training my ear to the sound.

"I'm so fucking thirsty!" he said.

"Which way?!" I demanded.

"There!" he said, pointing to an area of land that flattened out into slabs of pinkish rock.

We left the powdery dirt behind and made our way through a series of vast granite plinths. The sound of rushing water was always near, then far, scurrying away whenever we felt ourselves about to make the discovery. The end-of-day heat was reverberating off the grainy stone. It bounced back up into our faces with its intensity doubled. It did nothing but whet the palate for the eventual drink, but it was agony while it lasted. Our throats were as dry as the baked mud. The sound of water slipping all around us suddenly grew louder and stronger, rumbling with thunderous intent. We came through a large channel of boulders, stepping over fallen tree trunks until we reached a plateau. From here we realised we had come out at the top of a waterfall. The river pounded past us with venom, hurtling itself over the edge and disappearing below.

"Fuck," Diego said.

"It's just water. Come on. Just be careful at the edge, don't get sucked in," I said, helping him off the horse.

We scrambled up to the edge of a little clearing made by river debris washed down from further upstream. It had swirled around into a kind of rock pool. Not the cleanest-looking water, but not rapids either. We lay on our bellies toward the surface and brought eager handfuls of water up to meet our mouths. The feeling was pure ecstasy. I drank until my stomach hurt and then went back for more. When the horse snorted, I leapt to my feet and brought her over to the rock pool. I watched her drink, stoking her neck and feeling the muscle spasms twitch in recognition of this great new bounty. I looked over at Diego. He still wore the anguished expression of a man without hope.

"Why so glum, man? This is fucking beautiful!" I said.

"It's not good," he said.

"It's fine! It's river water. OK, maybe not the cleanest, but unless you wanna go walking out-"

"Not the water, Jack!"

"Then what?"

"We're at the wrong end of it. We're supposed to be down there," he said, gesturing a finger over the edge.

"Down there?!"

"Down there. I thought we'd come out at the bottom of the waterfall, not the top," he said.

"Fuck, Diego! I thought you knew where you were going?!"

"I'm not a fucking park ranger, ese! We do different routes all the time. I've only done this way once or twice. Plus it ain't so easy seein' where you going when you're tied to the ass end of a fucking horse."

"Shit. Any ideas?" I said.

"We could go around…"

"And how long is that gonna take?"

"I don't know! Like I said, I don't live here, it's not my fucking waterfall! It might not even be the one I was thinking of," he said.

"Come here and take a lookout. See if you can figure out your bearings from what's around, OK?" I said, helping him out of the rock pool and over to an outcrop protruding from the waterfall's edge.

"Fuck," we said in unison.

The waterfall made Niagara Falls look like a Sunday paddle down at the local Lido. Torrential flowing waters of several thousand cubic litres launched off the edge every second. It was a two-hundred foot drop below into a dark emerald pool, decorated with a necklace of pointy rocks. The view was nice, if you liked heights.

"Well, jumping's out," I said, "Can you work out where we are?"

"I think so... see that little clump of buildings? There, dark triangle rooftops…"

"Down through that wood there? Yes! Just beyond that little forest," I said, squinting.

"That's Trinco. The ghost town I was tellin' you about," he said.

"It looks a long way away..."

"And beyond it, you just follow that line straight, and you in America. The town's right on the border."

"Nice to know. But it does us no good here. Because, I dunno if you noticed, but... it's *fucking miles away*. And there's this little waterfall in the way too. Fuck! There has to be a way down..." I said.

We both scanned our eyes around looking for paths but there were only vertical rocks on all sides.

"I ain't never gonna make it am I, Jack? I ain't never gonna see my boy again," Diego said, dropping to his knees, tears glazing his eyes.

"Ah, Christ," I said, pitying him, "we'll figure something out, OK? Fuck knows how, but we'll figure something out."

"How, man? Not possible, not possible. Fuck, why'd I let you talk me into this shit?" he said.

"Me? How is this my fault? Don't go looking to blame anyone else for this shit, Diego. This is all your own making. Always looking to blame someone else. Never Diego's fault. No, it's Anton's fault, Jack's fault, the White Man's fault..."

"Jack, don't..."

"Don't what? You gotta take some responsibility for your actions! Shit, it's me that should be pissed with you! If it wasn't for you, I wouldn't be out here in the middle of fucking nowhere! With fucking holes in my shoulder! Standing around a fucking waterfall! And with no fucking way off it! Oh, and let's not forget - wanted for a murder I didn't commit! And, AND, on the hit list of some lunatic named Anton, who's gonna do everything in his power to make sure I end up being jailed for life - or better yet, churned into a burger patty in one of his twisted fucking meat factories!"

Diego had opened the sports bag halfway through my rant, pulled out the magnum with gooey powder stuck to its side, and pointed it at me.

"Perfect, Diego!" I said, "Your solution to everything. Well, go on then..."

"Don't tempt me," he snarled back.

"Do it! Really get some icing on that cake, eh?"

"It's not me. None of it's me..."

"If not you, then who? You're hardly the poster boy for tourism in Mexico, pal. But that's ok, I get it now. It's just how this country works. This is how scores get settled. It's not savage. It's no worse than back home, where everything happens in a sanitised way, behind closed doors, just out of sight. Whereas here, it's all out in the open, right in your face. Like your magnum, right? It's not the cops you worry about, but the cartels and the fucking pimps. It's harsh, but at least it's honest. I can't argue with that. So you do whatever you feel is right, Diego, because I'm here now, all laid out and with nowhere else left to turn. So you get to decide if I live or die. But it's you that has to pull that trigger," I said.

He lowered the gun with three simple words of defeat, "Ah, fuck it."

I was exhausted too. I wasn't convinced he really intended to shoot me, but if he had, at that exact moment, I honestly don't think I would have cared. I came around to sit next to him.

"What are we gonna do? Huh, ese?" I said, experimenting with his vocabulary.

"Ese? I'm your ese now...? Jesus, Jack, you're no longer the wet fish I met back at that party," he said.

"Exactly. I'm now an armed robber, a fugitive of the law, and a murderer. And I don't mean Sammy, I mean those guys back at the factory. Fuck. How am I ever supposed to live with that?"

"Just don't think about them. Ever. OK? They was gonna do the same to you. They was all set to! You did what had to be done. And really, I actually owe you, dog. I'd still be there now…" he said.

"I guess it doesn't really matter either way, I won't have to live with the guilt for much longer... So we're just going to sit out here, let nature do her thing? Let that hawk have a free meal? Or coyotes? Do you get them here…?" I said.

"We won't have to wait long to find out. Dark soon," he said.

"You got a smoke?"

Diego rummaged in his pockets and pulled out a squished packet of camels and a lighter.

"Two left," he said, with a wryly symbolic nod. We lit up. "Could double back... but not much point tonight. We'd just end up fuck knows where in the middle of the night. Maybe in the morning we could double back, find our tracks, go down somewhere into the valley. It's possible. Maybe we could get to Trinco by tomorrow night."

"You think you can last that long?" I said.

"Honestly...? I guess we just enjoy this last sunset..." he said, trailing off with fading belief.

The sun was all but sunk. A great, crimson, burning eye on the horizon. Sheets of ruby red light bathed the canopy with the warmth of a roaring fireplace. The sky was full of dark clouds, bubbling up like a cauldron. Vast swaths of watercolour beauty soaked in through our damned eyes and projected back pure into our souls. I stood up and walked the plank of rock.

"Or..." I said, pulling on my cigarette and allowing myself another look over the edge.

"You can't be serious homes?"

"What have we got to lose?"

Diego picked himself up and joined me at the edge. "OK, you first."

"Very funny." I glanced back at Marilyn, if she knew what we were saying and disapproved, now was the time to say something. She remained silent.

"You'll have to leave the horse," he said.

"Wait, are we really talking about this?"

"It's like you said, Jack, as fucked as it is, this is probably our best option."

"I'm not sure I can..." I glanced over again. A million litres of water moving thunderously over the edge felt like reason enough to stop this plan before it gained any more momentum.

"Need a confidence booster?" Diego asked, grinning and tilting the gun handle up at me to reveal the side glued with powder.

"Why are you always happiest when the shit hits the fan?"

"You'll never feel more alive than the moment before you die," he said, passing me the gun. "You take this, there's some gremlins at the bottom of the bag I can scoop out..."

"How much cash is there?" I asked.

"I did a quick count when we were riding. Around seventy thousand. Maybe eighty."

Diego ran his finger around the inside of the bag and came up with a few scoops of the anti-Ket. For my part, I snorted bits off the grooves in the gun, but it was more effective to lick the thing clean. I slobbered over it, finishing with sucking off the barrel in my mouth.

"Jack, you sexy gringo," Diego said, laughing.

"RARRRR!" I said, psyching myself up with a battle cry, the various drugs in my system smashing into each other like a hadron collider.

"Yeah bitch, Yeah!" Diego said, striding around the rock, the discomfort in his leg now fully removed.

I handed him back the gun and he threw it into the bag and zipped it shut. He pulled the bag over his head and under his arm in a sling. I looked again over the edge. It was still a bad idea. No matter how strong the hit was, the jump looked higher every time.

"How far do we go? How far do we jump out??" I said.

"Won't know that 'til we hit the bottom!"

"Fuck! Fuck! Fuck!"

"Are we doing this, ese?" he said.

"Yes. No. I think so. Fuck! Fuck! Yeah, we're doing this!"

"ARE WE FUCKING DOING THIS?!"

"YEAH, WE'RE FUCKING DOING THIS!!!" I screamed.

"Any last words for your horse?!"

"Marilyn, I FUCKING LOVE YOU!"

We took a few steps back and ran clean without breaks or hesitation to the edge and took our leap of faith.

"BIIIIIIIIIIIITCH!" Diego cried.

Despite all the shit that had happened over the last couple of days, I can say clearly and without a doubt that it was the most terrified I have ever been in my life. But once our feet were clear of that rocky ledge, when there was no going back. Nothing left other than gravity and the surging tide of the endless waterfall. Then I realised Diego was right. I felt something I hadn't ever felt before. Truly alive.

# 17

# MOTHER GAIA

Surging over the side, weightless and serene, wailing into a torrent of mountain-fresh water, an Englishman and a Mexican. Two most unlikely fish. We ploughed through the surface of the pool, plundering deep beneath its surface. The relentless cascading water forced us down ever deeper until my feet touched bedrock on the base, leverage for a kick-off. I was in urgent need of air. There were breathable micro-moments, before the swirling current whipped us back under for an extra few seconds of drowning. We had to thrash clear of the epicentre. A mess of arms and legs slapped the surface of the water, desperately gurgling our way to the edge. Diego bobbed up in my periphery. Utterly exhausted, he rolled onto his back and the tide drifted him to safety. I paddled over and pulled us both clear, dragging us over to an area of pebbles and cast-out driftwood. We lay panting, spitting out water, physically ruined but euphoric. Delirious and exhausted laughter followed. My face was stinging from the fall. My breath was cold as carbon. I wasn't sure if I was still feeling residual effects from our last parlance with the Horse Power but my body was roaring, emboldened by the sensory overload of the jump.

"HAHAHA! WHOOO! We did it, man!" I said, slapping Diego on the chest.

He didn't respond, other than slowly blinking in agreement. He still had the duffle bag tucked under his arm. there was no chance he would have let that slip away. I let him know that his black skeletal face makeup had finally washed off in the fall."You actually look kinda human," I said, talking loudly over the thunderous sounds of falling water, "I'm surprised. we've been through a lot of shit and it never smudged one bit! To tell you the truth, I was starting to worry that it was just your natural face!"

"I'm not Death, Jack," he said, panting for air, "I just needed a good bath."

"You're cleansed now, brother."

I laughed and patted him again for reassurance. Mine, as much as his. Without labouring the point on Diego, I felt genuine relief seeing him with a normal face, seeing something human underneath. There's only so long you can travel with the spectre of death at your side before you start feeling that lady luck may never show up.

There was little impetus to get up and start exploring our new terrain. I was happy lying there a little longer watching the twilight colours of dusk turning the cotton pink sky a paler shade of blue. We were in the shadow of the rock face, a giant wall of crumbly soft fuchsia stone, layered and fragmented. A wondrous mountain of sandstone, disappearing high into the starry abyss. I scanned the uppermost edge looking for the spot we jumped from. However, it was lost, too far for the eye to find. It was nothing shy of a miracle to have landed in the waters and washed ashore on the riverbank in one piece. The pebbles and rocks extended a few feet from us, bordered by a wood of soft green pines. Everything was laced with stillness and tranquillity as the daylight slowly dissolved. I watched as it slowly slunk back between the trees, giving way to the approaching darkness. Then I noticed something that required a double take, *a bear attacking a woman? No, a bear and a woman. A woman-bear.* I shook my head.

"What the fuck?!"

There was a figure made of black and brown fur shimmering out of focus, standing on a broad rock, as static as a scarecrow, with a wide frame and sagging shoulders. It took several more seconds for my eyes to piece together the illusion.

"Is that a woman dressed as a bear?" I said.

Diego sat up and considered. "Yeah," he replied.

"What the fuck is she doing?"

"Looking at us," he said.

"No shit. But why?"

What I really couldn't work out, beyond why she was dressed in a giant bear fur, was why she wasn't moving. She was just standing there, her little face poking out from under the jaws of her bear head. Instinctively, born of curiosity, I waved at her. There was some form of acknowledgement in a sharp head tilt, then she walked off.

"Does she want us to follow her?" I wondered out loud.

"Beats lying here. Fuck swimming, I'm done. Help me up, dog."

Diego and I hobbled over the various rocks and boulders, headed for a patch of dry grassland. It was a small clearing she appeared to be using as a camp. There was no sign of a tent or any other possessions of hers, other than a small leather bag propped against a stone, upon which she sat. There was an ashen centre circle with a few sticks built into a pyramid stack, ready for making fire. The outer circle had one or two more flat stones that looked passable for lounging.

"May we...?" I said, gesturing to the circle.

She waved a welcoming arm across the stones and so we sat, each taking our own. She had her head down staring at the fire pit. She murmured occasional and indecipherable words. It was a vague kind of chanting that I thought it best to allow her to finish before attempting conversation. I waited an extra few deliberate seconds after she stopped, just to be sure that she was done.

"I'm Jack. And this is Diego," I said. There was no recognition or response, so I continued. "Thanks for letting us sit... here."

"You fall a *long* way," she said, turning her head up to see us before laughing maniacally.

She had tanned leathery skin, stretched and weathered, yet soft and elasticated. When she smiled, the creases at the corner of her lips bowed outward like the ripples of a boat ploughing through still water. Her white and uniformed teeth were a contrast to the jagged jumble that protruded from the bear's jawline. She wore no makeup but her ears were decorated with an array of dangling bird feathers splayed out in a rich spectrum of colour. Around her neck, she wore a row of beads, white fragile shells spun in great intricate loops. Her eyes glistened with intent, her pupils searching for answers. She broke off her laughter as quickly as it had begun.

"Haha, yes, we fell a long way! You saw us?" I asked, tittering with laughter to try and build some rapport.

"Saw you. Heard you. Make loud bang," she said, smiling again, then stopping to look at Diego. "Who you?"

"That's Diego," I said.

"I ask him." She said bluntly.

"Diego," he said, waving at her with passing interest, before lying back on his rock to stare at the sky.

"Why you here?" she said.

"Swimming," Diego said, chortling to himself and passing exhausted air out of his lungs.

She looked sternly over to me, "And why you here?"

"Swimming," I said, grinning softly at her, hoping to show that by making light of our arrival it was not born out of deceit, but humour.

"You can't swim for shit!" she said.

This caught us off guard, sending Diego and I into a rapture of laughter that was easily ignited, given how giddy we were after surviving our great leap.

"She ain't wrong!" Diego said.

"I go to the woods, make a fire. If you want to stay, is OK, you can stay," she said.

"Really? That would be great. Yes, please," I said. "Diego, you hear that? That sounds great, thank you."

"Is OK. I go make the fire. You stay," she said.

"I have a lighter..." Diego said.

"I have lighter too. You think native woman don't have lighter? Stupid man. This is twenty-first century."

"I thought 'chu said you were heading into the woods to make a fire..." Diego said.

"To get stuff for fire, more wood. Not enough wood here to make fire like this. More people, more wood."

"That's great," I said, interjecting. "Do you need any help?"

"You stay here. Soon you be cold and need dry clothes, so you dry on the fire," she said, getting up. "Hungry?"

"Eh, yeah, I guess... but please, don't worry about us," I said.

"Too many words. I get dinner for three people. You like McDonalds?" she said.

"Erm...?" my confusion opened the door to possibility, *could we really be close enough to civilisation, or a roadside diner perhaps?*

"Ha! You so stupid!" she said laughing. Then she slapped her hand down on top of her other hand, palms colliding to replicate our jump. *SLAP!* "You fall big, big, big! Long, long way."

She walked off laughing to herself, and I called after her, "Hey, what's your name?"

"Ela."

"Ela?" I repeated, but she didn't turn back, walking off into the woods. "Funny woman."

"Got some mouth," Diego said.

"We're fucking lucky to have her. If she can get the fire going, we're laughing."

"I could'a done it," he said.

"Oh really? With your lighter? It must be soaking wet."

He pulled the lighter out and struck it a few times without success, just the damp rub of wet flint against metal.

"Huh. Well, hopefully she comes back with big Macs," he said.

"Really? After where we spent today, I don't fancy burgers ever again… certainly not this side of the border."

She returned, dumping an arm full of logs, lighting the fire, then heading back to get more. A woman of few words, she did all of this in silence, allowing us to enjoy a moment of calm. I noticed she was barefoot and completely at one with her surroundings. I wondered if she lived out here. I

306

asked Diego if that was likely and he saw no reason why not. When she came back the second time, she walked out of the wood nonchalantly, triumphantly, carrying a huge bird over her shoulder. Both her hands were needed to support the weight. Her fingers were entwined with large yellow leathery talons.

"Jesus!" I said, standing up in surprise.

"No - Ela. Haha!" She said, pulling the beast around her frame and throwing it down onto the floor.

"Oh shit. Diego, that's the hawk we saw earlier," I said, and then addressing her, "This guy's been following us for miles."

"Not hawk, kuntur," she said.

"Kuntur...?" I asked, raising her an eyebrow.

"Condor, yes? Condor," she said, correcting her language for our benefit, "kuntur is the old talk."

"A kuntur? Wow, it's a beauty. Diego, look," I said, kicking his leg to rouse him from a drowsy state. He was shivering aggressively and only partially acknowledged the bird and his surroundings.

"I'm cold," he said.

"Take off your jacket. Pants. Warm over fire. Here," Ela said, picking up two of her larger sticks and ramming them into the ground to create a makeshift clothes peg.

Diego stripped off, hanging his jacket and trousers up, then shuffled closer toward the fire. The dusk sky had turned sapphire blue as night took hold. The temperature sank rapidly in synchronisation. Ela paid attention to Diego as he stripped, watching him untie the shirt tourniquet to reveal the bullet hole in his leg.

"What happened?" she asked.

"Shot," Diego replied.

"Come out?"

"Yeah, out the other side."

"Oh."

Joining suit with the revealing of war wounds, I decided it made sense to check mine. I removed my once-white t-shirt and short-sleeved Hawaiian print shirt, flicking the water out and hanging them up to dry. I craned my head to examine my shoulder.

"And you?" she inquired.

"Also shot," I said.

"Ah hem," she replied, internally formulating her opinions.

"I think they went all the way through…" I said, turning my back to her, leaning toward the fire for better light and hoping she would confirm as much. She came over to me and prodded at my back with little remorse.

"Oww!" I cried.

"Huh.. looks like come through," she said with a muted level of concern before turning her attention to the sports bag next to Diego. "What's in the bag?"

Diego and I looked at each other but didn't speak. She took this as a response and sat back down. She stared into the fire and weighed up our situation.

"You two play with guns, is not such a good idea," she said.

"You're probably right, Ela," I said, trying to deflect attention from the deeper core of our past.

"And what about you, lady? If you ain't got no gun then how'd you kill that hawk?" Diego said.

"It's a *kuntur*, Diego," I corrected.

"Whatever. How'd you kill it?" he said, with an accusatory tone.

Ela dropped her shoulders and shrugged off her bearskin coat. Underneath she was more slight than she had first appeared, which was natural enough given that the bear added a healthy fifty pounds to her frame. Her clothes were a hodgepodge of genuine Native American poached animal skins, wedded with more familiar, western style fashion. A white denim shirt hung between her various inner layers. Over her shoulder, she had a bow and a sack of arrows, which she removed and rested on her stone seat. Diego made a nervous movement toward his bag, stopping himself before he made his paranoia too obvious. The atmosphere had suddenly become a bit uncomfortable. Ela looked again at the bag and then at Diego. She seemed to be adding up all the component parts and I wondered if Diego was worried she might turn the bow on us. She thankfully calmed the mood when she next spoke.

"You play with guns. You jump off waterfalls. You two are stupid." She started laughing again, poking the fire and rocking back with delight.

"Haha, you're right. We really are," I said, hoping to massage away any tension.

"You want to eat?" she said.

"Yes, that would be great," I said.

"Then you remove feathers. You know how?"

"No, sorry..."

"And you, mister, you know how?" she said.

Diego sucked his teeth, "It's Diego. D-ie-go, not mister."

"Oh, you want I remember you, huh? That why all the gang tattoos?" she said.

Diego's torso was littered with calligraphy, writings, quill-written names, and roman numerals. His body was scrawled with more ink than the Magna Carta. "She's got your number, Diego," I said.

"And you?" she said, to me.

"Me? No, I'm not in any gangs," I said.

"Hmm, strange. You pluck bird, OK?" she said.

"Yeah, sure. So you hit this thing with an arrow, eh? Must be a good shot..."

She ignored my compliment, instead picking up the condor and throwing it at my feet. Lying on its back, with his wings splayed out, I was able to appreciate its full size. It had the body of a large Alsatian dog and the wingspan of a man's arms at full stretch. "She's a real beauty. An offering from above?" I ventured.

"Like an Angel?" she queried. "Look at the feathers - only white inside, near the body, near the heart. After that, black all around. If an Angel, then it's surrounded by death." She glanced at me, then across to Diego. "You want me to fix wounds?"

"Fix wounds?" he said.

"Do you have medicine?" I asked.

"Some," she said, pulling a branch out of the fire, waving the cindered end around in intricate circles.

"Ah, I see," I said.

"You first, Jack!" Diego said.

"He's OK. He pluck bird, you need it," she said, turning her burnt wand in his direction.

Diego sucked his teeth again, weighing up the option.

"It's probably a good idea, your leg is still weeping," I said, unable to hold back a wry grin at the expectation of his extended anguish.

"I guess so.." he said, about to stand up but struggling to pull himself off the rock.

"You wait, I come," she said, toggling the stick back into the fire, then moving around to join him.

As she got closer, Diego moved the bag away from her approaching side.

"You think this is really a good idea? You done this before, right" Diego said, stalling.

"Of course," she said, looking at me and winking.

"What will you do, just poke…" he said, but before he could finish speaking she had rammed the flaming stick an inch deep into the entry hole on the front of his thigh. Smoke rose from the impact and Diego cried in agony.

"Now we do other side!" she said.

I got up and took off my jeans, positioning them over some sticks to dry out. I cheered on Diego, taunting him with encouragement.

"Fuck You Jack!"

"Come on, man, suck it up! Take the pain!" I said.

"Shh! You pluck, or you next!" Ela said, waving the burnt end in my direction.

I did as told, sitting down and pulling out feathers, throwing them into the fire. Ela treated the back of Diego's leg, cauterising the wound on each side. He declined to mention his manipulated genitals. I left that decision with him. When she had finished treating his leg, Diego voiced his need for a piss and hobbled off toward the woods. When Ela had her back turned he looked at me with a very deliberate gesture: *keep guard on the money bag.* I nodded softly. When Diego came limping back into view a minute later, he wore the ashen face of a man who's just pissed half a pint of blood. Ela was standing behind me, examining my shoulder again, picking at the skin holes.

"Hmm, you want burn?" she said.

"Erm, not really..." I said.

"Come on, Jack, what are you scared of?" Diego said, rejoining.

"Do you think it's really necessary?" I asked Ela.

She shrugged a non-committal response.

"Yeah, maybe I'll skip it then," I said.

"I have something, a medicine, to stop infection," she said.

Ela went over to her satchel and fiddled around with a few leather drawstring sacks. Then she produced a small wooden pestle and mortar, and began mashing herbs into a paste. She applied this paste to the front and back of my shoulder.

Then she took my newly dried t-shirt off the fire and wrapped it under my armpit, creating a makeshift bandage that held the healing herbs in place.

"Thank you, Ela, really. I think I'm done here," I said, passing her the bird with its amateur plucking resembling a badly shaved scrotum.

She scoffed at my efforts and finished removing more feathers herself, before gutting it and chopping off the head. She was incredibly resourceful, making a spit with two Y-framed sticks on either side of the fire, joined by a roasting pole between them. The bird hung there for a while crisping up while we made small talk. This was mostly Ela quizzing me about life in England. I told her about my previous job and my disillusionment with office life. I waxed lyrically on the subject of Rolando, my Mexican prophet, and explained the collapse of my nervous system. One panic attack, a dumped girlfriend, an abandoned job - and here I was, sitting around a Mexican campfire about to eat a condor.

"You know your problem?" she said, adding after a few silent moments of contemplation, "Man-made."

"You mean, modern man… the way we live now?" I said.

"Emails? That's not you, right? It goes far, far back," she said.

314

"Before emails?"

"Yes. Longer back. They are just what people use today, the modern way. Man has been lost for a long, long time. He's forgotten about all this," she said, looking beyond us.

I glanced around at the trees, the water slipping over the rocks, everything just visible in the remnants of light. The fire crackled.

"I can't argue with that... I can't remember when I last went camping. But it's hard. To exist in the world today means that you need a job and when you need a job, then I guess you're done for," I said.

"Just camping won't do it. Camping is for the weekend. I'm talking about life," she said.

Diego chimed in, "how's that bird doing, I'm hungry."

"You got a chance now, mister Jack," she said, ignoring Diego and pointing at my shoulder, "you got second chance." She looked back to Diego, "No chance for him though. He's right. Let's eat."

Ela had just one knife that she used to cut chunks off the bird and hand them to us. She explained that she had prayed for the condor after killing it, and told us about some of her other Native American traditions. She didn't fully divulge her upbringing, but it sounded like she had been raised traditionally, yet within a modern household. She ultimately rejected the temptations of modernity and left home, choosing instead to embrace the old ways of life.

"Condor tastes like chicken," Diego said.

"Tastes good?" she said.

"Really good. Thank you, Ela," I said.

"Not processed, you see? Natural."

"Definitely, I can taste that," I said.

"Wait, you sayin' everything processed is bad? Fuck that," Diego said. "Me, I like burgers. And this thing - damn it could do with a little chipotle sauce, eh?"

"You see?" Ela said, "no chance for him."

"Be real now Jack, you know a little sauce would be amazing," Diego said.

"Up until a few hours ago I was all set on being vegetarian, so maybe I'm not the best person to ask. But I know this is really good," I said.

"All processed things are the bad things," Ela said, "Burgers one thing, but same as government of United States. They are the process, the structure, that allows man to keep doing bad. Everyone just doing their job, so it's OK."

"Like the Nazis. Everyone was just following orders..." I said.

"Like Anton," Diego added, "He's a bad cat, but he ain't shit without his crew."

"Who's Anton?" Ela asked.

"My old boss," Diego said, "but not anymore."

"He's dead?" she said, anxiously looking at us.

"Kinda... he's gone away," he said.

"But, someone take his place?" she said.

"Yeah, I guess so. For now anyway," Diego said.

"Then nothing changed. The system remains." Ela seemed pleased with the neatness of how the argument had closed, humming comforting sounds to herself, much like when we had arrived. "You want peyote?"

"What's that?" I asked.

"Button tops? You sly motherfucker! Yeah! Yeah, I love that shit," Diego said.

"You do before?" she said.

"Once, at a party," he said.

She scoffed. "You do peyote at a party, then you don't do peyote before. It's for nature. For healing and for understanding. Be good for you two. They call it the Divine Messenger. I make us a batch."

Diego looked excited, taking his clothes off the fire and redressing. I did likewise, the goosebumps on my skin welcomed the steaming jeans back onto my legs. Toasty denim and buttons too hot to handle. I saw no point worrying about the peyote. It would just get chalked up alongside the plethora of other mind-altering substances so far consumed and actually I found myself looking forward to it more than the others.

Ela described it as a wholly natural substance, important given her aversion to anything touched by the hand of man.

"It's not like that other shit you've been taking," she said.

I glanced at Diego with those words and he simply shrugged. Neither of us had mentioned other drugs to her. She seemed to know instinctively. The cumulative effects were likely etched on our faces, possibly even for years to come.

"I'm making tea," she said, explaining for my benefit as I leaned over her watching the cactus buds get squashed in her mixing bowl. "Englishman like tea, yeah?"

"Yes, we like tea," I said.

As the night descended we passed the broth around the circle. With each sip, we delved into an altered reality, a psychotropic utopia. The visuals started slowly at first, the fire burning brighter and with flickering lucidity. The logs hissed as they cooked, yearning for us to listen. Ela had started up with her mumbo-jumbo chanting again. I couldn't say when she started, it just became apparent that she was and then I couldn't remember a time when she wasn't. The whole night went like that, time skipping backward, tripping over itself in a vacuum, surging from one moment to the next. It was nighttime when we started drinking the brew. Fully pitch black, but then the sunset would creep back in again, as though the sun rose briefly from the sky. If not that, then my mind was watching back loops of our previous evening, making me feel like we had been hallucinating from the very first moment we had pulled ourselves ashore. In that reality, Ela didn't exist at all. We were simply the slug-like origins of humankind, blobs of plant life, living organic matter, the very first primal shapes to be dreamt up in the void before existence. *We climbed ashore this...where? Where the fuck were we? When were we?*

Her chanting brought me back round, a rhythmic cycle.

She started to bang softly on a deerskin drum: *rummm dummm, rummm dummm, rummm dummm.*

I heard a hawk cry. The condor flew above our heads and I reached out for him but he was gone. Then, he was sitting on a rock next to me, his head still attached. He was plucked badly... *was this before we had eaten him?* He stared at me, not talking. Where I had ripped out feathers and torn the skin, they bled and became open sores.

I vomited.

"It's OK Jack, come back, come back," Ela was chanting.

It worked, soothing worked. It passed. The condor was nowhere to be seen. I wiped the vomit from my mouth and sat up, mighty and proud.

"Yes, yes... Feel Her..." Ela continued, drifting back into her ancient folklore jabbering.

"I do feel Her... I DO!" I said.

The fire rose higher, the coals raked over by Ela's stick. The embers fizzed and sparks of bright orange cinder danced up into the night sky. The purple, swirling roof above our heads was stained with a dizzying blur of opal stars. A galaxy of wonder and awe. The eyes of the animal kingdom were watching, chattering in distant approval.

"What *is* this?" I said.

"Nature.." she replied, *rummm dummm, rummm dummm, rummm dummm...* "All life is energy, it's the energy that is life. Everything else is the surface. We need to go beyond this surface, to see the energy. Do you see it?"

"Yes! Yes I do... I can *feel* it," I said.

"Everything man has created has served only to distance himself from this state of being. But you are here now! Enjoy it, feel it. This is nature breathing in death, breathing out life, one circle, going round and round..." *rummm dummm, rummm dummm, rummm dummm...*

Soon we were in the water, sitting in the shallows of the stream, Ela taking my hand and holding it under the surface.

"It's not the top of the water, but underneath, where you feel the energy…"

A moment later I was lying down under the water, my body and head submerged, the water rushing over my face. I did see it, I did feel it! But then a thought occurred: *"Where is Diego?"*

"I'M HERE!" he yelled from the opposite river bank. He was standing bow-legged, like a man riding a horse but with no horse present.

"What the… come back over here!" I said. I was out of the water, back on the rock. "Come here!" I was off the rock and now sitting squat in a tree like a bird. "No, wait, don't come here, come back to the fire, meet me at the fire."

Diego appeared next to me at the fire. This level of teleportation was hard on the senses. I needed to find a way to stay grounded, so clung to the rock with my fingertips.

"Don't fight it…" Ela said.

"I'm not!" I said, through gritted teeth. I was fighting it.

"We did a bad thing!" Diego said.

"Shut up, Diego, no we didn't. Stay in this space!" I said.

"You both need to calm. Calm, silence and listen to the drum" *rummm dummm, rummm dummm, rummm dummm, rummm dummm, rummm dummm, rummm dummm, rummm dummm, rummm dummm, rummm dummm…*

"I met an old woman on a plane... she had a cross around her neck.." I said.

"Do you seek religion?" Ela said.

"No... Mother!" I said.

"You seek Mother? You are here. This is Mother Nature. There is only peace and happiness here," she said.

"We did a bad thing," Diego said, his eyeballs burning with fear.

"He's right, Ela, he's right, we did a bad thing... many, many, bad things," I said.

"What you did was human," she said.

"We killed," I said.

"Exactly... human. They've been killing for thousands of years. Did you think they would stop with you? It is Human Nature. We are animals, we kill to survive."

"This was different..." I said.

"It always is," she said.

"The innocent died..."

"They always do," she said, "This condor was innocent. So was the mouse he ate for lunch. This is the circle of life and death. Right and wrong? Those are just man's words to explain the meaning when sometimes there is none. When a tree dies, its branches fall into the undergrowth, these become life for the insects. When one thing dies, another lives, this is the cycle of life and death in nature."

"Yes, yes. I can see it. I can forgive it..." I said.

"But the cycle of life and death within man is different," Ela said. "This is what we call War. War between man can never be stopped. But it is the war between man and nature, this is the one that will prove truly fatal, the one that threatens everything...Nature's greatest threat is man, and man's greatest threat is nature..."

The chanting stopped, I couldn't say when. We sat lost in the embers of the fire all through the night. The sun slowly began to rise, nothing more than a pinprick, but it heralded the end of the awakening.

"I did it. I killed Sammy," the words came from Diego's mouth.

I instinctively moved my hands over my lips to double-check they hadn't moved. *Could I have uttered it??*

"It was me. I broke her jaw... I strangled her." Diego's words. *Definitely Diego's words.*

"Diego, shut up, you don't know what you're saying. It's the drugs... we don't know what happened that night. It could have been anyone. Most likely, Anton," I said.

"It wasn't anyone, it was me. I remember it now. Maybe I always knew it. But I saw it. A memory that was buried - I saw it. I killed her because she had my baby in her and I'm too much of a fuckin' coward to admit it! That's the man that Ela talks about - isn't it? That's the mankind she describes! Everyone is right, I have fucked up everything I ever touched!"

"Diego, it's the drugs, it's the drugs! Don't talk this way!" I said, desperate not to have to comprehend the depths of his atrocity.

"It's not the drugs," Ela said. She stood up on her rock with each of us occupying one side of the fire. "The drugs don't lie, they just open the doors. He knew it. Like he said, he just needed to remember. I knew it too, when I first saw him, I saw the blood and murder in his soul. Your friend has death in his heart."

"No... say it's not true, Diego?!" I pleaded.

"It's true!" she said.

"Fuck you - you witch! Get the fuck outta my head!" Diego screamed, his face flickering red and yellow in the firelight, before submerging into the last remaining shadows of night. "You got what you wanted, now what? Now you want our fucking money! Well fuck you, you ain't getting it!" He stood up with the bag under his shoulder, unzipped it, and pulled out the magnum.

"Woooa, easy buddy, easy… let's all calm down. Let's take this down a notch."

"Do you see it, mister Jack?" Ela said. "Do you see the horrors of man, living in fear of nature, desperate to cling onto his fake little world? For that, he would do anything!"

"Please, Ela, let's calm this down and talk about it. Where's the drum, I'll play the drum," I said.

Diego pulled the magnum up at arm's length and pointed directly at Ela's head. The sun speckled across the treetops. Sharp white beads of pure cleansing light announced the start of a new day. Ela's hands moved from her navel to reach both arms outstretched, heavenward, as if feeling a beam of unwavering light entering her soul. I looked back at Diego. His eyes were a blaze of murderous fury, redraw, possessed, feverish. The effects of drugs, torture, and sleepless nights all combined to create a satanic rage that no words could exorcise. All reasoning was lost.

I heard a loud bang, and then Ela's head exploded like a watermelon thrown under a bus. A strangely comic voice spoke aloud inside my head: "*well, here we go again.*"

# 18

# E PARADISO

It took a while to process the events. Not more than a few seconds, but pressed through a time-stretching sieve that made it feel like hours. Ela's upright body, standing tall, minus one head. The blood had burst forth in all directions, showering Diego and I with brain fragments and miscellaneous cranial matter. There was nothing left on her shoulders to suggest any form had ever occupied the space. No skull, no hair, no face. Just Boom! Like C4 in a pumpkin. I turned to look at Diego, his face dripping in human residue.

"Jesus, Diego."

"It wasn't me!" he yelled.

"I WAS FUCKING STANDING HERE NEXT TO YOU!" I yelled back.

"I'm serious! I never pulled the fucking trigger!"

"What the fuck is wrong with you?! This is too much Diego, first Sammy, and now this? This poor, kind woman...You know, you really are a total fucking, psychotic, fucking, disaster zone."

Then a whip crack. A distant bang, not altogether unfamiliar from the last bang, sounded from somewhere off in the distance. The rock nearest us puffed up in a cloud of granite dust with nasty shards of loose stone flying up into our faces.

"What the fuck!?" I said, shielding myself from the debris.

"Something's trying to kill us..." Diego said.

*Bang! Puff!* This time the dirt exploded at our feet.

"There!" shouted Diego.

On the opposite side of the river bank, by the base of the waterfall, was a man wearing all black. He had a black stetson hat, silver handlebar moustache, and a long old-fashioned rifle that he had to reload between shots. I recognised him in an instant.

"Carlos!" I exclaimed.

He pulled back on the hammer and raised it toward us again. Diego grabbed my shirt and pulled me down to the floor. *Bang!* This round flew off somewhere into the tree line, the hollow sound of splintered bark echoing back to us. I lay with half my face submerged in the gravel, breathing out dusty clouds of fine grey soil. I wondered how Carlos had found us, cursing myself for forgetting his existence. The last we heard was that he was en route to Centaur Burgers, intent on finishing off Diego, before loading up the gringo to be returned for a prisoner exchange. He would have seen the burning factory from several miles away, then arrived there to find the place raised to the ground. Perhaps a quick body count later, deducting that we had escaped on foot. One horse bearing weight and one man walking alongside; simple enough tracks for an old gaucho like him. At the top of the waterfall, he would have found my horse peacefully licking up river water. With a sad twist of fate, she had then become the marker that helped Carlos to track our final movements. He would have scoured the ledge and seen the footsteps disappear, searching desperately around for their continuation but finding nothing more. *How long did it take you Carlos? How long to realise that we had the balls to jump? How long? You looked at it yourself, but didn't fancy it, did you, Tonto? You didn't have the fucking minerals! And that's why you're only showing yourself now. You've spent all night finding a safe footpath down - you coward - and then you shoot an unarmed woman, assassinate her from behind!*

I snapped out of my internal dialogue when gravity took hold of Ela's body and her legs finally gave way. Her torso toppled forward as she landed headlessly first into the fire. I tried for a fraction of a second to stop her body falling but it was too late. The fire was small, a mere gathering of ashen coals and charcoal logs, but it soon burst into a ball of flames when her bear fur caught alight. For a moment I thought I saw a spirit rising up from her body. A magisterial bird winged in a cosmic translucent fire, flapping vast wing beats as it rose ceaselessly into the dawn sky. I looked across at Diego to see if he had also witnessed this miracle, but he was gone.

"Diego?" I looked toward the forest and caught a glimpse of him buggering off into the tall grasses. "Bastard!". I glanced back at Carlos who was wading across the river, the gun held high above his head to keep it dry. I seized this moment to escape while he was preoccupied, popping up on all fours like a dog. I made eye contact with him for the first time since our meeting in bar La Luna. His moustache rippled in disapproval. Ela's small satchel of arrows and a fine white bow were next to me. I grabbed them and ran like hell toward the woods. Another rifle round fired behind me, whizzing through the undergrowth. I could see Diego's tracks clearly and kept hard on them. My mind was spinning with visions of retribution. I conjured up renewed vigour in the name of bringing Sammy's killer to justice. Diego's eventual confession played over and over in my mind, taunting me. I wondered if I had always known the truth, but somehow suppressed that reality within myself, just like him. It felt like old forgotten information finally remembered. The answer lay there permanently, just waiting to be rediscovered. Yet it didn't explain *why* our lives had been tangled together by that murder, *unless it was for this, to enact justice upon him, to track him down, and kill him. And what would Ela say to that?*

I ran harder and harder, pushing past branches and scrambling over shrubs. I felt the shadow of Carlos on my back chasing me down. He ebbed closer, gaining with each step. I had lost sight of Diego but his ungainly running technique made his tracks easy to follow. Occasionally these revealed him as a fully splayed-out body print where he had fallen into the dirt. After a short while, I noticed a faint trickle of blood in the dust. I now tracked a wounded beast, his loins no doubt burning with the pain of reignited rectal bleeding.

We ran for what felt like an hour, the forest rising up into a steep unforgiving hill that made the hamstrings burn. The sun became fully established with great shadows peeling off the trees and the sounds of animals waking up to the morning's hunt. I stopped to reel in some desperate breath. I scanned back down the hill for a sight of my pursuer and prayed that I might have lost him. However, I would catch a glimpse of his dark figure swooping from one shadow to the next, morphing and shape-shifting ever closer. I realised to stop now would be to finally accept the hand of death. I rallied and ploughed on higher, my stomach retching and my head screaming blue murder in all directions. Eventually, the ground levelled off into a clearing of a few shabby trees scattered about in a fecund clearing. Beyond this was a cluster of several collapsed timber buildings, the ghost town of Trinco.

I took another nervous glance down the hill. There was no sign of Carlos. Diego's tracks vanished at the edge of town, somewhere around an old broken wagon cart that lay fallen on its side. I strode on and into the main gully of town. A single wide road with buildings lining each side. It was a ramshackle town that had been preserved in time by snowy winters and warm summers, mummifying its wood with a silvery sheen that created a weary sort of nostalgia. Each building was fronted by a porch, connected together with a decrepit boardwalk that crumpled semi-submerged into the arid soil. A series of these boardwalk planks rose and fell like the keys of some great piano, rupturing out of the dry earth, playing one final tune for the closing of time. I walked slowly up the main avenue, staring into the broken windows of these forgotten lives. The gun shop, the pharmacy, the blacksmiths, the saloon. Each seemed to remember the presence of man, but none wished to speak his name. Wind chimes rattled and the odd door clacked softly back and forth within its casing. I kept going. My eyes winced at the morning sun as I desperately searched for signs of Diego. He chose not to reveal himself, instead letting me plunder further into the lifeless vacuum of town. Reaching the end of the main drag, I stood briefly in the shadow of a white-rendered church positioned next to the water well. The roof was lined by a parapet wall, and rounded masonry pleated around a central bell. Cracked plaster revealed glimpses of brickwork peppered with bullet holes. I tried to imagine where Diego might be hidden and whether he wanted me dead too. *Did he know I was hunting him? Would he care, or would he simply hope Carlos and I punched each other's ticket? Then he would be free to continue on his way. But Not today... Not today!*

Realising that I was too exposed in the street, I ducked across a hollow raft of boards and took cover behind a dilapidated log store that propped up the corner of the sheriff's office. Opposite me was the saloon. To my right was the old white church. I glanced left, back down toward the entrance of town, which was now occupied by the unmistakable figure of Carlos. His black outline shimmered in the tide of the rising sun. He brought the gun up to his shoulder and fired a shot at the church bell sending it into spasms of clinging and clanging, while he proceeded to march up through the scorched desert floor of Trinco. Tumbleweed bumbled around with mindless perversion. The dust swirled through broken window panes, wheeling with delight, while the old heavy doors hung desperately onto their hinges to witness one last showdown.

"Diiiiiiego!" Carlos called out in a piercing cry.

I scanned all the buildings and their windows, keen to see from which he would emerge. But nothing stirred. Carlos walked on, the dirt under his boot just audible under the final hollow rings from the old church bell.

"Diego!" Carlos cried again, "Let's talk about this, OK, ese? Let's see if we can come to some kind of understanding…"

Diego still didn't budge, increasing the likelihood of any final showdown actually being between Carlos and I. These were odds that I didn't fancy.

"You wanna do this the hard way, eh? How many chances do you want me to give you? How about this… you come out now, and I don't kill your lady," Carlos bellowed.

I gulped back a mouthful of air which was made of at least one-quarter sand. My eyes squinted under the harsh rising sun. Sweat beaded my brow, wiped away with the back of my dirty brown hand as it held a pristine white-feathered arrowhead drawn from my satchel.

"Or your boy?" Carlos continued, "If you come out now, you can choose which one of them lives! You bring me the gringo, and you have my word, they both live! I won't even need to go to Arizona…"

He let the final words ring around the hollows of every building, the purpose of them designed to let Diego know the game was up. *He knew where they lived.* Carlos had almost reached the end of the street, standing just a few feet from the well in front of the church. He turned to address the words back down into town, wondering if he had passed a cowering Diego in one of the boarded-up shops. I wondered too but redoubled my efforts to stay hidden.

"Did you think I wouldn't find out, Diego?" Carlos said, "I know all about Marianna. And Santi. How old is he now... eight? I know all about them, ese. I'm gonna be *real* nice to your boy... maybe I'll go visit and play daddy. I can be like the daddy you never was... and I'll get that bitch Marianna working for me! You didn't think Tito would give them up, huh?! Come on, man, you know me better than that. Once a man's got two knives in him, he'll tell you anything you want."

Carlos took a little slip of paper out of his pocket and started reading aloud to the street.

"Sixty Seven, Fair-Mount Drive, Ari-Zona, 64578...."

The swing doors of the saloon sprang open and Diego came charging forward with a Devil's fire in his eyes. He was holding the magnum out ahead of himself as if charging with a fixed bayonet.

*Bang!*

He fired a round into Carlos, which hit his shoulder and span him like a spinning top.

*Bang!*

Carlos returned fire, shooting from the hip. Diego sucked the round into his belly and collapsed down the final few steps of the saloon before staggering ungracefully down into the parched earth. I swallowed a final gulp of the hot desert air then burst from my cover with the bow primed. I fired an arrow. It whistled through the air, burying itself into the thigh of Carlos. He yelped, then instinctively began reloading the bolt on the rifle. I pulled out another arrow, but was too hasty, clumsily thumbing it around, followed by a mal-coordinated attempt to line it up with the bridge of my knuckles. I knew my moment had passed. I glanced up to see Carlos locked, loaded, and aimed at my head. His moustache curled into a horseshoe grin.

*Bang!*

Diego had rotated himself in the dirt and fired his last magnum round into the back of Carlos whose chest tore outward into a thousand ribbons of shredded organ. He sank onto his knees and dropped face-first into the dust. His stetson popped off his head and rolled away down the street, off into some long-forgotten era of sepia-tinted fable.

Diego lay coughing and spluttering out handfuls of blood. When I reached him and saw the stream of claret flowing from his belly, I knew it was the end.

"Might have known you'd be in the saloon… Anything in there?" I said.

He shook his head and pointed at the well. "W-water," he said.

"You want me to get..?"

"T-take me…"

"OK." I reached down and pulled his arm over my shoulder, carrying him, yet only ever getting his body a foot or two off the floor. I slumped him against the well, then tossed the bucket down and began hauling it back up. The bucket came up sloshing full of crystal clear water which I helped tip forward into Diego's blood-filled mouth.

"T-thanks... Jack."

"I don't even know why I'm helping you... after Sammy," I said.

He winced at the mention of Sammy, visible even though the anguish of his physical pains, the impact of my words seemed to rival, just for a moment, the agony of his intestinal bullet hole.

"I didn't mean to," he said.

"Enough, OK? We've played that game. You beat a pregnant woman to death. There's nothing else to say."

"Anton would have killed me if I didn't," he said.

"That may be, and perhaps it's the way it should have played out. Was it your baby?"

"I don't know... I told myself no, I told myself no... Oh god, I just kept getting so fucked up. I stopped knowing who I was, what I was capable of... p-please, don't tell anyone, Jack.."

"And let Anton do time for a crime he didn't commit?"

337

"Fuck Anton. I told you, he's a fuckin' b-bad guy… he deserves what he gets. Fuck what Cooch said, Anton didn't care if Sammy lived or not. After all, I killed plenty for Anton before. It's all just business to him…"

"So that's the code of the streets you live by? Anton knew what he was getting involved in, and all that shit? Look, I ain't exactly about to head back to Mexico City and try explaining the whole situation. I've done too much to get this far… besides, I would need to explain my role in everything…"

"I ain't gonna make it," he said.

"Yeah, I can see that. Shit, Diego, you want me to try and-"

"Ain't gonna make it, Jack!"

I realised he was right, his gut was bleeding profusely. He had a hole in his leg the size of a Valencia orange and his undercarriage had undergone a total rearrangement. Some kind of base-level human empathy made me persevere with one last token offer.

"I could get some wood, make a stretcher…"

He simply shook his head and pointed to Carlos. "The note."

I went over and prised the piece of paper out of his dead hands. I gave it a quick read, it was the address of Marianna and Santi in Arizona. I tried giving it to Diego but he shook his head and pulled the green bag out from under his armpit.

"Take this," he said, "Take it and give it to Maria. Please Jack, please take it…"

"Fuck. It's never quite over with you, is it? Always one more test. OK, I'll take the bag, but only 'cos you're getting blood all over it…" I said.

"Please, don't say how… don't say nuttin'. Nuttin' about Sammy, OK?"

"I won't say a word. She'll be at this address?" I asked.

"She'll like you, Jack. Just don't say a word… and tell my boy I love him, will you? Tell him… tell him to be your own man. Be… your… own man…"

"I'll tell him. You OK out here, in the open?"

"Yeah, I'm good. You'll get there, won't you, Jack?"

"I'll follow the sun."

*"Be… your own man, Jack…"*

Diego's eyes faded. I stepped away, wanting what little memory he had left in the world to be all his own. I took a few heavy swallows from the water bucket and steadied myself for the final march. Alone, this time. I had the money bag over my shoulder and little else. I had found the freedom I was after. Not in the shape I was expecting, but I had revealed the rawness of my primal condition. I looked at the trail ahead and then at the burning, radiant sun, which danced in my eye. Through the blinding light, I saw nine hexagonal rings spiral out of a pure hollow centre. I stood mesmerised in the burning glare, the crimson sky broken only for a second by the passing of a huge bird. A screech came, long, hard and hollow.

And I murmured, "Kuntur, Diego, Kuntur."

# THE END

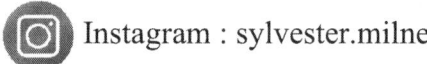 Instagram : sylvester.milne

Printed in Poland
by Amazon Fulfillment
Poland Sp. z o.o., Wrocław

31632316R00195